THE PAPER EATER

LIZ JENSEN

D0332908

BLOOMSBURY

First published 2000
This paperback edition published 2006

Copyright © 2000 by Liz Jensen

The moral right of the author has been asserted

Bloomsbury Publishing Plc, 36 Soho Square, London WID 3QY

A CIP catalogue record for this book is available from the British
Library

ISBN-10 0 7475 8533 4
ISBN-13 978 0 7475 8533 6

10 9 8 7 6 5 4 3 2 1

All papers used by Bloomsbury Publishing are natural, recyclable
products made from wood grown in well-managed forests. The
manufacturing processes conform to the environmental regulations
of the country of origin

Typeset by Palimpsest Book Production Ltd, Polmont, Stirlingshire
Printed in Great Britain by Clays Ltd, St Ives plc

www.lizjensen.com

FOR MATTI

. . . Who would have thought my shrivell'd heart
Could have recovered greennesse? It was gone
Quite underground; as flowers depart
To see their mother-root, when they have blown;
Where they together
All the hard weather
Dead to the world, keep house unknown . . .

From 'The Flower' by George Herbert

The topography of the seabed consists of a circular
plateau of porous rock, two hundred kilometres in
radius, making the ocean here as shallow as a coastal
reef . . . it is not hard to imagine an artificial land-mass
geophysically welded to this plateau, sustaining a
society with its own infrastructure and economy. The
technology is available. But is the vision?

From an article by Gilles de Ferrer in *The Oceanographer*
Translated by Colin Harbutt

BOMBSHELL

If there's one thing to be said about life in captivity, it's that you get to travel.

Welcome aboard the *Sea Hero*, a former Attractionworld cruise liner rescued by the Liberty Corporation from the ship-breaker's yard and converted at a cost of squillions into a floating fibreglass cage. Two male humans per cabin, and trans-hemispheric incarceration conditions apply. The pros of this include human-rights entitlements to craft-hobby materials and language cassettes. The cons: curtailed freedom of movement, seasickness, no smoking, and a Babel feel. Human detritus being big global business, you can be sure the profit margin looks crakko. That's the backdrop.

The hero – me.

Bonjour. Harvey Kidd. Forty-four, balding, ink-stained and alone. Divorced, beclobbered and unfree. A defective product of society, a nobody, briefly and catastrophically catapulted to somebodydom against his will. Not a real hero, but the opposite: a coward, a human ostrich. Prone to nightmares. Sometimes I'd rather not sleep.

But I must have done last night because this morning I'm woken by a vigorous electric crackle from the tannoy. Showbiz being in Captain Malt Fishook's blood, he doesn't drop his bombshell right away. He introduces the concerto first.

– Hi, folks, his voice ring-a-dings through the static. Beautiful day out there. (Like bollocks. It's grey and dank, dishwater sea, sky like ectoplasm.) Today's composer is Hugo Alfvèn, a Swede whose work flourished in the 1930s, particularly on cruise liners.

Fishook's a former Attractionworld man. Like the duvet covers, he came with the ship as part of the package. You can see why a leisure conglomerate would want shot of him; there's a side to him that would unsettle the kiddies.

– Well, Voyagers, he goes on in this global drawl he's got. Before this morning's musical entertainment, let me tell you that the next port of call is one that some of you know well.

A bad feeling germinates inside me. For weeks the ship's been jazzed up with nerves, whispers, fear. Our navigational rota dictates that we ricochet from one territory to the next, so as not to stay in anyone's back yard, and the latest rumour's been that –

– We're heading next, he says, for the island of Atlantica.

Boom. The rumour's true. The bad feeling sprouts to life, like a manic fungus that blobs up in the dark. Fishook must know what kind of wounds he's opening. What can of worms. It gets worse.

– Our arrival on the island in ten days' time, he goes, all nonchalant, will coincide with the national festival, Liberty Day. You can hear him smile in the little pause he gives. Smell the cigar smoke as he puffs. – There'll be fireworks, experience simulators, and a Final Adjustment, among other attractions. All the major retail outlets are offering unprecedented discounts, some of which will be available at our on-board concessions. Which as you know accept both dollars and euros. So get ready to party, folks!

John's shape in the bunk above, like a nylon pregnancy, bulges to the left, then stiffens. *A Final Adjustment, among other attractions*. For a bloke on Death Row, that is not a happy thing to hear. I shudder. Us Atlanticans are all on the list, but John, being an actual killer, is right up there

2

at the top, with the geologists and soil physicists they keep in solitary.

– So now for our Swedish concerto, goes Fishook. Happy sailing. And please – enjoy!

Then the tannoy gives a burp and some swoony music kicks in; a tricksy jazz rhythm, with big-band trumpety stuff complaining in the background. Atrocious.

My cell-mate doesn't move. Cabin-companion is the official term. The Captain's term. Fishook has brought with him from Attractionworld a penchant for theming, which afflicts his terminology. Voyagers. Crew. Journeys, as in, I see from my records that you are booked on a lifelong journey, Voyager. On behalf of the crew, let me welcome you aboard. Likes to hawk the lie that we're all on a happy cruise, taking a break from the pressures of society, with him, Cap'n Malt, triumphant on the poop, superintending our romantic odyssey through the waters of the northern hemisphere. The media back home view it differently.

They call us floating scum.

Finally, John groans through the music.

– You know what that means, for me, he says.

– Not necessarily, I go.

I'm feeling jittery, ragged, claustrophobic, a bit sick. For once, I'm grateful for the musical racket dinning through the sound system.

– You'd have been notified, I say. As firmly as I can. Has Fishook called you to the bridge yet? I can't see John's face from here, but I guess he's just staring moochily out of the porthole at this point. – Well, has he? I say. No.

– No, John echoes.

– Well then, I tell him. Hang on to that, is my advice.

But I leave the cabin as soon as they unlock. Experience has taught me that emotions are for losers. Feel a thing for a fellow-human and you're dead meat.

*   *   *

3

At breakfast, the canteen is strangely silent. The Euro tables are filled up, and I spot a few stray Yanks, but the Atlantican section – more than half the canteen – is almost empty. Then word starts going round that one of the blokes in solitary, some soil physicist, has thrown a wobbly and got himself frogmarched to Dr Pappadakis, who zonked him with a jab. And that a structural engineer, helicoptered in from the island last month, started yelling out a string of mathematical equations from a porthole, then tried to chuck himself overboard. Personally, I know how to deal with my own demons. I go to the Art Room and come back with a sheaf of scrap paper to fuel what Dr Pappadakis calls my neurotic hobby.

It's not neurosis, it's survival, I've told him many times. Why *not* strive for numbness? He has no answer to that. Through certain techniques involving the jaw muscles, and paper, I have managed to paralyse my entire brain for long stretches of time.

Don't knock it.

I make my papier mâché in the traditional way, by actually chewing the paper myself. Like most people, I can cram a page of A4 in my gob, no problem. Cooped in a cabin, a year after a certain knitting machine went haywire, I've had time to chew things over.

Like this: Chew, chew, chew.

Spit.

And plop, into the pulp bucket!

Loose-fibred craft paper or newspaper is undoubtedly the best material to use, but I have a range of redundant criminal dossiers to recycle. (To get technical for a moment, we're talking upwards of ten thousand computer-sprocket pages, medium-stiff, and tolerably rich in rag content.) I began chewing paper shortly after I came on board ship, in the wake of the first Mass Readjustment. Initially, I started the chewing to keep myself from blabbing the true story of my rejection by society, but soon it developed into a comforting habit. It helped blank things out. Memories, mostly. And now, a year on, although the ink's turned me as grey as concrete, I wouldn't be without it.

Sometimes I read the papers, before I chew them. But sometimes I just chew them. Pages like this:

I certify that this is my own statement, that I am not an Enemy of Liberty, have no criminal record, am of sound mind, and own a loyalty card. I am aware that anything I say may be used as evidence in any forthcoming Libertycare trial of the Sect member or members. I am willing to appear as a witness of terrorism, attempted terrorism, enablement of terrorism, moral backing of terrorism, or financial compliance with terrorism. I hereby declare that I am not masquerading as anyone other than myself————.

And there's a space, for the customer to write his name. Or hers.

Mrs Tina Willets, in this case.

And who is she? An Atlantican. A model customer. Nobody.

Chew, chew, chew.

Spit.

And plop!

At the end of each session, I swallow a mouthful. I need the roughage.

There are hordes of customers like Mrs Willets who feel invisible and unheard. As a certain woman once showed me, the daily human impulses of every man, woman and child on the island – from religious cravings to retail habits – can be plotted on a graph. As a junior associate, she processed some of the figures herself.

Chew, chew, chew.

There is much to be said for routine. A man with a well-designed timetable is in control of at least part of his destiny, isn't he. Aeons ago, when I lived in a white semi with a green door in Gravelle Road, South District, Harbourville, I always ran business to a strict timetable. I had to. In my unique line of work, if you missed the opening of a stock market, or the renewal date for a passport, or the deadline for a payment, you were history. Every job has its occupational hazards, and fraud's no exception.

My circumstances dictate that my timetable is different now, though it still involves paperwork.

Of a kind.

After masticating each mouthful sixty times (the enzymes in saliva play a big role, I discovered in the ship's Education Station, where I am a regular visitor) – after doing that, I spit the pulp into a green plastic bucket (capacity, five litres), and when it's half-full, I pour in two litres of hot tap-water and stir. Then I leave my raw material to soak overnight, and the next day gloop the pulp out into my small storage vat. Next I add certain specific quantities of whitewood glue, flour, wallpaper paste, and oil of cloves. Then I whisk it with a metal hand-whisk. This part's important, to achieve the right consistency. The finer the pulp, the stronger the paper paste. John calls this mixture my cud. There are short-cut, gimcrack methods. You can buy the kind of cat-litter that consists of recycled newspaper pellets, which you soak in water, before adding the other ingredients. Or you can get hold of so-called 'craft kits'. Or wood pulp. But as I explained at length to Dr Pappadakis, I believe in using authentic materials in the time-honoured way. Actually, being detained as an Enemy of Liberty, I don't have any choice.

Paper has played a large part in my life.

It's because of paper that I'm here.

Chew, chew, chew.

Spit. And plop!

* * *

As cabins go, this is the usual meat-and-two-veg. Standard bunks, a toilet cubicle, a wash-basin. A fold-out table, for meals and craft activities. A shelf laden with my home-made chess-pieces, and the knick-knacks we've accumulated between us, my cabin companion and I. Duvets on the bunks, with Attractionworld designs on the covers. This month I have the Funky Chicken. John has Stegoman.

It's the last day of July, according to the Alpine calendar John's stuck to the wall. If it weren't for these boxed months, with snow-capped mountain ranges behind, you'd have no way of telling that it's been a year since we left Atlantica. When you're on a ship, there's no sense of seasons. Back home, the year had a natural retail rhythm, with Christmas giving way to the January sales, followed by Valentine Week, Mother's Day, Easter, Father's Day, the Silly Season, Liberty Day, Back to Skool, then Hallowe'en, the pre-Christmas season, Christmas itself and then the whole shebang again.

You knew where you were. And now in ten days' time –

Don't think. Head in the sand. Chew!

– Ugh, John goes, picking up his embroidery. He's a needlework man.

John and I, we've been together a month.

If I'm short and squat, which as a matter of fact I am, then he's the opposite: a towering, scary man, lumpy-featured. He's a murderer, or so the story goes – though you never know who's truly guilty here. You won't hear the Sect mentioned except by the new arrivals. And they soon learn. John has glinty little eyes like chinks in a wall, and a talent to hone in on weakness, which gives weight to the rumour that he bullied three of his neighbours into a suicide pact.

We have our arguments over my papier mâché indus-try. He claims it turns his stomach to see me sitting here in my thermal vest, masticating. And sometimes he'll give me a grim look and try on his special blindfold, the one he's planning to wear for what he's now calling the Big

7

Fry-Up. But we have more in common than you might think.

– Do you support capital punishment?

That was the first question he asked me, when he came to join me in the cabin, after the previous bloke, Kogevinas, got transferred to the half-way facility on Gibraltar. Not Hi, John's the name, or So gimme five, mate, or anything normal. It threw me.

– Capital punishment, no, I told him.

– Torture, then? he goes.

Now he had me there. You see, I'd been thinking in some detail about this issue, and I'd decided that some people deserved to be tortured, psychologically, for their crimes. An eye for an eye, a psyche for a psyche. Plus a little physical discomfort doesn't go amiss. I was thinking of my own personal torturer, Wesley Pike, of course, and the ways I'd like to fuck with his head and cause him grief if I got the chance. Call me childish, but what I'd do is I'd shut him in a glass box, stopper his larynx, make him wear special confusing glasses, and stuff bat-shit up his nostrils. I'd make him drink salted lemonade from a baby's bottle. I'd smear him with chilli-oil and jeer at his dick. When you're cooped in a cabin, you find yourself having thoughts like that. Quite normal. So when John asked me for my views on torture, I found myself hesitating.

– I said torture, he goes. You oppose capital punishment. We've established that. But are you in favour of torture?

– Under certain circumstances, I confessed, I have to admit I am.

He thumped me on the back, then, hard. I was frightened for a moment, given his reputation as a man specialising in unprovoked violence, but it turned out the gesture was friendly.

– Correct answer, he said.

8

Torture became an issue we returned to often, after that. It was the nearest we had to common ground. He was an expert on the physical side of it. I favoured discussing the psychological. We'd talk for hours, sometimes, playing the game first developed in a children's playground, sometime in the fifteenth century probably, the game called *Which Would You Prefer?*

This is how it goes.

– Which would you prefer, I'd ask, for example, standing in a vat of rancid margarine watching all the forcies who ever nicked you making love to your ex-wife – *and her enjoying it*, or having to listen on headphones to two hundred hours of *Così fan tutte* played backwards at ninety decibels and at the wrong speed?

– Watching the wife, John might decide, and hoping she'd shag herself to death. And which would *you* prefer, being boiled alive, or being forced to eat nothing but your own excrement until you died of salmonella?

– Boiled alive, I'd say. Quicker. Which would *you* prefer, seeing your favourite weathercaster skewered through the liver, or –

You get the picture.

– D'you reckon they put *us* together as a form of torture then, mate? John said after lunch, as I sat down to work. Because you sure as fuck drive me round the twist. Prisoner 1-0-0-8-7, guaranteed to have you howling at the moon within twenty-four hours or your money back. That Malt Fucking Fishook.

You shouldn't have applied for a transfer, then, dung for brains, I thought, but I didn't say anything. I can't, when my mouth's full.

Then he changed tack.

You'll be sorry when I'm gone.

He was smoothing out his blindfold. He's embroidering plastic pearls and little glittery sequins on it – an elaborate task for such a hulk, about as unlikely as a walrus filling vol-au-vent cases.

– Believe me, he went, charred remains are no substitute for the live version.

Miss him? You must be joking. He tried on the blindfold, and the sequins winked at me.

– See no evil, he said.

I kept on chewing. Fifty-five, fifty-six, fifty-seven.

Speak no evil, I thought, chewing.

Fifty-eight, fifty-nine, sixty.

Spit.

And plop, into the bucket.

Atlantica, Atlantica.

Some dark chronological force has dictated that today, twenty-four hours after Fishook's bombshell, should be John's birthday. My cell-mate is fifty. Looks sixty. Acts eight.

There's a rattle at the door as Garcia unlocks.

– Here arrive you mail, he announces, and flings it on the floor. The metal door slams behind him with its usual *ku-klung*, followed a second later by the reverberative *du-dunnnggg*. John manoeuvres his weight off the upper bunk to pounce on the mail – a few letters and a parcel – but I don't move from my leprechaun position on the bunk, next to the pulp vat, because the bottom line is that I never get letters.

– A letter for you, goes John.

A second bombshell: it hits me like a punch.

I gulp, and accidentally swallow a mouthful of paper pulp, which feels and tastes much as you'd expect – sawdust, metal, printer's ink, I needn't elaborate.

– How d'you know? I ask through the aftertaste.

John can't read.

– The number on it. It's your number. I know numbers.

– Hand it here, I say, willing my hand not to shake.

John's podgy face changes shape, like malicious putty.

– What do we say when we want something?

He can be a scary bastard.

– Please, Mr Henderson. He hands it and I grab, swoop my eyes across.

It's a cream envelope. My name, number and address are in large handwriting that loops and clambers to the right-hand edge of the rectangle. Writing with no discipline, like someone learning or re-learning how to do it by hand. Bright-red biro, and more flabbergasting to me than blood.

Fortunately, John's too busy with his own mail to bother with mine. He's a family man, so he has greetings from his mum and his ex, though not his kids. The mum's card has a chip in it that plays Happy Birthday To You. We listen to that a few times, and I read him the messages in the cards. There's a gift, too; his step-nephew, Jacko, has sent him a parcel tied up with coarse yellow string. The stamps – exotic flowers – are Namibian. Jacko's a satellite engineer, so he travels the entire globe.

– Go on then, I say to John, buying time to recover from the shock. Birthday boy. If there's a catch in my voice he doesn't notice.

– Still don't know why he does it, says John, scrutinising the package.

I can't fathom it either. The gifts started arriving last month, out of the blue. Generous, considering John's never even met this sister's ex's half-brother's son by marriage or whatever he is. Didn't even know he existed.

– Maybe if you're a satellite engineer, saying: My Uncle the serial killer on the floating international penitentiary makes you look the big cheese, I tell him.

– Jealous?

– Slightly, I admit.

And it's true.

When John opens the parcel, something blocky and beige

11

falls out and bounces on the floor. It looks like a loaf of home-made bread – irregular, with seeds and chaff in it. I pick it up, weigh it in my hand. To my surprise, it's as light as polystyrene. It smells spicy. Organic. Like compost. I pass it to John, who puts it to his fleshy nose and snuffles at it like a professional truffle-pig. Boggles me, mate, goes the look on his face.

– Read me the postcard, then, he orders, like he's a prince with a personal slave rather than an illiterate moron.

Happy Birthday, Uncle John, I read. *Some genuine rhino shit for you. A souvenir from the savannah. Hope to meet you sometime! Regards, Jacko.*

John chuckles.

– I like him, that Jacko.

– The fairy step-nephew. You're his charity case, I tell him.

– I reckon he's the success of the family.

And he puts the dried turd on the bedside table along with his cards, gently, like a monarch's crown razzled with sapphires.

– Now you, mate, he goes. How long's it been?

– As long as a piece of string, I tell him, inspecting my letter, trying to sound cool as a cucumber but all choked up just feeling the envelope, because despite my best efforts to banish her, my first thought's been of a certain woman, and my heart's going *thunk* like someone's aimed a sledgehammer at it and swung. Memory's a forceful thing, I'm right to avoid it.

The envelope's so light it could be empty.

Harvey Kidd, Voyager no. 10087, Cabin B 52, Prison Ship Sea Hero.

My insides are in freefall. You don't wait for eleven months and twenty-three days to hear from the outside world, and then get a pleasant surprise, do you. The decision's so simple it makes itself.

– I'm not opening it, I tell John.

He laughs.

– What, never?

– Probably, I say, standing back from the idea and approving. I'd say, *probably* never.

– The ostrich position again, goes John, spitting on his palm and smoothing his hair down in the mirror.

– It's a good position, I tell him. I'm comfortable in it.

Red biro. And whoever wrote it isn't used to addressing envelopes. I can't work it out. An Atlantican stamp, post-marked Central Post Office, Harbourville. No clues there, except that it's home – and also, suddenly, the place we're headed. Somehow, I don't like either element of this combination.

– Best to leave it, I go. No news is –

I stopped. That choking thing again. My heart felt dangerous, like I had a pacemaker and it'd been put on a setting that was too fast and fibrillous for a human. I could see John's bulbous face in the mirror. He was looking at me sideways, like he does when he's wondering whether to buzz the crisis button. But he won't, I thought, not after last time, when we had an ethical disagreement about chastity belts, and he ended up in solitary for false-alarming. So I just stuffed some of his Namibian wrapping paper in my mouth and began chewing.

Chew, chew, chew. Chomp, chomp, chomp. Chew, chew, chew. Et cetera.

– You know what that is, goes John, straightening himself up in front of the mirror, and indicating my papier mâché pulp with a jerk of his head. That cud of yours. That spitting habit. It's what teenage girls do, isn't it. Bulimia.

And he opened his birthday card again, to make the chip play the tune.

That night, as we passed the Straits of Kattegat, I propped my unopened letter on the shelf alongside my Garry Kasparov autobiography, the forget-me-not condolence card, my papier mâché chess-pieces, and John's bric-à-brac, which included the dried sea-horse from the Philippines, the plastic figurine of an Atlantican terrier whose collar bore the message: GIVE A DOG A BONE, and the mass-produced Egyptian papyrus covered in phoney hieroglyphics. Jacko the mysterious step-nephew again.

The boy needs shooting.

Then came the first nightmare, which did its usual thing: starting as an innocent dream and then turning nasty.

I'm the Bird of Liberty, and I'm flying over the ocean, with the rest of my family following silently in my wake in V formation. I guess they're Birds of Liberty too – in fact I get the feeling we're a smallish flock returning home after a trip away.

Suddenly, there it is. Down below, look. The familiar fried-egg outline of Atlantica, cushioned on the sea, its lush flatlands and lace-frilled shores exhaling a purplish haze of mist. You can picture the seabed below, where the artificial land has been grafted like a tooth in a jawbone, the waste craters like blood vessels feeding the porous rock, mingling fathoms deep with minerals, calcium and hot brine. Feeling the organic genius of it, I feel a nudge of pride, a nudge that turns into a loud yell.

– Home sweet home! I cry out.

And my voice rings happy through the clear blue sky.

From up here the geography of Atlantica is scaled down to toytown, a 3D map. Hovering high, you can see Groke to the north, Mohawk to the south, St Placid to the east, all ringed by farmland – pineapple fields, guava orchards, the bright red hoo-ha of tulips. And spread below, the leisure centres, schools, malls, golf courses, and retail parcs of Harbourville itself. As we swoop down, spiralling lower over the capital, the yellow-grey skyscrapers leap out at us

14

like pop-ups, unpacking their mazes of detail, crowding us
with the machine hum of the twenty-four-hour city. I love its
thrill, I love its energy, I love its hope.

We've landed now, on a sea-less beach – a flat vista of
sand, peppered with small boulders and clotty hanks of
bladder wrack. Here, a big bonanza of a picnic spreads
out before us: chive-and-onion kettle crisps, whole lobsters,
processed-cheese triangles, lychees, choc-o-hoops, devilled
peacock eggs. What you might call The Works.

My mother Gloria sports a sparkly evening dress of turquoise chiffon, protected by a homely kitchen apron – for
thrills and spills, she says. She's busy doling out home-made
granary baps with a large pair of surgical pincers. Us kids
first, then Dad and Uncle Sid. The next part's blurry (there's
a live crab in it, and a five-piece chamber orchestra) then
abracadabra, somehow I've collected a mass of driftwood
for an al fresco fire, where my big sis is char-grilling some
freshly caught mackerel thrust upon her by a local fisherman
struck dumb by the sight of her fantastic naked breasts. Lola
always goes topless, so she often gets perks like this. We've got
used to it as a family. Sometimes you can stop a dream in its
tracks, but this one kept rolling on, filling me with its bliss.

We're on to business matters. I do the talking, as usual,
fast and furious, while they listen. I've got a proposition
for Uncle Sid, I'm saying. His assets are out of kilter. We'll
have to sell a consignment of Chinese water pistols and other
novelty toys to Lola's comfort-ranch empire, via a subsidiary
of one of Dad's loan schemes, so as to set off a chain
reaction in Cameron's leisure-and-armaments-related stock,
knocking up the value of Mum's petrol shares. And bingo,
the water-melon transaction we began back in March will
come full-circle. The bottom line, I tell them, is a humungous
profit for the family business.

They don't get it, of course. They're not so quick on the
uptake finance-wise, which is why I'm managing our affairs in

the first place. But they all cheer happily at the news, even my brother Cameron. And the smile Mum gives me says it all.

I, Harvey, am her favourite child. Ah, the happy chords she twangs in me, my mum! She takes a strawberry from her basket and pops it in my mouth. I catch sight of Dad and Uncle Sid exchanging a look – I've wowed them with my business smarts again, hooray – and my heart bangs with pride.

But when Cameron bares his perfect orthodontics to bite the fruit Mum hands him, I feel a horrible stab of jealousy at the thought that his strawberry might be bigger than mine. And watching the fruit's sweet juice trickle across Lola's breasts, I feel the usual surge of desire mingled with shame.

Slowly, depressingly, my strawberry turns sour. I taste paper, glue, and bitter ink. Above us, the sky blackens and dies.

Still chewing, I wake on the *Sea Hero*, bereft again. *Atlantica, Atlantica.*

Outside through the porthole the sea is grey and flat as a strip of sheet metal, the sky a greenish wash, the horizon a menace now I know what's lurking beyond it. John's been having nightmares too. That's no surprise. He's woken three times and yelled and farted, then gone back to sleep. We're both raddled and jagged and raw.

We've been lying there in silence for a while, thinking our morning thoughts, which are always the worst ones of the day, because they're tangled in the freedom of sleep.

– Tell me how you did your fraud then, he goes. His voice is small and lonely like a kid's.

I play along sometimes to soothe him. But today we both need it.

– There's worm-holes in the system, just like in the galaxy, I tell him. (If I shut my eyes, I can remember the joy of it

16

and forget what it led to. Remember the dream part, not the nightmare.) Wriggle through one, and you're in a different dimension. The Fiddling Zone. There's only two occupational hazards, I tell him: arrest and repetitive strain injury. Every five or six moves, you slice a piece off someone else's salami and add a zero to your personal equation. It's one of the oldest scams in the book. But you need to be the dedicated type.

– Wouldn't suit me, then, murmurs John, lumping over on the bunk.

– No. But it suited me, I said. Ricocheting money back and forth. Shimmying to and fro over the International Date Line. I got very good at the pan-hemispheric transactions, I told him.

– What are they when they're at home?

– They're robbing Peter to pay Paolo. Then borrowing from Paolo to pay Hans, and ripping off Hans to satisfy Marie. Plundering Marie's savings to fob off Josef, who owes Gretchen, who owes Randy, who in turn owes Peter. You can start with next to nothing. One bloke I heard of, he was actually a million in debt. By the end of the year, he'd whipped up a fortune, bought a fish farm near St Placid, and married a gas heiress. True story.

John grunts; he can't help being impressed. These *violenti* don't know their arse from their elbow when it comes to fraud.

– But how d'you get going, like?

– I had a thousand. It's doodly squat, but it was enough to buy my dad a car.

– A *car*?

– Yup. A car. The whole thing began with a humble Mitsubishi Supremo. It didn't really exist as such, but there's people on line'll sell you anything. I didn't want the car, see. I just wanted the electronic paperwork.

– Uh.

– So I used the *A-Z* and picked a street, then staged this fake accident, a big smash-up, with the car a write-off. Noted the time and place and then electronically weasled into the local copshop's computer and dumped in the details. I got my dad to claim the insurance, which was double what I'd paid for the car documents.

I felt proud, remembering it. I was a bright kid. From John's silence you could tell he was impressed.

– Then I made Mum decide that my brother needed a brace because his teeth were wonky. It was the most complicated and expensive kind of brace that existed on the market, it was state of the art, at the time, with rubber bands and copper spring-work and pressure-pads and implants. Anyway, I whipped together this huge orthodontist's bill, and got Mum to claim it off the Social Office. That was in the days before Libertycare. I think Wickham was the President, at the time. Or maybe even Malone. So then I had Mum set up her own import-export company. And then Dad too. That's when we started trading in earnest. You can shunt their money about and add to it, see.

John began to snore.

I feel nostalgic every time I think about the life I once led. It was good. It was solitary, but there was glamour to it, big-time. It was a game, a drug. There was a gambling element, but mostly it was skill – technical skill, that paid off, if you kept your eye on the ball, stayed up to date with the anti-fraud technology. By the time I was nicked, my family members owned six off-shore companies, each with its own bogus board of directors – concoctions, the lot of them, names fished from the phone book. No one checks.

I miss my family. How I wish I could talk about them – I mean really talk!

I'm always careful, when I mention them, not tell John their names. Careful not to say anything that might raise an alarm, and link them to what's happened on Atlantica.

18

Careful to give no hint of what I led them into. While he's snoring up there, I'll let you into a secret.

I grew up an orphan.

An orphan, with a family?

It happens.

By the time I was a teenager, my parents, uncle and siblings were as natural to me as . . . as . . . as . . . *yoghurt*. We all have ways of coping, don't we.

The Hogg family was mine.

It was my mum who arrived first.

She made her debut when I was nine, but I have a hunch that she'd always been there, waiting in the wings, for when I needed her. I'm sure it's a common fantasy among orphans – just as children from normal families often dream they are adopted. I'd never had a dad, see, and my real mother drank bleach when I was three. I have no memory of her. I was living in Harbourville Junior Welcome Centre – my third institution – at the time it all started. And as usual, the bullies were after me. I'd always been the kind of kid other kids picked on; perhaps my experiences, the ones I have no memory of, turned me inward. But I wasn't consciously unhappy, and I did have friendships, of a kind. You're never alone with a computer, are you. I was the one who'd spend a whole day getting to grips with a piece of software, or circumventing a tricksy firewall – the kind of idle, voyeuristic hacking that ends up giving you an education. (It was back then, as I scrutinised the electronic paperwork of some of the world's leading companies, that I realised how easy it is to conjure up cash out of nowhere.) Yes, I had brains but – well, probably no charm. And certainly no social skills of value in a Junior Welcome Centre, where the kids with clout smoked heroin and made their own bombs. Next to that, my bubblegum skills looked like a joke. In the first home, in Groke, they said I smelt of fish. In the second, in north Mohawk, they started a rumour that I had an extra arsehole hidden in my armpit. Here, in Harbourville, the largest children's facility on the island, they said I was infected. But it was one boy, Craig Devon, who made my life a misery. If I was at the bottom of the food chain, he was right at the top. He boasted that he'd amassed enough explosives to smithereen the whole centre by blowing it sky-high.

– Know why you've never been adopted, Harvey Kidd? he'd go.

Innocent grown-ups loved him because his face was angelic, rimmed with bubble-curls. He had actually done advertisements for soap, and had his own bank account, and he's now a famous TV commentator. His nose was thrust right up to mine, now; the rest of the gang stood a little way back, mocking me with the usual taunts.

– Yo, Harvey Kidd, the human virus!

– Zap him with germ-spray!

– Quarantine alert, amigos!

I always dreaded the early evenings, when the computer room was locked for the night and we kids ran loose before tea and bed. What I'd do is, I'd keep a low profile, wait till Craig and his gang were occupied with their bomb-making experiments, and sneak off to look for squirmy water creatures in the biology pond. I liked looking at the tadpoles best; over the course of the year I'd watch them hatching from their blobby eggs, and swimming about until they grew dwarf legs and abracadabra'd into tiny orange frogs. I'd been safe from Craig and his gang here in the past. Not any more, though – because suddenly here they were, massing up on me, ringing the pond.

– Ever wondered why you've never even been with a foster family? goes Craig, smiling.

My mouth twitches feebly and I fiddle with the small stick I've been using to poke in the reeds.

– Know why nobody wants you in their home?

That's his sidekick, Charlie Lockhart. His claim to fame is that he's blown off the end of his thumb. I look away.

– It's because of your social infection, goes Craig.

I don't know what a social infection is. They're always on about this. I ran a search for it once, but no joy.

– I haven't done anything, I go.

– You don't have to DO anything, to be infected, goes Craig Devon, pretending to be patient, like he's talking to someone thick. You just ARE.

I stood very still. I watched the air breathe itself on Craig's bubble-curls, waft them round his pretty face.

– You need a disinfectant purge, he goes. Like a douche. Do you know what a douche is?

The boys behind him giggled and snorted.

– No. I don't bloody fucking well know what a douche is.

– Voyage of discovery coming up!

They laughed at that too.

– The question is this, goes Craig, pretending to look thoughtful. Will the subject to be disinfected go into the fluid willingly, or will force be needed?

He was quite clever. They admired his way with words.

The pond was small, but deepish, and throttled with chickweed. The water in it black, stinking of rotten stalks. I took a deep breath and closed my eyes tight, till green cracked shapes danced around.

– Well? goes Craig.

I fell in slow motion, and with an extravagant bathroom splash that I heard from under the chilly filth.

I can't remember much after that, except seeing tiny strings of bubbles fizzle from my mouth and wondering if it was the end. But the black water shocked my heart into a frantic pumping and when I got my face out and my breath back I was gulping whole mouthfuls. I pulled my torso out and looked about me. I saw the boys running off, the fluorescent soles of their trainers winking green.

A few minutes later, there was a small explosion from the direction of the Sports Hut. The boys had moved on.

I don't know how long I lay there, but I know I felt her before I saw her. My memory of it is, simply, that a feeling began to sluice over me, calming my shivers and coating me in warmth. So that I knew when I looked up, I'd see something good.

And I did. So good, I had to keep blinking to stop it draining away.

She never looked so extraordinary as that moment when I first laid eyes on her. She was always beautiful, but her beauty sort of fizzed at that moment, like a soluble aspirin. I remember her clothes, because they were biology-pond clothes – salamander clothes, to be precise. A tight-fitting green dress with the exact markings of a salamander. Anyone else might have mistaken her for a hallucination but I knew exactly who she was even before she spoke.

– Don't worry, Harvey, she said gently, in that beautiful caring voice that I will always love until I die. It's me. I'm here.

– Mum! I breathed, choking on it. My mum was here, at last! And a huge weight lifted from my chest.

Bear with me. Psychology's involved.

This miraculous, beautiful, fizzing mother in the salamander dress – more real than the real-life unremembered one ever was, I assure you – had wrapped me up in love. It was weird; she was sort of internal and external at the same time – a bit like God, I guess, or a good marketing message.

– This is what you do, she said. You're to go straight to the matron. Now.

I was going to object, but she held up a hand to stop me. Her nails were painted a delicate peach. As we walked back towards the low red-brick building that was home, Mum told me I had a dad who'd duff Craig up, if he tried to threaten me again. And she let me know – quite how I'm not exactly sure, the memory's hazy – that Dad was as strong as a tanker, and tough like cowboys in old movies. She also told me that

Dad's elder brother, Uncle Sid, was rooting for me too. So by the time I reached Mrs Lardy's office, I was feeling quite euphoric about my new situation. I knocked hard on the door, high up, where a grown-up's hand would knock, then strode in and sat down on the big chair in front of her desk. Mrs Lardy couldn't hide her surprise at seeing a kid sitting there, dripping on to the floor.

– What are you doing here? Is that – she's peering at my collar – is that *Spirogyra*?

– I've come to complain, I go. The charter of this facility states clearly that it's your job to look after the children in your care, and I'm afraid you are failing in your duty.

Her eyes widened as I carried on. Weird, but I don't quite know, to this day, where the grown-up words were coming from. It was true, I'd studied the charter the same way I'll study any piece of paperwork, I guess. But quoting it at her like that – well, she must have thought I'd aged ten years in ten minutes. I knew better, of course, than to tell Mrs Lardy about my mother (who had dissolved for now, but was, I knew, on standby), but I told her the rest of the story, in a way I never could've done before.

– So I want something done, I said after I'd done this long spiel about the charter. Meanwhile I shall be sending an e-mail to the local authority about the standards of care in this institution.

She was pretty gobsmacked, I can tell you. But I think she was pleased too, because when I'd finished, she smiled, and said she thought I'd turned a corner.

Mum was as good as her word about Dad and Uncle Sid. They came to me that evening in the dormitory.

– I'm on your side, son, whispered Dad. And I always will be. Remember that.

– You're our special boy, said Sid. Craig won't lift a finger against you again.

And the funny thing was, he didn't. The moment my family

23

stepped out of the wings, I became immune to bullying. Nothing touched me. Nobody could hurt me. It was like I carried a bubble of safety around me. Craig got on with his career in commercials. He didn't pick on me any more. He ignored me. No, more than that: he avoided me, like he was scared to come close.

It was the vibes.

It was only years later, when I got hauled into Head Office, that I actually had to go into the psychological mechanics of it – which were simple enough. How could any child grow up in a children's home and not know that something big was missing? How could you avoid it, when you saw mums and dads with their shrieking kids in the open air, getting tangled in a kite and swearing, fighting over the last peanut-butter sandwich, or chucking a stick for a drooly Labrador? I knew happiness when I saw it. It didn't all happen at once. It was organic, my family tree.

It grew from that one magic acorn of shock.

My older sister and younger brother first appeared about a year after I'd met Mum, Dad and Uncle Sid. I must've felt pretty much adored by the grown-ups in the family to risk introducing other kids who were a potential threat – but overall, it panned out pretty well, once I'd learned to keep my brother in his place.

The money side of things evolved organically too.

It was a labour of love deciding what they'd all look like and then doing the biz with my photomontage graphics package. For Mum, I first scanned in Mrs Lardy, and morphed her with a very skinny nurse from a TV soap, then superimposed the Tragic Princess. Somehow, through some further nifty palette-mixing, I ended up with a face that was pretty close to that of the ravishing salamander-woman I'd first seen by the biology pond after Craig Devon had administered his 'purge'. Although I should really have called her Gloria, her official Christian name, to me she was just 'Mum'. Dad was called

Rick, and he was a combination of St Francis of Assisi, from an oil painting I downloaded from my Medieval Art CD, and a footballer I cut out from the back of a cornflakes packet, and scanned in. Uncle Sid was much older than Dad, more like a grandfather really, and I generated his picture from the policeman on the Say No To Drugs campaign. I swapped the left and right-hand sides of his face around, and relocated his eyes to make them friendlier. Then just added a moustache, took away the uniform, gave him a pumping-iron sort of body – too young for his age, really – and stuck a big scar on one cheek.

My sister Lola had freckles and pigtails and all the usual big-sister stuff. I scanned her in from the 'after' picture in an advertisement for spot cream, and superimposed a girl from a centrefold. I left the breasts in, so I guess from the start there was a hint of incest. Although I'd reckoned I always wanted a brother, once I had Cameron up and running, I never quite warmed to him, and often thought about killing him off altogether. He had a nerdy, I-haven't-got-any-friends sort of face. The basis was a kid in one of Mrs Lardy's ancient knitting patterns, but I morphed it with three separate baseball players. I made him smaller and skinnier than me, and then gave him crooked teeth, because even then I was jealous of him. Sibling rivalry. It's pretty much normal, I think.

It was plain sailing after that. It's easy enough to convince a set of machines that somebody exists. You trawl through old newspapers to get hold of dead people, resurrect their identities, generate their birth certificates by back-dooring into the Statistics Office, kick-start the automatic posting system, change their names by deed poll, generate a new set of paperwork, and Bob's your uncle.

Or in my case, Sid.

Once I'd established their identities on-line, we were in business.

*   *   *

– Which would you prefer, begins John after breakfast.

We're back in the cabin. Him sewing, me chewing A4 sheets torn from the criminal dossiers by the bed.

– Being stripped naked by Captain Fishook, who barbecues your goolies over red-hot charcoal pellets, or a JCB comes along and lifts you up on its arm thing and hangs you upside-down in a bath of piranha fish that gobble up your eyes and leave like, just the hollow sockets?

– Goolies and pellets, probably, I sigh. But actually, mate, I'm not really in the mood.

– Atlantica, he goes. He's embroidering again. – Liberty Day, he breathes. Harbourville.

He knows how just the sound of things can knot up my intestines.

– And other stuff, I say. His Final Adjustment, is what I mean. – So can we just not talk, for a change? Can we just shut the fuck up?

He doesn't like this. His voice changes to wheedling, but there's menace behind it.

– C'mon, kiddie. Let's have a conversation. Or a story. I don't mind which.

He's looking at me steadily. Sometimes I think he might kill me one day, just for something to do. He's stood up now, his belly jostling about under his T-shirt. He smiles and I look at bad gums and the botched dentistry of his teeth.

– Question One, he says. (He's pretending to be a teacher, which I guess appeals to him.) – When are you going to open your letter?

– I'm not.

– Question Two. Why?

I'm scared to, is the truth. I look away, chew some more paper. But he won't let go.

– Question Three. Who d'you reckon it's from, then?

– Dunno.

I don't want to know, either. The letter, the news about

26

Atlantica, the words *Final Adjustment* . . . Head in the sand. But John's persistent. It's boredom does it.

– Question Three. Might it be from the wife?

It takes me several chews to remember that I was once married. That's how distant my life on Atlantica seems now.

– If you're talking about Gwynneth, I go, after I've spat, she's not my wife, she's my ex. And apart from some stuff she wrote on a form once, I don't think I ever saw her handwriting.

It was true. Who uses handwriting, nowadays?

– Question Four. Your daughter, then?

– Tiffany? He must be joking – If it weren't for her – I begin.

Then stop. Why do I let him do this? I reach for a sheet of paper and crunch it into a ball.

– I've heard that she's the one . . .

But by then I've stuffed the paper into my mouth, and I'm back to chewing.

The best, and most honest thing I could have done, once the Hogg family had custom-built itself around me, was to stick to their company exclusively. Not get involved in any other relationships – especially ones that meant practical commitment. But I couldn't, could I? I was human. I had physical needs. I don't just mean sex, I mean the day-to-day stuff you do as a couple, like sharing a tub of popcorn at a drive-in, choosing which texture wallpaper for the utility room, microwaving something Thai.

Gwynneth seemed like another godsend, at first. In an odd sort of way she reminded me of my sister Lola. She loved to laugh, live for the moment, act on impulse. She'd drag me off to places I'd never dreamed of going on my own – clubs, rollerblade races, and live TV shows that required audience participation, where dysfunctional families slagged each other off. She was always getting tickets for this or that.

I met her in a queue.

It was at the Taxation Centre, as it was called back then, before you did everything online or by phone; I was there sorting out some family business. Gwynneth was ahead of me, but she was dithering about, grappling with the usual problems posed by Section 9(g) of the YB408 self-assessment reclaim clause. Anyway, the long and the short of it was, I helped her with it, and she asked if she could buy me a coconut milkshake to say thanks.

– Or there's a new diet drink with cinnamon? she goes. If you're not too busy?

That's when our eyes sort of met and locked. Hers were very round and wide, like Pacific Ocean shells with mother-of-pearl in. She had a nice body too. By nice, I mean it was a sensible size and shape that looked welcoming. Not madly sexy and outrageous like Lola's – just well, OK. I liked that.

One thing led to another, and in a little bistro, on our third Mexican beer, I realised how badly I wanted her to like me. Soon I found myself pouring out all sorts of stuff to her about my folks, and the computer consultation service we ran as a family concern. I was enthusing about them, like you do when you're proud of something and it's all yours. She was very impressed with the business side of it (I didn't use the word 'fraud'), and our complicated deals. It was obvious from the way I spoke that I had money. That's never a turn-off for women, is it? But I think I genuinely appealed to her too. You got the feeling she'd maybe had a hard time with men, and that I might be an experiment in something different.

– So what do you call yourself, exactly? she goes. I mean, when you're talking about your job? I mean, mine's simple, I just say beauty therapist.

I hesitated. Technically speaking, I was a criminal.

– I'm a flexecutive, I went.

That seemed to hit the spot. And it wasn't a complete lie; it's a broad church.

One thing led to another; tickets to a show, a Korean restaurant, more talking, some rather fumbling sex. It was odd, doing it in the flesh for the first time, rather than in my head. I had trouble keeping my eyes open, even though I was keen to see what was going on. I was so used to imagining things. But Gwynneth's hotness and wetness and – well, fleshiness – they really drove me wild. There were all sorts of things I hadn't expected – the grappling with clothes, the grunty panting that goes on, the tropical nature of the atmosphere you somehow build up between you, the urgency of it all, and the whoosh of release. What a fandango!

– I love this! I blurted to Gwynneth, as I exploded into her – joy of joys! – on the turquoise leather settee of the three-piece suite she called her Best Bargain.

– I love *you*!

I couldn't help it. It was my first time doing it for real. And I *did* love her. I loved everything that she brought me. I loved being normal. I even loved going shopping with her! She was a true Atlantican that way; it's in the blood. She was a choosy and discerning consumer. She knew what to buy to suit her mood, knew when to purchase, and when to window-shop. She liked theming, she liked self-assembly – or rather, she liked to buy things I could put together with an Allen key while she made us something from a sachet. It was a kind of a foreplay thing.

The trouble was, as things progressed, she wanted to meet my parents.

– And Lola and Cameron too, she goes, all pink with enthusiasm. And your Uncle Sid! They sound just brilliant! God, Harvey, you're so lucky! My parents are awful. My brother's an arrogant jerk, and I haven't spoken to my sister since she deliberately smeared taramasalata on my basque.

Well. All relationships have their sticky moments. Gwynneth

was shocked and disappointed when I finally broke the news to her about my family only existing on paper.

– And in my heart, of course, too, I added, trying to smile winningly. In my heart, they've always been very much around. I can hardly remember a time when I didn't know them.

She didn't like this one bit, though. In fact, she said, she was *shocked to the core.*

– Frankly, Harvey, she says, I'm just a bit worried that you might have a mental illness. I've never come across anyone inventing a whole family before.

– How many orphans d'you know? I snapped. Look. My real father was just some bloke with sperm, as far as I can gather. No record of him. And my real mother drank bleach when I was three. Can you blame me for craving a spot of normality?

She looked at her nails for a moment. They were impressive, because they were made of acrylic that was stuck on, and then decorated with twirly sea-horses and glitter. When she looked up, she blinked tears.

– I'm sorry, Harvey. It's just I mean, have you ever thought about seeing someone – professional?

This hurt, but strangely enough, in the end I managed to sway her. It took time, but I knew she wanted to give me a second chance. What I did was I persuaded her to come and see things for herself. Back in my apartment, I showed her my CD ROM, and all the downloaded paperwork that had accumulated over the years, and talked her through it.

– So they're a business really, I concluded. A family business.

The paperwork was my salvation, because slowly, the Hogg family's transactions, which represented real money, persuaded her to imagine a set of scales, with my financial wizardry weighed against my possible madness. The dosh won out, and I thanked my lucky stars it did. When I asked her to marry me, she said could she think about it for a while. Then one week, two days and five hours later she said yes.

I was over the moon. At last, I was going to be a normal bloke after that bad beginning I'd had. Not only did I have a girlfriend, I was going to keep her! That's what marriage is, isn't it? Having someone exclusively?

I was wrong there as it turned out.

I've wondered many times since then what Gwynneth thought about during those nine days and five hours when she was making up her mind to marry me. Was it because she was self-employed at the time, doing nail extensions, and needed someone to sort her paperwork? Was it because she wanted to get away from the boring parents, the arrogant brother, and the sister who attacked her with taramasalata? Was it because she loved me and wanted to stay with me for ever, forsaking all others?

All I know is, things seemed fine. They really did.

And then, not long after our marriage, something started to buckle and turn hopeless. Sex is always one of those dodgy things, isn't it? I'm no expert, I'll be the first to admit, but for every high, it strikes me, there seems to be a low. A sort of depression, even. Things were fine, to begin with – no, more than fine, they were crakko! We'd go at it with gusto, in that bedroom of mine with the dressing-table that had the angled mirror that, if you accidentally opened your eyes, reflected interesting parts of the anatomy as you were doing it. But then one day, soon after we'd bought the house in Gravelle Road, things went wrong. Just like that.

One minute we were at it, the next she'd wriggled off, leaving me bobbing about in thin air like a divining rod. She turned to me with this fierce and frightening light in her mother-of-pearl eyes. Angry tears glittered at their edges, then spurted to her cheeks.

– You were thinking about someone else just then, weren't you?

How do women discover these things? Telepathic surveillance? We'd been married less than a year.

I covered my poor vulnerable genitals with the nearest thing to hand – a foam-filled slipper in the shape of a lobster. We had matching pairs, twenty dollars from Dreamworld.

– No I wasn't, I go.

– Yes you were.

Impasse.

– Gwynn, I beg, pulling her back towards me with my free hand.

– It's her, isn't it? she says. You were thinking of *her*, weren't you?

– Who? I go, like I don't know.

She blushed. She didn't want to say it, she was ashamed of even thinking it, I guess.

– Her, she mutters.

We both stare at the bulgy lobster slipper. It's got these nylon feelers.

– Lola. Your sister.

– No! I say, with force.

At least it's the truth. I *haven't* been thinking of my sister.

– I swear on my life, I say. I was not!

Actually, I was thinking of my mum.

The telepathic surveillance thing must have kicked in again, at that point, because Gwynneth's look turned to disbelief, then horror. Then revulsion.

– God, Harvey, she murmurs. So it's even worse than I thought.

What could I say, except sorry?

We argued about the ethics of it for weeks after that. She went out every night, without me, on the razzle, and came home with wide, wild eyes and lemon Hooch on her breath. Sometimes, as she trundled about the kitchen liquidising tinned fruit and slamming cupboard doors, she'd call me a 'pathetic worm' and a 'sicko'. But fantasising about the female members of my family was more a question of habit than malice, I pleaded. And anyway, it wasn't as though they were there in the flesh, as true-life rivals to Gwynneth.

– Look, you know I don't have any experience of relationships! I pleaded. I've had to make it up as I go along!

But that only riled her more.

– It's them or me, she'd say when we were in bed, and turn her back on me, her smoky hair fanning on the pillow. You decide.

– It's you, I went. It's you!

– Then drop the Hogg family, she said. If you don't – *exorcise* them – then I'm leaving you. You watch. One day you'll see my bum shrinking, and it won't be Weightwatchers, it'll be me going like thattaway. Outa here. Gone.

But when you hear a threat repeated more than a few times, you realise it's going nowhere. Which was just as well, because by then Gwynneth was pregnant. I'd read in *True You* about women's hormones. It makes them weepy, having an embryo inside them. She cried when she told me. But I was thrilled. Thrilled! A family, at last!

– You want me to keep it then? she asked, snuffling into a Wet One.

What a question! When I came to put my arm round her, she sort of crumpled.

– Of course I do! I said. Of course!

I was completely baffled. Why on earth wouldn't I want a baby?

– You know I've always wanted a family, Gwynneth! I'm *longing* to be a dad!

I couldn't work out why she seemed so grateful about that.

The house in Gravelle Road was on the new estate near the site that was to become the purification zone. The road was actually going to be called Gravel Road, because the planners had put gravel on it. But they changed it to Gravelle to give it class. Another example of their imagination: it was on the junction with Tarre Street, near Pension Road. Anyway, it was a semi-detached with good feng shui, and we used the money from my family business to buy it. It was an up-and-coming area.

The property market wobbled for a while, when the Liberty Corporation was voted in, and work began on the waste crater which was going to feed directly into the porous rock on the seabed below and kick-start the economy. There were voices of dissent, I remember, but after a while you stopped hearing from the geologists and things went ahead. Once the economic success trickled down to us customers, living close to the source of Atlantica's wealth suddenly became a positive plus, real-estate-wise. It was similar to being parked near any big man-made structure – like the Taj Mahal, I guess, or an Egyptian pyramid. I'd voted for the Libertycare package myself, I should say at this point. I was personally all for it. The fewer humans to screw things up the better, in my view. Plus I had a hunch that it would be good for trade, and I wasn't wrong. The average Atlantican didn't need much convincing. We'd always been willing to give new ideas a whirl. If a free sample came through the door, we'd try it. No one was sorry to see the death of politics.

Gwynneth chose a cherry theme for the lounge, and we went for marble-effect in the kitchen, with inset halogens above the hob. I installed a power shower in the bathroom and drilled holes for hooks where she said.

The new 'hands-free' system was even better news for me, business-wise, than I'd dared to hope, because by the time Liberty was servicing Atlantica, my fraud network was practically invisible. I even began to feel that, in my own small way, I was contributing something to society. If you'd asked me to put my finger on what, exactly, I might have had trouble, but I know that as Atlantica began to thrive I felt I was playing a role in keeping the economy buzzing.

As Gwynneth had builders come in and make a couple of alcoves in the hall, so she could put little fibreglass cherubs in there, backlit, and as I ordered turf, I began to feel proud of the way Atlantica was turning its fortunes around with the purification thing. When I was a kid, the rest of the world had looked on us with scorn. To live on reclaimed land was similar, in world terms, to inhabiting a trailer park. Atlantica was one of those forgotten places before; too small for the media to bother with, too remote for tourism. We had no role to play.

No one can say that about the kidneys of the northern hemisphere, can they?

Thanks to Atlantica's unique combination of porous bedrock and porous landfill, no container would be turned away. All waste – be it industrial, organic, or nuclear – would be welcome, no questions asked. That was a pledge.

Gwynneth hesitated for a long time over the kitchen tiles, and eventually settled for a mock terracotta that was easier to maintain than real terracotta, and you couldn't tell the difference unless you were an expert, plus it was wipe-clean and low-maintenance.

Once the crater was functioning, the first thing we noticed was the climate change right on our doorstep. Gwynneth's window-boxes went ape. We planted a banana tree on either side of the patio area, and her mum gave us a bougainvillaea. There are certain water creatures that do what Atlantica does, I thought one day as I gazed across at the zone from the Osaka Snak Attak, where I sometimes went for noodles. You pass muck through them, and they decontaminate it, send it back into the atmosphere, the filth strained out. It makes you feel proud.

– You should come and visit, Gwynneth urged her cousins

in Canada. They're calling us the Hong Kong of the Atlantic. It's a shoppers' paradise!

The weeks passed. Gwynneth battled with morning sickness and gave the spare room a makeover in the acid palette that was the big thing at the time. The Canadians came, and saw, and were impressed. They left with bulging suitcases.

Soon Atlantica was dealing in human waste too. I had no objection: commerce is commerce. The floating penitentiaries thrived. Those were honeymoon times. The world brought its problems to Atlantica, and Atlantica – a geophysical miracle! A tiny artificial land-mass in the middle of bloody nowhere! – fixed them.

But if things were going well for our little island state, they were going from bad to worse for Harvey Kidd as a family man – bougainvillaea or no bougainvillaea. The friendly lull we'd had after Gwynneth told me she was pregnant didn't last. Always, as I headed back home from the Happy Eater or the Snak Attak, I knew there'd be grief waiting. As soon as I walked in the door and made for the Family Room, Gwynneth, her belly footballing bigger every day, would start up again.

She never accepted the family. And she particularly hated the surname Hogg. An ugly name, she said. And it was true. It was an accident of paperwork, I told her, I didn't choose it. When you're constructing an identity from a set of laundered birth certificates you've –

Well, it was like talking to the wall.

Some couples just rub along together, as far as I can tell. Not us. Mum, Dad, Uncle Sid, Cameron and Lola remained a big problem in our marriage, even after Tiffany was born. It emerged that one of the Canadian cousins had nosy-parked his way into my Family Room when I was out, and seen what he called my pin-ups. That hadn't helped, to have Gwynneth's prejudices confirmed by a third party.

I didn't watch the birth, because Gwynneth told me the

Customer Hotline advised not to, but I saw her minutes later. Boy, was she a funny creature. She had a grumpy face and grown-up ears, and when she grabbed on to my finger with her tiny hand with its tiny perfect nails, I fell in love. I'd never had a pet and had always wanted one but this was miles better, I could tell. I had founded a family! A real one!

– It's Daddy, I told her. Say hello to Dad!

But Gwynneth said I was talking too loud and it'd make Tiffany cry, plus she'd catch a chill, and what did I think I was doing, leaving the door open, and couldn't I see I'd give her all sorts of germs, and they say the father should keep his distance in the first year. And she shooed me away.

– Go and make money, she said. Go pow-wow with your Hoggs. You're earning for three now.

That was the beginning of it, and it didn't stop. It was Gwynneth's way of getting back at me for the Hoggs. If I was going to have my own private family members, she was going to have hers.

– You can't argue with the logic of it, she told me.

And she was right, I couldn't.

So I did what I knew how to do; I made money, and Gwynneth spent it. She dressed Tiffany in little themed outfits and changed our three-piece suite once a year. She bought novelty garlic-crushers, garden rakes, designer sweatshirts, the same kind of shoes in three different colours, travelling irons, espresso machines, teak coffee tables, opaque plastic salad bowls, self-seeding window-boxes, holidays for her and her mum and Tiffany in Ghana or Lanzarote, bathroom makeovers and exercise videos. She bought wedding presents for her friends when they got married, and sympathy lunches when they divorced, and took Tiffany to Florida for her fifth birthday, to swim with dolphins. When Tiffany was nine, they both joined the Feel Real Club and started doing parachute descents and bungee jumps and white-water rafting.

And Tiff was a crakko little kid. I'd watch her out of the window wobbling about on her big bike and feel these huge waves of love.

But me and Gwynneth, we were always dogged by the same old conflict that we dragged around behind us like a ball and chain: money versus the Hoggs. You couldn't have one without the other, as far as I was concerned. She disagreed. Like all regular arguments, ours took the form of a vicious circle.

– I just want you to get rid of that family, Gwynneth'd say.

– But it's a family business, I'd go. And what would we live on? Thin air?

Then she'd say something like – You could find a proper job. You're clever with paperwork, you can do computers and admin and whatever. You could do anything.

And I'd say – I'm not trained. I'm self-employed. I can't have a boss, it's against my nature.

And she'd say – Well if you don't, I'm leaving.

– And Tiffany? I'd go.

– I just want you to get rid of them, she'd go.

– And what would we live on? Thin air? I'd go.

– You could find a proper job, she'd go.

Etc.

It would be fair to say that I frustrated Gwynneth. When Tiffany was about ten, she persuaded me to see a stress-management consultant called Geoff, whose sister's nails she did. I'd sit there in his sissy consulting-room that stank of aromatherapy, trying to understand what Geoff called my 'demons', and listening to his suggestions. Such as, I could take Gwynneth to the Odeon once a week. Buy her flowers that came from a proper florist's. Stop trying to muscle in on her relationship with her daughter.

Geoff's stress-management consultancy didn't strike me as a particularly professional service. His bookshelves were stuffed with creepy self-improvement manuals, and he banged on zealously about a weed called St John's wort, 'for moods'.

What I couldn't get through to Geoff was the idea that there was nothing wrong with being loyal to your original family, and enjoying their company. I told him how fantastic Mum was: how well she'd always cooked, how much she loved me. I told him about Dad, and what a great, straight guy he'd been, full of sound advice to a boy growing up. About Uncle Sid, always game for a laugh. About how clever Cameron was, and how Lola had the boys falling over themselves because of her animal magnetism.

But like Gwynneth, Mr Stress seemed to have a blind spot about the whole subject.

Atlantica, Atlantica.

The next nightmare's even worse. Me, Mum, Dad, Sid, Lola and Cameron, we're at Liberty Head Office, walking down corridors and up escalators, searching for a certain woman. I have to see her again, I have things to tell her, things I couldn't say when we were together, because there wasn't time and I didn't have the words, things about how if only we could've had a shot at living a normal life, as normal as you can when you're people like us, who have trouble saying things, so much trouble that it's only in your head you can do it . . . But the words get mangled up and the corridors go on for ever and –

– Wait!

My sister Lola has stopped in her tracks. She turns to face us.

– I know where she is! she says. We've been looking in the wrong place! Hannah Park doesn't work here any more.

– So where is she? I go.

As I wake, a freezing wave slaps across my heart and I remember the pure white concrete of the crater.

*   *   *

39

– Bad night then? asks John, after Fishook has tannoyed his morning message. The Swedish music is sweeping through us like a chilly wind. – You were talking in your sleep, you were.

– I'll sleepwalk next, I warned him. Come and strangle you. I'd have indemnity. I read an article about it. You can do anything you like, if you're unconscious.

– You were saying someone's name, he goes. It sounded like Park.

– It wasn't a name then, I said quickly, busking it. It was about parking.

He looked doubtful.

– I have two types of dream, I said. Sky dreams, which are about flying through the sky with my family, and dreams about parking. Which are about parking.

That seemed to satisfy him.

Later in the day, he said – Multi-storey, or kerbside? and I said – Both.

You try to paralyse your brain with chewing, keep things on an even keel, but then something comes along, and you can't. Like now. The news of our return to Atlantica I could have handled. But on top of it John's execution, and the letter, and then a certain woman nightmaring her way back –

Well, there are limits, aren't there. So I'm helter-skeltering to Dr Pappadakis now. I'm not the first to request a visit. He's seeing Atlanticans at five-minute intervals. As Garcia opens the door to let me out I try to avoid looking at his chunky jaw, his long front teeth.

– You stay walk on red line, he says. Or I no hesitate shoot, hokay?

On the way to the surgery, Garcia follows five paces behind like a traditional Japanese wife, apart from the stun-gun. As I pass the mirror on the poop, I catch sight of a squat, balding grey man. It's always a shock seeing the colour. Like concrete. It's as if my skin's dyed from the inside. I

40

drag my eyes away, but not before noting that my face has changed shape since I last saw it. My cheeks have become so muscular they now look like the buttocks of a male ballet dancer. I shudder. Bulging spheres in grey tights. Swan Lake. My tongue is black.

– Your entire epidermis, goes the doctor, examining my skin with a magnifying glass, indicates high levels of ink in the bloodstream.

That's not what I came to see you for, I say. I want drugs.

But he's not listening, he's on his hobby-horse again. Dr Pappadakis is on sabbatical from the Papandreou Hospital in Crete, and he's done a thesis on cancer risk.

– Printer's ink, he goes, it's highly carcinogenic.

Dangerous particles have leached into my skin, where they could decide to wreak havoc at any moment, warping my cells, turning them maverick.

– I must do blood tests, he says all Mediterranean and mournful, preparing the needle.

– Must you? I don't like the sound of this. – If there's something bad, I tell him, I'd rather not know. (This approach has worked for me in the past.) – Look, I came here for some Prozac. Or could you just give me Valium? Or a few Libbies?

– You have visitors arriving, is that the problem? You are Atlantican, no?

– No. Yes. I'm Atlantican. But no visitors.

– No parents-brothers-sisters?

– Not any more, I go.

– No wife?

– We're divorced.

– Children?

Mind your own business!

– Daughter. Tiffany. Not visiting. Estranged.

– Friends?

That's when Hannah flits back. I thought I'd banned her for good.

– Drugs, I beg again. Look, it's my cell-mate John. He's going to be finally adjusted. It's kind of stressful.

Pappadakis looks up sharply.

– Your *cell-mate*? he goes, and the question hangs in the air for a moment, till I realise it's a language thing.

– Cabin-companion, I correct myself. My cabin-companion, John. He's on Death Row.

I roll up my sleeve and he finds my vein. We watch as the syringe fills with a blackish maroon. When he's finished I hold the cotton wool over the puncture. Pappadakis sighs, looks at me oddly again.

– You have thought, lately, about death?

– Quite a bit, I confess. What with John.

– John? Pappadakis looks away, then. Shuffles about with some papers, glances at the clock.

– My cell-mate. Sorry, cabin-companion.

– And you are sure – about your, er –

– Cabin-companion, I say. I have an odd feeling we're going round in circles. – No. Not sure. Just, it's likely. He's right up there on the list.

– He is dissident? Geologist? Soil physicist? Structural engineer?

– No, a serial killer, apparently.

– I see, he says, sort of edgy.

There's a bit of a silence.

– Have you seen how you look? he goes finally, fiddling with his worry beads. You were off-white when I first met you. Now you are really quite grey. Soon you will be the colour of the burnt wood for sketch-drawing and for barbecue, what you call it, of the *charcoal*, and the whites of one's eyes, what we call the conjunctiva, will turn yellow, you follow? You too are – I mean your own er, prospects, they are . . . somewhat similar, no?

42

It takes me a minute to see what he's getting at.

– Oh, sure, *technically*, yeah. But there's a quota, remember? Libertycare policy states two a year, maximum, as a deterrent.

(I've done my sums. There are a thousand Atlanticans aboard, and you can count on the dissident scientists and those accused of violent crimes, i.e. John, being top of the list.)

– I could die of old age first, I tell him. Some Libbies, OK? Just to see me through?

He sighs.

– A small amount, he says, handing me a plastic cylinder with a child-proof top. Bear in mind that since yesterday's announcement I have increased the amount of placebos that I issue. Your chances of this being genuine are therefore only one in five. Goodbye, Voyager.

And he ushers me out to the corridor, where the chipmunk-faced Garcia awaits me, gun poised.

– How d'you know you're swallowing the real thing, then, John's asking.

I've explained the placebo theory.

– You don't, that's the beauty of it. If you believe it's working, then it'll work, see?

– Like Libertycare, says John.

I look up. It's not like him to talk of home.

I'm too unsettled to sleep. Too scared of more nightmares. In the semi-dark, I eye the letter again, with its crude mosaic of red lettering. Yes; crude. Disturbing. It seems to scream at me: *Atlantica! Atlantica!*

The past spilling back like that. It's bad management. It's bad manners. It's bad for my heart. If it breaks again – if there's any disturbance – any kind of resurrection –

If –

43

I'll get lockjaw, that's what.

Who would use red biro, to address a letter? I'm not used to colour. Who would write in that stagey way, all loops and squirls?

A woman, that's who.

A marauder.

I chew over this thought, and others: dreams, fears, ghostly detritus, stray memories, and wild wishes; my mental cud; the unfinished and unfinishable business of a graunched heart.

THE FESTIVAL OF CHOICE

Hannah Park's brain was different from other people's: her mother was sure of it. It made her incapable of certain things. Love, for instance: the romantic love you see on television or read about in books; that was one of them. Social grace was another.

By the time Hannah was eleven, she'd lost track of how often she'd heard Tilda tell the specialists, in the hushed whisper reserved for embarrassing information, that her only child was unfortunately not quite right.

– But I *feel* normal, Hannah would object. Normal-*ish*, anyway.

– Is it 'normal-*ish*' to draw rude cartoons of your own mother? Tilda would snap back. Is it 'normal-*ish*' to wear a giant cardigan day in day out? Is it 'normal-*ish*' to collect thirty thousand peanut-butter labels?

The setting for these prickly discussions was usually a hospital canteen, following another fruitless consultation with a man in a white coat.

– Would I be normal if my cardigan was smaller? Hannah would ask, as she divided and sub-divided the food on her plate into the usual categories: Protein, Roughage, Carbohydrate, Things I Don't Like. Cool colours to the left of each section, warm to the right. Would I be normal if I collected stamps instead? Would I be . . .

– Those things are just symptoms, Tilda would retort,

fumbling in her little green handbag for her pills. For a clever girl, Hannah, you can be stupid beyond belief.

It was a recurring theme of Tilda's. How was it possible for a child with an IQ of 148 to prefer disfiguring glasses to contact lenses, and read encyclopaedias in the way ordinary people read mail-order catalogues? Having an abnormal child had taught her the meaning of exasperation. Oh, for a proper diagnosis! How much longer would this thankless odyssey grind on? Hannah had been wondering too. Her whole childhood was a blur of waiting rooms, interspersed with trips to the orthodontist to get her teeth fixed, in case she started smiling. If she bared her metal brace in the mirror of a darkened room, she looked like an oncoming train.

Tilda heard of Dr Crabbe by word of mouth. He was a retired psychiatrist in Groke, who had written several works on disorders which fell within the spectrum of autism.

– Come up to Groke, Dr Crabbe had urged on the phone. Let's suck it and see.

His surgery was housed in a small portable bungalow made of the new recycled cardboard, which scored marks with Tilda. As Hannah and Tilda sat in Dr Crabbe's waiting room flicking through style magazines, they could hear his voice booming through the wall. Hannah strained to listen, but couldn't make out the words.

– Well, he certainly *sounds* authoritative, remarked Tilda, not lifting her eyes from the gazebo spread in *Sweet Home*.

Hannah sighed. Her mother always built the doctors up in her mind beforehand. She stared out of the window at the big shock of pampas grass in Dr Crabbe's front garden, plonked in the centre of the lawn like a failed hairdo. Something about the way the pale tips of its feathery brushes waved in the breeze stirred up an unaccountable but familiar current of melancholy inside her. The feeling was called *Weltschmerz*, according to the psychiatrist they had seen last week.

Everyone gets it.

Hannah was just beginning to feel an asthma attack coming on when the booming stopped suddenly, the door opened, and Dr Crabbe emerged. For a retired psychiatrist, he was surprisingly young. Short and square, he had a powerful, muscular face, and a dark moustache. He reminded Hannah of a keg of explosives. She fingered the little mask attached to her oxygen inhaler.

– Mrs Park? And this must be Hannah!

He grinned and shook their hands forcefully. Hannah bared the oncoming train.

– I was just talking to my voice system, said Dr Crabbe.

Tilda made a little impressed grunt and nursed her crushed fingers.

In his office, which was decorated with bloodthirsty hunting pictures, Dr Crabbe scanned through Hannah's medical record on his little laptop, and made knowledgeable noises as he recognised names of doctors and hospitals they'd visited.

– I see she's done the rounds, Mrs Park, he said. Quite a strain for *you*.

The tears sprang to Tilda's eyes as though he'd tweaked the plumbing of a secret tap.

– How can I help? he asked gently, as Tilda dabbed at her eyes. She took a deep, careful breath.

– All I want . . . Her voice caught and Hannah looked up sharply. Dr Crabbe had talent. – All I want is for someone to –

– To take you seriously, he said, nodding slowly. And you *deserve* it, Mrs Park, he said softly.

That did it. When he patted her arm, Tilda began to sob. As she snuffled into a hanky, Hannah looked at the wall, where a bloodhound was mauling a rabbit next to a dead pheasant. Dr Crabbe said it must have been very distressing, and he couldn't promise a diagnosis but he would see what suggested itself; autism had a far wider spectrum than anyone realised. There followed the usual background questions, the testing of the

47

reflexes, the chat about feelings. How depressed did Hannah get, on a scale of one to ten? Did being the product of donor sperm make her feel stigmatised? Had she ever thought of taking her own life?

– Well, said Dr Crabbe, after Tilda had replied to all the questions at length. I have a diagnosis.

Tilda stiffened, and gripped the armrests of her chair. Even Hannah was taken aback.

– It's a very rare syndrome, he said. Known as Crabbe's Block.

– There was a tiny silence. Hannah wondered if her stomach might gurgle.

– Crabbe . . . as in, *Doctor Crabbe*? asked Tilda faintly.

Yes, he affirmed: having discovered the disease himself – only very recently – he had awarded it his own name. It was the norm in medicine.

– How many people suffer from this, then, Tilda asked him anxiously, as he wrote down the name of Hannah's disorder on a piece of paper and stapled it to the bill.

He looked up then, his face grave.

– Mrs Park, your daughter is . . . *unique*.

Tilda instantly began to glow with pride.

Life improved after that. Hannah felt less guilty about the time she spent on her peanut-butter-label collection, less self-conscious about her need to wear the cardigan, less inhibited about her habit of popping bubble-wrap blisters when she was under stress. She studied hard for her multiple choices, and did well. Tilda thrived too. She developed a plethora of small ailments which kept the diary chock-a-block with doctors' appointments. Then, when the Liberty Corporation took over the management of Atlantica, she joined a shoppers' circle, collected loyalty points, and soon climbed the ladder to become a VIP Customer.

– Meet my daughter, she would smile to new members of the shoppers' circle. She suffers from a rare syndrome.

Hannah felt like a new product that had hit the market. One with special features. She would smile slightly and show her flashing teeth.

– She's got agoraphobia now too, Tilda would add. This development was a recognised component of the syndrome, according to Dr Crabbe. – It doesn't bother her though, said Tilda. She's never liked outdoors.

And it was true. She hadn't.

Now, fifteen years later, Hannah Park sits on a swivel chair in an open-plan office sectioned with low Perspex screens and phalanxes of potted ficus plants on the nineteenth floor of Liberty Corporation's Head office, doodling a cartoon of the man who diagnosed her. She had a strange dream about Dr Crabbe last night, in which she was married to him, and had taken on the name of Mrs Hannah Crabbe. Without ever having had sex, she and Dr Crabbe had produced a baby that Hannah wheeled about the pedestrian walkways of Groke in a state-of-the-art buggy. In actual fact, according to a pink fluorescent message that gradually wrote itself across the sky, the baby belonged to another man. She must return it immediately. But she couldn't, because a chasm full of boiling water and geranium-scented oil had opened up in front of her. It split the city of Groke in half. She would never be able to cross it. Dr Crabbe knew about all this, and did not hold it against her because he was a trained psychiatrist.

As Hannah began drawing the individual hairs of Dr Crabbe's potent moustache with small experienced flicks of her pencil, the Customer Hotline droned in the background. The call she was half-listening to was from a regular, who liked to play games. Hannah recognised the customer's voice. A wheezy, smoker's voice with cracks in it. Sometimes he'd pretend someone was strangling him.

– I woke up this morning with a bad feeling, he said.

Hannah took a sip of her coffee. Warm and vile, but in a familiar way.

– And how did your problem begin? asked the Hotline responder in the female medium-register voice known as 'Dolly'. The machine used the Dolly mode mostly for men. Dolly was highly effective. From complaint to confession in five minutes flat, the Hotline co-ordinator liked to boast.

Silence.

The machine moved on to the next question.

– How about giving me a call back later, when you're more in the mood for a chat?

– Hey, sweetheart, said the customer. Don't hang up on me. I've got a problem here.

Hannah began shading Dr Crabbe's cheeks, but she pressed too hard and her pencil broke. The cross-hatching was too thick and tight, turning the doctor's complexion a smudgy black. Customer Hotline duty made her tense. She reached for a sharpener.

– Do you have a worry that you'd like to share? asked Dolly.

Silence.

– Do you suspect anyone of sociopathic or criminal activities?

Hannah took another sip of coffee, replaced the cup on the daisy coaster her mother had made in her pressed-flower phase, and began scribbling a dark background to Dr Crabbe with her newly sharpened pencil.

Monitoring Hotline calls was considered 'core work'. How better to make use of the flood of customer comments, ran corporate thinking, than to haul up all calls containing trigger-words and their variants – kill, hate, cheat, steal, blackmail, etc, and then laboriously fillet them in case one contained a diamond? It cut out the usual middlemen of paid informant and forensic evidence. It rendered hunch obsolete.

This customer, whose ex-wife Kelly had 'poisoned his

life', was one of the classic attention-seekers, sufferers of that great contemporary ailment, Social Munchhausen's Syndrome: over-zealous citizens trapped in nobodyhood who'd do anything – fake their own murders, suicides or muggings – to get noticed. There were twenty, thirty such callers per shift. More, at certain times; pre-Christmas, the Silly Season, and now, the Festival of Choice. On the door of the cabinet where data on the calls was stored, Hannah's colleague Leo Hurley had scrawled a caricature paranoiac in marker pen. Googly eyes, flared nostrils, jug ears, flying droplets of sweat.

The customer was still playing hard to get with the responder.

– Are you choosing by phone today, Dolly pursued, or will you be going to your local shopping mall? Hannah had programmed this line of questioning specially for the Festival of Choice. It wasn't a festival, so much as an electoral referendum, but it embodied the spirit of the day better, according to Strategy.

– Look, sweetheart, said the customer. This isn't easy.

– I'm listening, said Dolly. I value what you have to say.

– I'm in danger, the customer blurted. His voice shook slightly. Dolly attracted masturbators.

– Does your problem relate to the Festival of Choice? asked Dolly. Her voice had gone husky and soft. She *encouraged* masturbators.

He took another deep smoker's breath.

– I'm in danger of putting my cross –

– In the wrong box? Dolly responded, after three seconds of silence. I can help you with that. If you'd like to tell me more . . .

As the customer droned on about his phoney indecision, Hannah considered giving Dr Crabbe glasses. But like hands, they were hard to do.

– Nice talking to you, sweetheart, finished the customer finally. I feel a lot better.

– You've made the right choice, said Dolly.

A nice touch, that. Hannah had thought of it herself. As the next call kicked in, she lowered the volume and let her eyes flicker to the window. The forecast for the Festival of Choice was good. *Clear blue skies and clear blue water*, the weather channel said. From this floor the panorama was never less than stupendous. The big, shining coil of the Hope River snaking into the estuary, flanked by the Makasoki bubble-buildings, translucent egg-boxes of reflected light. Above them, dancing rainbows, condensing and dissolving like pastel sugar, pale and buffered by distance. The light they cast – a pellucid yellow – spread with a shimmer out to a glassy sea dotted with ships and tankers bringing in cargoes of waste. Even from this height, separated by fathoms of glass and chrome, you could still feel the city's electric zing like a shiver in the blood; and still subliminally hear the distant honk of ships, the sing-song whisper of the Frooto wind-mills, the smooth hydraulic whish-whish of trams. The island tattooed itself on you; a great techno-organic edifice in per-petual motion, its infrastructure jewelled with sports centres, malls, and waste facilities, its simple geography zigzagged with transport systems, and fringed with lush plantations of coconut, pineapple, and lemon grass. Beyond Harbourville, the fried-egg island lay circular and gently humped by the swell of St Giddier's Mount. Beneath the crust of the artificial land-mass, the deep invisible mechanics of the waste-disposal system, feeding the hungry rock below. And all around, the clear blue ocean – wide as the sky.

The phone rang.

– Customer Care? answered Hannah.

– It's me, said Tilda. Have you chosen yet, or aren't associ-ates allowed to?

Immediately, Hannah's thoughts contracted and she began drawing small, tight squiggles next to Dr Crabbe on her pad. It looks so unprofessional, being phoned at work by your mother. If someone came in – someone like Wesley Pike – it would be embarrassing.

– I'm just about to, said Hannah.

– I did, first thing, said Tilda. And they were round an hour later with the most gorgeous bunch of flowers – they're giving them to all their VIP Customers, to say thanks. *And* I got a box of chocolates! Tilda couldn't hide the pride in her voice. So are you coming to St Placid? Better hurry up, before I've eaten my way through them.

– Yes, sighed Hannah. While other departments worked overtime, staff in Munchhausen's had been given a half-day off. She had promised Tilda a visit.

– I'm on my way. I'll be there by lunchtime. Must go now. Got to choose.

Unlike the customers heading for the malls and parcs today, Hannah preferred to do her admin electronically. It saved time, and it saved bumping into people. She typed in her password, and the questions appeared on screen.

A. *Do you want Atlantica to continue being serviced by the Liberty Corporation for a further ten years?* There was a box you could click on.

Keeping human error out of people-management, was their Festival slogan. Actually, Hannah's memory of the time people called 'the bad old days' was pretty fuzzy. Strange, the way history had become a bit of a blur, and you needed TV documentaries to remind you how poor the island had been, how full of violence and despair, how similar to the frightening, other world you thought of simply as 'Abroad'. Strange, the way the past had just sort of stopped being a factor.

Perhaps that's what happens when you're finally in safe hands.

B. *Do you want Atlantica to slide back into the control of a potentially corrupt political system, run by ambitious but flawed men and women?* Another box.

Swiftly, she clicked A, then switched to the news, where the angel-faced commentator, Craig Devon, was talking facts and figures.

– *The latest Festival polls show the choice for Libertycare is 95 per cent in Harbourville itself, with 93 per cent of Groke also choosing yes, and Mohawk and St Placid, 97 per cent.*

He was pointing at some graphs. Craig Devon was one of Atlantica's most trusted pundits. Tilda said there used to be a boy who did soap commercials who was his spitting image. She'd like to have had a son like him.

So a resounding victory for Libertycare's customers, I think it's fair to say at this stage, said Craig Devon. *And although a Corporation spokesman stressed earlier that they're not being at all complacent, it would be a surprise to us all, I must say,* he blahed, *if the no choice were to increase by any significant . . .*

More blah. Hannah switched channels. Here they were doing vox-pops; there were *Shop 'n' Choose* promotions in the malls, with fifty extra loyalty points if you polled.

– Yes, I've been very happy with them, especially the complaints procedure . . .

– I remember what things were like before. That documentary the other night reminded me – I mean the corruption was just so rife . . .

– The way they'll send back a whole lorry-load of produce if it's sub-standard – little details like that really make you respect it as a system. We've certainly benefited as a family from some of the special offers . . .

– The thing I like is the way the rest of the world's had to really pay attention to us in recent years, and the loyalty scheme really does . . .

Hannah flicked channels again; more news. This time there was an item about the US response to the Festival of Choice, featuring a taxi driver from Michigan, called Earl. He'd been popping up on TV quite a lot recently, as the leader of a new campaign to get the Libertycare system servicing the United States. The clip showed a man in his fifties, in a blood-red shirt and checked golfing pants.

– OK, so call me a mug, said Earl. His supporters jostled around him, grinning and waving banners. – Or correct me if I'm missing something important. The camera panned in on Earl's earnestly perspiring face. – But it isn't communism we're talking about here. It's *cap*italism. And I *like* what I see over there on that island. And I'm thinking, heck, that could be us! We don't want another asshole President! We don't need all that human error bullshit! There were cheers.

Hannah switched off.

She had heard about this Earl character before, in-house. Leo Hurley reckoned he was a Libertycare initiative, an ambient plant, disguised as a grass-roots punter. But Hannah was less sure. A hypermarket model of people management was fine for parcs, complexes, penitentiaries and small territories like Atlantica. But containability had always been at the heart of its success. There was no way you could apply the same software system to a superpower.

– So who d'you think's behind Earl, then? Leo had asked her.

He'd been behaving oddly lately – jaded. He'd better watch it, Hannah thought. Personnel will pick it up on his next need-profile.

– No one, said Hannah. He's an ordinary American. He's seen us on TV, like everyone else on the planet. People are beginning to see the results. They're impressed, that's all.

Leo's problem was cynicism.

As the tram slid out of Harbourville, the nerviness Hannah had been experiencing since her first glimpse of ground level became shot through with pure panic. It was six months since she'd left Head Office. It gave her a shuddery sense of inverse vertigo to be this low down, a stab of danger, as though the ground might chasm on you, suck you in: whoop, gone. Flushed down, like waste. A gaggle of elderly people at the front of the tram were chattering excitedly and waving scuba equipment. Members of the Harbourville Over-Sixties' Feel Real Club, according to their sweatshirts. Hannah's mother had toyed with the Feel Real Club, but decided her health wouldn't allow it. She approved, though. It showed that you didn't have to go to Florida, she said, to live high on the hog.

Hannah stared out at the flat farmlands. This was pineapple country, the fruit growing in spiky rows. When the tram passed an ostrich farm, a whole flock of flouncy-bummed birds scattered in panic on muscular legs. Their brains were smaller than a chicken's. The nerviness wouldn't flatten itself. Hoping for a distraction, she opened her laptop and trawled through the transcripts of a few more Munchie calls. There was a woman accusing her step-daughter of stealing her artificial nail kit. How had that got through? A man whose twin brother refused to enter into a timeshare, threatening fratricide. A crater worker complaining of skin eruptions and balance problems: Hannah marked it for referral. There had been a lot of those lately.

Mass hysteria again, like the geologists.

As the tram slowed, and the pineapple fields gave way to okra and lemon grass, the agoraphobia inched upwards, constricting her lungs and throat. She clasped her mask and applied it to her face.

– All right there, love? asked the tanned, dapper gent sitting next to her. He was clutching a wheeled caddy filled with golfing clubs.

Hannah nodded through the translucent mask that covered her nose and mouth. Breathed rhythmically. If she stayed that way, she wouldn't have to talk to him.

– I chose this morning, first thing, he said eagerly. Cos I want to make sure they finish that golf course, I do! The thing that puzzles me is (he leaned closer to her, conspiratorially, and looked at her with bright eager eyes set deep in his tanned face) who are they, these people?

Hannah looked blank. What was he on about? What people? She tried to convey her question with an eye-movement above the mask.

– Who are they? he repeated. Who are this five per cent lot? The ones choosing B and not A?

She'd wondered herself, in an idle way, but knew she'd find out soon enough: Munchhausen's would be processing their questionnaires, afterwards. They'd probably turn out to be the usual suspects the 'difficult customers' classed as Marginals. You can't have winners without losers.

– Mystery, said the man, more to himself than to Hannah, and sighed. One of the seven wonders of the world.

He got off at the next stop, his clubs chinking.

Hannah took off her mask, yawned, and peered out of the window again. She could smell the lavender of St Placid.

– Much have I travell'd in the realms of gold, she murmured, echoing Wesley Pike.

Her boss liked to quote poetry. Outside she could see pylons, and the air-crystals glittered mauve.

Tilda was smaller than Hannah remembered. Hannah spotted her through the window, on the platform, scanning the carriages. Her tilted face was the narrow, questioning shape of a papaya.

– Hello, Ma, said Hannah, stepping out into muggy warm-ish air.

An awkward moment followed: Hannah bent to kiss Tilda's papery, powdered cheek but somehow bungled it because of the crush around them and it turned into a fumbling embrace which they both shrank from.

– I came under my own steam, said Tilda, taking a step back and smoothing her mauve shell-suit. She nodded in

57

the direction of an electric buggy parked on the kerbside, its disabled sticker prominently displayed.

– How are you health-wise? asked Hannah dutifully.

– Well, the laparoscopic investigations continue, sighed Tilda. We're coming up to the tenth anniversary of the start of that. I've got more keyhole surgery booked for March, but in the meantime the doctor who deals with my connective-tissue question is taking long leave. And d'you remember that polyp I told you about?

It was after Hannah was diagnosed with Crabbe's Block that Tilda's health problems came into their own. Internal organs, usually. Nothing visible. It was only when Hannah was head-hunted into Head Office's Munchhausen's Department that she realised her own mother counted as a classic seeker of attention. Munchhausen's by Proxy, to begin with. Then the real thing. The Liberty Corporation, it dawned on Hannah, had known about her Munchie mother from the start. That's why they'd recruited her.

She wasn't offended. She was pleased to have been spirited away from home like that. Pleased to have been given a role.

As Tilda continued the story of her latest medical adventures – the scheduling of appointments seemed to be a key feature – Hannah looked round at the neat fuchsia'd borders of the tram station. The pressed rubber chips of the platform felt different under her feet, as though they were full of packed energy.

– Anyway it's my kneecaps now, finished Tilda. The plastic's fatigued.

– I don't remember it like this, said Hannah. Something's changed.

– Well, what d'you expect? Tilda ducked into her buggy and gripped the little steering wheel.

It made her even smaller, Hannah thought, like a toddler in a pretend car.

– St Placid's had more makeovers than any other city, Tilda said proudly, starting the ignition. Even *we* can't keep track!

But it wasn't a makeover thing – it was something else, something less tangible than a revamp, Hannah thought, oddly aware of a springy feeling underfoot as she trailed her mother's electric buggy on foot down the residential streets past rhododendron hedges, mail-boxes, and tidy lawns dotted with miniature wells, windmills, and bird-baths with plastic ivy. Water features were big this year, and lawn furniture with pop-up parasols. The lavender smell gusted out from the gas pumps. It seemed more potent than usual, as though it were fighting a competing perfume from a rival source.

Tilda's ground-floor apartment comprised a box shape within the larger box of the block itself, which was painted in variegated pastel shades. Inside, Tilda had chosen lilac as a theme, to complement the lavender. Here the smell seemed more voluptuous and luxuriant, like a bath-house.

While Tilda fussed in the kitchen with her little percolator, Hannah glanced around the living-room. Her mother's latest craze was for Japanese flower-arranging, and the occasional tables were cluttered with cut palm leaves, wires, secateurs, dried-out sticks and other Ikebana accoutrements. On the shelf by the CD rack was a hologram of Hannah as a child, clutching a Marilyn doll in one hand, and in the other, a plastic monster, a gorgon with multiple heads. The small face overwhelmed by glasses, the pale eyes not meeting the camera's stare.

– You probably can't even remember what it was like before, said Tilda, returning to the living-room with the coffee and re-arranging her flowers, a big bouquet of blue irises and orange tulips. See? They're in Liberty colours. That's a nice touch, isn't it?

– What? asked Hannah. The heat in Tilda's apartment was already making her sleepy and confused.

– You can't remember politics. D'you still drink it black?

You were barely an adult. All that incompetence. I can't believe we put up with it. Look at the Americans. Look at the mess *they're* in. Then she lowered her voice and whispered proudly – Have you seen how jealous they're getting?

She reached for a plastic box, with twelve individual drawers. Pill time. She had labelled the little drawers neatly, in felt pen.

– You remember I phoned the Hotline when the neighbours were making all that noise with that idiotic mixing desk?

Hannah forced her eyebrows to make a questioning shape.

– Gone.

Tilda arranged a row of five pills before her, then poured a glass of spring water. She gulped the first pill, swished it down with water, and covered her mouth to give a small ladylike burp.

– Gone?

– Transferred. The second and third pills. – The rep was on to it straight away. Next day, literally, they were gone. They were borderline Marginals, he said. He said you were right to call us, Mrs Park, it's people like you who enable us to do our job, and on behalf of all of us at Libertycare, I'd like to take this opportunity to thank you personally.

Hannah recognised the wording. The Hotline used it.

– I'm a satisfied customer, I told the rep, Tilda went on. You can guess how *I'll* be choosing!

Through the triple-glazed window, a clutch of fit seniors jogged by in masks and pastel track-suits, goldfishing laughter.

– HRT trash, snorted Tilda. That's my tax dollar. I'll fix us lunch, shall I? I ordered the Gourmet Special, two minutes in the microwave. They do me a daily delivery, with my knees.

It was a platter for two, with plastic knives and forks: something white with plenty of fat and carbohydrate, and sprinkle-on vitamins from a sachet. Comforting.

– Breaded turkey escalopes, Tilda said after they'd finished it. With cauliflower *dauphinois*.

Hannah pictured a bird in the shape of the country called Turkey, flattened like a lumpy pancake.

– Can they fly? she asked Tilda abruptly.

– I think they're like ostriches, said Tilda, after a moment. Talking of which, Chunky Choo-Choo on tomorrow's three-thirty at Mohawk. Fancy a flutter? You can borrow my code. You need to watch her form though, she laid an egg on the track last season!

She laughed, throwing her head back, then looked at Hannah and stopped smiling. She sighed – a small, pained exhalation. In the silence that followed, Hannah had a sudden, sinking sense of what was coming next. She could almost see the words forming themselves in her mother's brain.

– I don't know how someone like you ends up as a psychologist.

Hannah folded her arms, pulled back from the table.

– I've told you before . . .

– Well, I don't understand the difference. Psychologist, statiwhatsit. You need to know about people for that, don't you? Don't you? And you're hardly what I'd call a people person.

There was no real point in replying. Slowly, Hannah pulled at one of the elastic bands on her wrist, then let it snap sharply against her skin. It hurt.

– Industrial psycho-statistician, said Hannah.

She looked away from her mother, out through the window at the rhododendrons and the camellias. *Go*, she thought. *Go now. Escape. Out.* Clouds freighted with the beginnings of rain.

– You don't need people. I've told you. It's all on paper. Or on screen. Or on CD ROM.

She took the elastic band off her wrist and swiftly scrunched her wispy hair into a little ball. With the elastic around it, and bits sticking out, it sparkled like nylon hay.

– So what are you working on now then?

– It's confidential, said Hannah, reaching for her mask. Using the inhaler was a tactic she'd adopted in childhood, to gain – quite literally – breathing space. Sometimes the need was genuine, and urgent, but often, with Ma, it was more complicated.

– You could give me the gist, Tilda reproached her plaintively.

Hannah felt a flash of anger. Her mother always did this.

– Just Hotline duty, she said reluctantly.

– Oh really? asked Tilda, smiling. It's a lovely service! I get special rates.

Hannah felt the annoyance mounting.

– Do you realise that when you ring up it's a machine asking you the questions? she blurted. Then instantly regretted breaking protocol.

Tilda flushed deep red.

– Well, they're very clever, aren't they, these computer programs, she said finally, twisting in her seat. A good sight cleverer than real people, I reckon. They've done an excellent job.

But she looked slapped. A small itchy silence.

– Nice arrangement, tried Hannah, indicating some red sticks emerging from a flat vase on the television cabinet.

– It's not finished, said Tilda defensively. It needs pods. She pulled off a fluffy slipper, laid it on her lap and stroked it like a cat. Her lips puckered into a knob.

– What happened to that young man at Head Office then, she asked, the technical one who you were on that course with?

Hannah fingered the plastic tube of her inhaler. She should have seen this coming.

– Nothing happened, Ma, she said tersely. You know that. We're just friends.

– Friends, spat Tilda. That's very trendy, isn't it, to be just friends with a man.

Hannah said nothing. Looked at the Ikebana. Wondered what kind of pods you'd –

– I expect you're still a virgin then, blurted Tilda. She flushed. Looked shocked with herself, but pleased too.

Hannah swiftly shoved the small mask over her nose and mouth and inhaled deeply.

A terrible silence flapped its wings between them.

An hour later, Hannah was back in Harbourville, breathing in the zestful, wake-up smell of peppermint. Walking from the tram station along the estuary embankment, watching the reflection of Head Office ripple out in broken stars, she felt a little zing of relief to be home. In her small apartment on the tenth floor of the ziggurat, she watched the news. The yes choice had been over 95 per cent. The nos would be questionnaired.

The departmental celebration party was at six.

As she cut herself a strip of bubble-wrap from the big roll by her bed, and then fought with the flaps and zips of her yellow party dress, she again tried to picture a turkey. Annoyed at her lack of recall, and curious, she flicked on the encyclopaedia and ran a search. And there was a bird-creature called a turkey, its bottom-feathers arranged in a curious flip-out fan at the back, its wattles red. She clicked to hear its cry, and the turkey jiggled its red wattles and opened its beak to release a low chattering bark rising to a squawk.

The bird-creature looked nothing like what she had eaten at lunch.

Life kept doing this.

*   *   *

She shared the lift with a tall blond man, youngish, wearing earphones: a field associate. He was handsome, with the soap-sculpted face of a mannequin, but he had a defeated look about him. His strong jaw swivelled as he chewed gum. When he asked her which floor, she could see the crinkled blob of it in his mouth: a bright, frightening green.

– Nineteen. Please.

– Festival party? he asked. His eyes were blue.

She nodded and looked at the floor, feeling his eyes on her as they shot upwards. Always too fast; she hated the lurch of it. Yet you were never quite sure when you were in motion, and when you'd stopped.

– It's Hannah Park, isn't it, he asked. She saw the blob again. I've seen you before, he said. Planning meeting. You're in Munchhausen's, right?

– Yes, said Hannah. She felt uncomfortable. She never ceased to be puzzled by the ease with which her colleagues struck up these mini-encounters with each other. She'd seen it happen time and again; people beginning a conversation with a virtual stranger, like this, and ending up friends, or enemies, or lovers. Fleur Tilley had slept with fifteen people in Customer Care alone, according to e-mail gossip. In lunchbreaks. On office floors. Someone from In-house Surveillance tipped her off about the spot checks in return for –

Hannah reached in her pocket for her bubble-wrap.

– This may be the last time you see me, the man volunteered, chewing more fiercely. I'm being questionnaired.

He must have done something or said something quite serious. Hannah wondered if he might be drunk.

– What happened? she asked reluctantly. The lift stopped. She wasn't used to this.

– I said we were drones.

– Drones? she asked, as they stepped out.

– You know. Like worker bees. Servicing the queen. It was just a quip. But I said it to the wrong guy.

– Uh-huh, mustered Hannah. Drugs maybe, she thought. You could get them.

– Catch you later, he said, sauntering off ahead of her.

Just a boy really, she thought, seeing the way his jacket hung limp on him.

– Hi, people person! Leo Hurley greeted her hoarsely.

Hannah started, jolting her tonic water. Some splashed out and fizzed on her wrist, and she reached for a napkin. It had the Festival logo on it – a big square with a bold cross in it, the Bird of Liberty flying above. She always felt ill at ease at these functions. Leo had a crisp-crumb stuck to his beard. His hair was dishevelled, and there was something restless about his eyes. They were gleaming, like he was asleep, and she was the nightmare.

– How are your Munchies? he asked. Hannah sensed he was just making small talk; his glance kept shunting about the room. They were standing in a corner, away from the throng that crowded round the stainless-steel bar. The place was rapidly filling.

– Irritating, replied Hannah. If I hear one more faked suicide, I'll scream.

– Fleur told me about one today, threatening to kill his whole family with dry-cleaning fluid, said Leo, still scanning the room. But there must've been a programming error, or a mis-route, because Dolly kept asking him about brands. What brand of dry-cleaning fluid he was planning to use. Whether he'd like it delivered, or would he be going to his local parc. Was he aware of the loyalty discount.

This wasn't new.

– So what happened?

– Don't know. He hung up. Leo gave his barking laugh. He said it was like talking to the wall. He –

Hannah followed the line of Leo's eyes.

The room had hushed.

65

Wesley Pike stood framed in the doorway. Some people have a magnetic presence. They inch their way into your subconscious and you think about their bodies more often than you'd like to.

He was taller than almost everyone else in the room, but not only taller; broader, bigger. It was as if he were built on a different scale, out of different materials – not banal gristle and blood, but something more potent, more valuable. Just looking at him – he'd begun working the room now, up and down, like the shuttle of a loom – made Hannah blush. It was unnerving that she could so easily picture his torso beneath. Hairless, muscular. He spent about twenty seconds on each interchange, clutching an arm just above the elbow, patting a shoulder, gripping a hand for a tight, stimulating second. It was like receiving a small electric charge – one that was weirdly prone to trigger a sex thought. He flashed his smile like a fat wallet. It made you feel special. She knew she wasn't the only woman to feel violently attracted to him. Men were too, apparently. Even those who weren't usually that way inclined.

– He uses a pheromone spray for sexual charisma, murmured Leo, picking up on her train of thought. Someone saw him in the Mens', once, doing his armpits.

She laughed, then cupped her hand over her mouth, embarrassed. The idea was bizarre, ridiculous.

– Why would he do that?

After all, Wesley Pike was famously celibate. The only rumour about him that remained consistent was that he had a relationship with the Boss herself. Not a physical relationship, obviously. Something more mysterious. Almost spiritual.

– Just for the hell of it, said Leo, smiling crookedly. It's the only power he's got really, when you think about it.

He didn't look powerless.

He was making his way to the small platform now. As the

chatter dipped and faded to a respectful hush, all eyes rested on the Facilitator General's flat, smooth face.

– Well, he began, smiling. A big wide smile, and at the same time he stretched out his arms as though to embrace them all. The customers have spoken. Euripides said – he signalled quotation marks – that mobs in their emotions are much like children, subject to the same tantrums and fits of fury. He might have added that when they're pleased they'll shout it from the rooftops.

A small cheer and a bubble of murmurs.

– We at the Liberty Corporation are honoured to have been chosen to service this island for a second ten-year term. None of us is surprised by today's result.

He gave another wide smile. The room seemed to froth with the chemistry of it.

– But it's gratifying nonetheless. He paused.

Hannah wondered whether he was about to get lyrical. He was capable of it. Sceptred isles, enchanted paradises and whatnot. Might he choose this moment to voice the word that hung at the back of Atlanticans' thoughts, more and more? Or was it too early, even after ten years, to talk about Utopia? No; instead, he was praising 'the organic hermetics' of the Liberty principle. What other service had gone so far in pleasing all of the people, all of the time? You only had to look at history. The system was nothing more than a blueprint for freedom. Freedom *within* freedom. Freedom *to* and freedom *from*. Freedom *that nourishes itself*.

– We take pride in our customer-care programme, he continued. Those of you who work in Munchhausen's will know just how valuable our customer feedback is. The customers like to see those figures published.

He smiled.

Yes; they liked to see those simple graphs. Up for good, down for bad. She'd heard it all before – about how it made the customers feel safe, to know that what they said counted. About how feedback helped keep Marginals off the streets, put hard-core losers offshore, didn't threaten the fragile physics of the eco-climate. Et cetera et cetera.

– People need a system they can trust. A system that doesn't let them down, Pike was saying. With Libertycare, what you see is what you get. Which is why other nations – he paused, looked meaningfully around the room – are now beginning to take an active interest in adopting the software.

More cheering. People were getting quite drunk, Hannah noticed. There was a feeling of well-being, relief, joy even. Life at Head Office had its moments.

Wesley Pike was grinning now, the pleasure radiating out, blessing them all with its warm glow.

– So this is an important victory for what may one day become – why not? – a new world order. And I'm sure if the Boss herself could join us in a drink – a smile quirked at the corner of his mouth – she would.

There was laughter. Yes; people were genuinely happy, thought Hannah, relaxing slightly. We've worked hard for this.

– So I'm going to propose a toast to Libertycare, he finished, raising his glass. And the principle of the greatest happiness of the greatest number.

A cheer went up, and Hannah caught sight of Fleur Tilley, sozzled, lifting her glass. Soon the room was awash with babble.

– Listen, Hannah, said Leo. He was easing her towards an area of the room where the crowd was thinner. Still darting his eyes about, as though looking for someone.

– There's something I found out.

Hannah wondered what was different about his eyes. They seemed to sit at a tilted angle in his face. Uneasily, she felt for the strip of bubble-wrap in her pocket, and popped two blisters.

– What?

– It's a . . . gossip thing.

A gossip thing? Leo didn't gossip.

– What d'you mean? What's up?

– I was on the top floor earlier, with the Boss, and –

But suddenly he was gone.

When she turned round she saw why: Wesley Pike was heading towards her, smiling and purposeful. He moved like a car. A big smile; next thing, he'd parked and his hand was on her shoulder, thrilling and frightening.

– The Boss is pleased with you, Hannah, he said. Your Profile's up.

Hannah felt her face redden and she reached for her bubble-wrap. More than anything else, she wanted to pop another blister. His hand on her shoulder felt like a heavy sexual moth.

– Go ahead, he said. If it makes you more comfortable.

He noticed everything.

– It's a bad habit, she muttered, shoving it back in her pocket.

– There are worse ways to deal with tension, he said.

She followed his eyes. Fleur Tilley was already well past the tottering stage.

– At least we won't have to send *you* to rehab, said Pike.

He had made a joke, Hannah realised. She tried to make a noise like laughter. Then gulped at her tonic water.

– Anyway, I have good news for you, he said.

His eyes were grey, clear like glass. She wondered how he could see through them. She felt the sweat prick her armpits. He smiled, his glance whizzing expertly across the room, then returning to her and resting – surely just for a brief, flickering moment, actually resting on her breasts? She felt a burning sensation, low down.

– The Boss has decided to move you.

Her heart caught, and she moved her weight from one foot to the other.

– *Reward success, questionnaire failure*, he said, smiling at the quotation. She was being praised as well as flattered, she realised suddenly. She stared at his chest and pictured running her hands all over it, like a blind person feeling a wall.

– There are going to be some changes. Now that the Festival's behind us.

– Changes? She immediately felt stupid, echoing him like that. But what did he mean? What was she supposed to say?

– You'll be part of a new venture. A short-term project. It's beyond your normal remit, but the Boss reckons you can cope. He smiled. Big, broad. – So how d'you feel about doing some people-work?

What?

She felt panic rise within her like vomit. She clutched her bubble-wrap fiercely, feeling the air-pockets strain with the pressure. She felt trapped, conned. No, she thought. Not that. *Reward success*, you said.

– I don't have the experience. I can't –

– At Liberty, there's no such word. He smiled, his eyes floating over her.

– But my Block –

– It's nothing threatening. You'll find it interesting. What do you know about Multiple Personality Disorder?

Not much, thought Hannah, trying to focus. Almost nothing.

– It's quite rare, she said, searching her brain for stray knowledge. I mean, hardly anyone gets it. It's a – she fumbled for the words – a rare delusional thing. That's all I know.

– Well, you'll be discovering a lot more. He paused. – It'll stretch you, socially.

Hannah felt herself not stretching, but shrinking. She supposed that she felt flattered, deep down, below the inappropriate sex thoughts and the panic. *Reward success*. So why did it feel like a punishment? She looked into her glass. At the bottom was a lonely sliver of lemon.

Multiple Personality Disorder. That was when a person thought they were lots of other people. Ran several identities in their head at once. She couldn't remember the statistics, but it was an unusual condition. You had to be pretty disturbed. There was a proxy version too, where you imagined the people were semi-independent of you. Orphans were prone to it.

– I'd better say yes, then, she mustered.

It came out gobbly and savage, like the noise the turkey made.

Leo Hurley must have been waiting, because as soon as Pike had powered off he was there next to her, clutching his drink, the crisp-crumb still sticking grimly to his beard. Hannah was popping the bubble-blisters, one by one, not caring now who saw her, her mind churning miserably.

– What's up?

She gulped air. Forced herself not to look in Pike's direction, so as not to stoke it up again, that awful invasive thing he'd done to her.

– Nothing. I don't know. Some new project. I'm off the Munchies. Look, I don't want to talk about it. It's people-work. The words tasted like poison. – You said there was gossip.

Leo's eyes slid sideways, and he coughed, then turned his body to shield them both from the rest of the room. The tall handsome man from the lift came to the table to reach for a drink. Odd, thought Hannah, the way he wore headphones at a party. Perhaps it was a field-associate affectation. The young man nodded distractedly at Hannah.

– I was in the Temple earlier, said Leo. His eyes were gleaming again. He looked slightly mad. – Just after the Festival.

The Temple was where the Boss was housed. On the top floor.

71

– And?

Leo lowered his voice.

– You mustn't say anything. But she's switched modes.

– How d'you mean?

Hannah wasn't aware the Boss operated in modes in the first place.

– Altered focus.

– How? What to?

– Well, the last ten years, she's been running in default mode. Democratic auto-pilot.

– And now? Hannah realised what had happened to his eyes, now. They were frightened.

– A new code's kicked in. He licked dry lips, and swallowed. – I'm pretty sure she's switched to damage limitation.

And then he was gone.

Damage limitation.

Next to Hannah, closer than she'd thought, the pale man with the headphones was pouring himself a drink.

– More tonic water? he offered Hannah.

– No thanks.

She'd popped all the bubbles by now. She'd have to go back to her apartment, and cut another strip from the roll. Or better still, go back to her apartment and climb into bed and try not to think about what Wesley Pike had said.

– We meet again, the man said, holding out a hand to shake. Benedict Sommers.

He'd got rid of the green gum somewhere. His eyes were the palest blue. Like swimming-pool water, the shallow end. She hated this. Leo understood, only because he was the same, or sort of. But no one else did. Benedict smiled, and held out a packet.

– Gum? he offered. Hannah shook her head.

– No thanks.

He put the packet away.

– I'm sorry, she blurted. But I can't talk to people I don't

72

know. I just can't do it. I have a sort of – allergy. It's not you. It's – me.

– Hey, he said. It's been a long day. I understand.

And he flashed her a rueful smile. Hannah couldn't think of anything to say, or any reason to say it, so she turned and walked off.

Benedict Sommers watched her.

Everyone knew about Hannah Park. The brilliant mind, blocked by the antisocial personality, and trapped in a body she hadn't a clue what to do with. Not a bad body, in actual fact, he observed. But she wheeled it about like it was a trolley for her head. An interesting case, but not so unusual in Head Office. The Boss had a talent for targeting the right brains to fit the right task. The Munchies, in Hannah's case. Her mother had used her as a proxy all through her childhood, apparently. There was something pitiful about her.

But if Hannah Park had problems, she wasn't alone.

A bad attitude to authority, was the phrase being memo'd about, following his remark earlier today. The questionnaire was going to focus on that. The whole thing had been blown out of all proportion. But there it was, a black mark, and one that wouldn't be erased easily. He'd have to work hard. Show willing.

Or bugger off altogether, he thought suddenly: leave Atlantica. Get rid of his terrible Munchie flatmate in St Placid and sell the place. Seek his fortune in the big wide world.

He adjusted his headphones thoughtfully.

Activating them at parties was a little game he played. Wear your surveillance gadgetry on your sleeve, and they all assume it's something else. Even people who should know better. You get to hear all sorts of stuff.

Tonight, Benedict had picked up Hannah's conversation with Leo Hurley by accident. But the content of it interested him. He knew about Leo Hurley. His screen-maintenance work gave him access to the nerve centre beyond the firewall. He'd be one of the few people who regularly saw the Boss.

A mode-switch, right on the heels of the Festival. That's what he'd said. *Damage limitation*. And he was worried. Useful information, if you knew what to do with it.

Which Benedict didn't. Yet.

But slowly, as the conversation between Hannah Park and Leo Hurley began to settle in his mind, the sense of possibility grew. It formed a ball of energy inside him, made him feel handsome, successful, proud. As he smiled, he felt the energy shine from his mouth like a child's pumpkin blazing a serrated grin of fire. Outside, in the fading light, a glittering plane scraped the orange sky. It could be going anywhere, thought Benedict, weighing up the day. Anywhere.

He was getting steadily more drunk. From fast track to questionnairing, just like that. It wasn't fair. Fine, OK, have rules, but hell –

He must have been thinking about Melissa subconsciously before she even touched him, because he got an instant erection when he felt the palm of a hand pressing in the small of his back, through his shirt. She was from Human Services. An appropriate department, for someone with her talents. Talents which he'd be more than willing to put to the test, now. Right now. *End the day with a bang*. He swung round, grinning, his mind still sore from the day's defeat, his prick aching with greed. But it wasn't Melissa.

– Think of me as your fairy godfather, said Wesley Pike.

A PLACE FOR IDIOTS

The ship's Education Station is widely held to be a place for idiots, but I am drawn to it nonetheless. When I first came on board and was searching for the meaning of existence, I stumbled across a yellow philosophy book that contained a theory about the universe by some bloke whose name I can't pronounce. It's just a great big knitting machine gone haywire, he reckoned. Now, that makes sense to me. It's a thing that gets started for no reason and reproduces itself in a mad and uncontrolled way. Like cancer, or the plastic bags in the cupboard under the sink. Ever since reading about this knitting machine, I've thought about writing a pamphlet called *Power for the Powerless*. Thought One: The more mysterious the system, the more the mystery excites you, the more it is bollocks. If it's nice and simple and you can understand it, beware. And if you respect it, run a mile. Actually that's three thoughts for the price of one, which is a typically Atlantican bargain.

Chew, chew, chew.

From what is old and ugly, bring forth the new. In the Bible or some such place, Judaea or Galilee or Aesop, a rotten old lion-carcass became home to a hive of bumble-bees, geysering up a glorious fountain of honey. From the strong came forth sweetness, di-da di-da. And likewise, from the dossiered evidence will come . . .

What? Vindication? Explanation?

No. Something more practical. A chess set. Sixty-four squares. Thirty-two pieces. Queen's Gambit. Schliemann's Defence. The Killer Grob.

It passes the time. I have already manufactured the sixteen pawns and all the main players except one, so I should be finished by the time we dock in Harbourville. Today I'm starting on the last black piece: Tiffany. She belongs on the front line of the opposition along with Pike, the Machine, Gwynneth, Geoff the stress dickhead, Keith the cat, Malt Fishook and Hooley the Social Adjustment associate. I decided long ago who'd be what. Tiff hasn't the imagination to be a knight or the brains to be a bishop. She's blinkered and defensive enough to be a rook, though. I haven't forgotten my daughter's face, and the angry hunch of her shoulders. A dumpy turret of a girl. I'll give her a nice little portcullis, and make her the same height as the other main players, about twenty centimetres tall. The pawns are smaller. They're just customers.

Hot breath on my neck.

I turn: John's bulbous doggy eyes are fixed on my modelling. He's been getting jumpier and less predictable ever since Fishook uttered the words 'Final Adjustment' on the tannoy, and who can blame him. At mealtimes, I've noticed how guys keep slapping him on the back, treating him all friendly, making rueful faces, thinking, thank Christ it isn't me.

– It's Tiffany, I tell him. My daughter.

– You want her dead then?

I can feel another conversation about torture revving up. But funny, I'm not in the mood.

– No. Course not. She's my flesh and blood.

– So why the effigy, he goes, like he's a shrink or something.

– I've told you before, they're not effigies. This is a rook. See the crenellations round her neck? This isn't magic, John. It's art.

He makes a face.

– But she's a black one, right. You told me before, she's on the baddy side. Now what I'm asking myself here is, how come?

I hate this. I hate the way he tries to prise stuff out of me, like I'm an oyster. I feel like saying, there's no pearl in there, mate, it's just the same sad, cringing guk that's inside everyone.

– I want the whole story now, he goes. What you did, how you got busted, how you ended up here, the whole lot. Before the fry-up.

Something inside me goes cold, like my heart's been shoved in a freezer.

How's he to know that I've spent the last year forcibly keeping my mouth shut? If I tell him the real story, he'll probably blame me for his downfall, and rip my head off. He's big and brutal enough. But on the other hand –

Suddenly, his hands are round my neck. See what I mean?

Am I his Scheherazade, spinning out my tale to save my bacon?

– If you don't, he says.

Calm down, I tell myself, fighting the panic. John is actually just John. Even killers like him know how to whistle a tune, can appreciate a joke, won't say no to a round of table tennis, are perhaps capable of normal relationships. And fortunately, he's thick. I can leave bits out. I can tell him a version, and then he'll be dead anyway, so he won't be in a position to . . .

– OK. Deal, I rasp – and he's loosened his grip, but he's still there next to me, a solid mass of flesh. *Power for the Powerless*: Rule Two. If someone's bigger than you, and violent, remain his friend.

– I'm waiting, says John. And starts drumming his fingers on my head.

– I was living in the house in Gravelle Road, in Harbourville,

I sigh finally. (It was so long ago, it felt like hauling up an old corpse from a river bed.) I'd moved in there with Gwynneth when we got married. We'd been there eighteen years when she and Tiffany left. I didn't notice them go. In fact it was a whole day before it dawned on me that they weren't there any more. That shows what separate lives we led by then. I was always in. And they were always out. Shopping and whatnot.

John gave me a look, and I could tell he was thinking about the whatnot part.

– How did you find out, then? he goes.

– I ran out of coffee, and that's when I saw Gwynneth's note. She'd left it in the coffee tin. She'd written it in capital letters, on her crappy little PC.

– What did it say?

– I don't remember, I tell him.

But I'm lying. It said: REMEMBER YOU WERE MAR-RIED AND HAD A LOVELY DAUGHTER? WELL, NOT ANY MORE BECAUSE TIFF AND I HAVE MOVED OUT. WE'VE HAD ENOUGH OF PLAYING SECOND FIDDLE, WE DESERVE BETTER THAN THIS. G.

It was that line about deserving better that made me wonder if they'd moved in with some other bloke. The thing about Gwynneth was, she wouldn't've done it without somewhere to go. She'd have planned it.

– It wasn't spontaneous, I told John. That's for sure. I mean, she didn't just wake up one morning and think, hey, I'm suddenly fed up with the husband who has provided for me financially for the best part of two decades. She thought about it beforehand, worked things out. She even set up one of those Internet divorces: one click and our marriage was history.

– So what then?

– So I haven't seen her since. And it was another three years before I saw Tiffany again.

78

And then when I did, I wished I hadn't.

– So what happened, after they went?

– Nothing, I just carried on as usual, living my life, working away at being me, doing my thing, making money. Just me and Keith.

– Who's Keith?

– The cat. Burmese. Intelligent. Knew which side his bread was buttered. He quit too, little bastard, when the shit hit the fan.

– How come you didn't notice they'd left? *I'd* have noticed, if it was me.

– Well, like I said, Gwyn and Tiff were always out. G and T, I called them.

John looked puzzled, the way he always does when you mention letters of the alphabet.

– G and T, to us literati, stands for gin and tonic, I explained. It was their favourite drink, as it happens. Or sometimes I called them Ice and Lemon. Quite appropriate, if you knew them. One was cold, the other was bitter.

John said – Women, darkly, and picked up his embroidery.

– Anyway, I said, I was busy working. Making money for them to spend. Too busy being a good husband and father. Paying for their gin and tonics.

And their boyfriends' lagers too, no doubt, I'm thinking, but I don't say it. Sometimes I ask myself: will I ever understand women? *Power for the Powerless* was conceived at home.

– The human slot machine, I called myself.

– Hey, Harvey babe, John's chuckling, suddenly cheerful, threading purple silk on to his needle, wetting a finger and selecting a silver sequin from his sewing box. Bring out the violins.

– Yeah, well, the family business was making a lot of money, as it happens. We were a hot little team.

– But – he's looking all puzzled – I mean, what I don't get is, like, when you got married and that. Why didn't you drop the family business then, do something else?

He really can be gormless.

– For Christ's sake, John, you don't just drop your own flesh and blood!

– But I thought you said they weren't real!

I wish I hadn't let him in on that now. I've never felt comfortable, admitting it. I poke at my paste with the wooden spoon. It looks lumpier than usual. I feel myself sort of bristle.

– They were to me, I say.

That really was the problem, I realised, as I read Gwynneth's note from the coffee tin. Ice and Lemon had left because I preferred my pretend family to my real one. I remember sighing as I put the kettle on. Feeling bad, because they had a point.

– Well, Keith, I said to the cat, who was snaking round my legs, vibrating hunger. Just you and me now, boy.

The thing is, I thought, as I opened a tin for him, I knew where I was with the Hoggs. We never had any arguments. I was very much the head of the household. They did my bidding. And by doing it, in their own limited way, they showed proof of their love.

Yes: love.

Keith meowed, and I lumped out his portion: it was tuna and cod in jelly. Then I stood up with the empty tin in my hand and breathed in its horrible fishy fumes. It made my eyes water. If it weren't for Keith and the Hoggs, I thought, from now on I'd be completely alone.

But I didn't tell John the bit about loving my family. He wouldn't have understood, any more than Gwynneth and Tiffany could.

– You can't relate to real people, that's your trouble! Gwynneth would squawk at me.

– Yeah, Tiffany would echo, what about us? D'you think we're a couple of plastic replicas or something?

– So what happened? went John. Who busted you?

I sighed. The papier mâché was drying on my hands. Picking off the little lumps can be very satisfying. You crumble them into a heap, or flick them individually. Picture the port-hole as the target. I've stuck on a little red sticker, dead-centre, for the bull's-eye. I hit it, once. *Power for the Powerless!*

It was a cloudy day in July; I remember the month, because it was just after the Festival of Choice, and there were still these tatters of paper floating about in the air from the celebrations, and shrivelledy-looking helium balloons in the shape of the Bird of Liberty tethered to people's dish aerials. With G and T long gone, I was alone in the house, apart from Keith. He was purring on my lap while I clicked away. I'd trained him to knead his claws on the fabric of the chair, rather than in my flesh. I liked him sitting on me, while I worked. It gave me companionship, and a nice warm feeling in the groin.

– I'm in my office, transferring ten thousand from my uncle's account into my mum's, I explain to John, before ransacking one of my kid brother's off-shore companies to pay for the money that's owed to one of Mum's companies in the Cayman Islands. This is *after* she's borrowed at exorbitantly high interest from my big sister's Costa Rican offshore development loan scheme. Which in turn owes it – plus interest – to one of my uncle's Martinique outfits.

– I think I'm with you, goes John. (As if!)

– Anyway, the point is, thirty K's at stake this morning.

– Right, he goes.

– Then there's a ring at the doorbell.

– You opened it?

I wish I could have said that I had a hunch, an instinct not

81

to respond to it. But the doorbell rang a lot. Dispatch riders, takeaway deliveries, the ironing service, the weekly tele-shop. Keith jumped off my lap at the sound of the doorbell, hoping for pepperoni and pineapple pizza, his favourite.

– I thought it was a bike delivery. I was expecting some cash after the last transaction, I say.

– And who was it?

– My daughter.

I add an extra lump of papier mâché to her bum, and grit my teeth.

Yes: Tiffany. In smart orange-and-blue Libertyforce uniform.

Tiff had always been her mother's daughter. From the moment she was born, they were a little female confederacy, plotting oestrogen-type stuff together while I concocted cash. Girly kitchen things at first, gingerbread men and so forth, then women things, men of the non-gingerbread variety. It was pretty much an open secret. What could I do about it? As a family man, I was a failure. I'd never got close to her. I loved her but I didn't know her. Gwynneth behaved as though she was the only parent, and I was just a . . . oh, just a feature of the home landscape. It was weird, I thought – but what did I know about family life? *Perhaps* it was normal. Perhaps, I thought, if Tiffany'd been a boy, it would've been different. We'd have gone to ball games or ostrich races or whatever the big thing was. Anyway, the more Gwynneth resented me for my lack of 'social skills' the more I retreated into my shell.

As soon as Tiffany was old enough to understand, Gwynneth told her that Daddy preferred another mummy and daughter. It wasn't strictly true, not in the beginning, but the saying of it polluted everything and after a while I thought, well, sod it, so what if I do prefer them. Who wouldn't? After that I kept myself to myself in the loft conversion with the Hoggs.

At least G and T can't hate me for funding their shopping trips, I thought.

Wrong.

– You're under arrest, says Inspector Tiffany Kidd, still parked on the doorstep by the banana tree and the dwarf Alpines. She's bigger, more substantial, harder-faced than I remember her. Canteen food. It's bulked her up. There's a Libertyforce van out in the road behind her in the road, Fraud Squaddies tumbling out on to the front grass. She flashes a plastic-covered search warrant at me, and an ID card showing an unflattering hologram of her own face, and I have time to think, what crappy paperwork.

– Don't think you don't deserve this, she says briskly.

It crosses my mind that I might be hallucinating. Computers can frazzle you that way, short-circuit your nodes.

– What the fuck d'you think you're doing? I yell at her. What is this stupid game?

As the forcies pile out of the van, she shucks me off like an old raincoat.

– Common Assault, Article 5D, Libertycare Customer Charter! she yaps. Impound his computers! De-activate his hard discs! Confiscate all CD ROMs and floppies!

And the uniformed gophers swarm through the house.

– That family paid for you to go to that posh school with the netball and the oboe lessons! I yell at her.

She just stands there, her eyes flashing with a hatred so pure that it could be bottled and sold as a multi-purpose repellent.

– That family paid for your snow-breaks and your designer labels from all those fucking boutiques!

A spotty youngster joins her at this point.

– All right, there, ma'am?

I throw in my last card.

– Not to mention your abortion!

I make sure I say it loud and clear. The young forcie looks at the Lemon, and then at the floor.

– Slap him in cuffs, she spits.

And lo, it came to pass that, like a common criminal, I was shoved into the back of a Libertyforce van stinking of junk food. I was in shock. I felt numb.

– All right there, mate? asked the spotty forcie who was now attached to me by handcuffs, like an outsized and gormless gnome dangling from a charm bracelet. With his free hand he was feeding himself Chicken McNuggets from a greasy cardboard bucket.

– All right? My entire family has just been wiped out. Do YOU reckon I'm all right?

I thought *Inspector Kidd* was your family, he goes, all jovially. He's munching an evil-smelling nugget. *She* seems to be alive and well.

The Lemon was sitting in the front of the van; I could see the back of her head through the glass.

– She's not family, as far as I'm concerned. (I said it loudly, hoping she could hear it.) – Real families are loyal. Real families don't fuck you about. Real families honour and respect their dad.

The forcie laughed aloud.

– See you've got a good sense of humour then, mate, he went.

I couldn't think of anything to add that was in words, so I spat on the floor. And on that note we drove off.

It was one of Tiffany's subordinates who interrogated me at the copshop at Staggerworth Junction in South District. He wanted names, dates, all that stuff.

– It's all on the discs, I told him.

– And your password?

– Moron, I said. He noted it down without a flicker.

– What's the prognosis then, doc? I asked him.

He looked at me questioningly for a moment.

– Oh. This type of fraud, you're usually looking at ten years, in my experience.

– *Ten years?* Cue the classic line from me, about wanting Libertyaid. Knowing my rights.

While I waited to make the call, I learned more from the forcie: the Lemon had been an inspector for two years, here at Staggerworth, just a mile up the road from the house. She was ambitious. This was her first major fraud bust. That figured: stepping into the van I'd heard another forciewoman congratulating her in a booming, lesbian sort of voice.

– Nice one, Tiff! Vengeance, yo!

– You have to hand it to her, I told the forcie miserably. It takes balls to shop your own dad.

Then she walked in.

– How's your mother? I asked, trying to disarm her.

Tiffany smiled.

– She's very well. She's *happy*. Living with a lovely bloke. Geoff. (I felt my eyes bulge.) – He's a stress-management consultant.

Then she added, smirking – I call him Dad.

Sissy curtains and St John's wort.

– Well, I call him Wanker, I said, and thought, I should have guessed. Gwynneth was right. I don't notice things.

– Well, thanks for the update, I said. Now where's my Libertyaid representative?

– You don't want one. There's a proposition for you. Unless you'd prefer a twenty-year Adjustment, she smirked.

– The other forcie said ten years.

At which point Inspector Tiffany Kidd looked suddenly pissed-off. Like a kid again. I remembered her at five, throwing a tantrum after she'd melted part of her plastic kitchen set with Gwynneth's hair-dryer, and put the blame on Keith – who was only a kitten at the time. She didn't like being in the wrong.

– Well, I say twenty. It's my bust, I researched it. I know how much you've made over the years. Starting with fifteen hundred dollars for a state-of-the-art brace for your imaginary brother, and finishing with the sale of five offshore mini-islands – which are actually just large rocks – for a hundred and fifty thousand each. I've seen the evidence, she goes.

– So how come you don't want me to go to jail? Don't I deserve it?

– You *do* deserve it, she stabs bitterly. You deserve it for the way you tried to *fuck* up our lives by making out we were *second-best* to some *other* family that *didn't even exist*. Then, perhaps realising the childishness of it, she stalls herself. After a pause, she says, looking at her shoes – But I'm under instructions from Them.

Well, that knocked me sideways. Head Office? What do they want?

She looked from her shoes to the wall. It was an unremarkable pale green, decorated only by a dribbly splotch of what looked like dried Nescafé, no doubt hurled there by another detainee at his wits' end, but it seemed to interest her quite unduly.

– I don't know, the Lemon confessed, clearly irked at having let herself mention it at all. They were looking for a fraud like yours. A family like you've got.

– What for, for Christ's sake?

She looked blank.

– Dunno, she said. They didn't say.

– So you shopped me to advance your career?

– Nothing wrong with that.

I sighed. There'd be no getting through.

– So what do I have to do?

She was looking down now, picking at her nails just like she'd done as a turbulent teenager. It made me sad to see it. I wanted to tell her to stop.

She said – There's a man called Wesley Pike.

*   *   *

86

John whistled. – The black king, eh?

– If you think they're out to get you, I said, it's because they are.

And that was where I left it with John. He went back to his sewing for a while, and I chewed the rest of it through, quietly.

The rest of it? Oh, the bit I hadn't told him. The tail-end to that scene.

Why didn't I tell him? Because of what Gwynneth would've called 'stupid masculine pride', I guess. Shame, a bit – not at what happened, but about being too gormless to have spotted it. And an inability, no, a refusal, even now, to come to terms with that final slap in the face.

It was just as she was leaving. It was me who prompted it. I don't know what came over me. The memory of her as a kid, I guess. Not the teenager and then the woman she became, but the cute little girl wobbling about on her bike in the back garden, looking so sweet and innocent and adorable in her little white cowgirl outfit with tassels.

– Tiffany, I said.

– Yes?

– How can you do this? (My mouth was hanging open.) – I mean – I mean – I mean –

– What? What d'you mean? she snapped.

I nearly stopped then and there. I should have. But I didn't.

– Well, I said hopelessly. I just mean, how can you do this? I'm your dad!

She looked blank for a minute, then puzzled. Uncomprehending.

– No you're not, she said.

It was like a slow-motion experience. The long, long delay from ear to brain. While things were sinking in – more sort of slumping into place – I let my hands drop loose by my

87

sides; I could feel them swinging free like a puppet's. A noise hatched in my throat, but it got stuck, and hung birthlessly in the silence.

Then, watching Tiffany's face – the face, I now realised, that looked nothing like my own, and never had, but belonged to some other man, whose name I didn't even know, who'd been with Gwynneth on one of those nights she'd come back drunk and smoky from the razzle – you could see the thought dawn on her. It spread across her face, blooming into a sweet pink smile.

There was a kind of shocked laughter in her voice when she spoke.

She said – You didn't know?

GOOD MORNING

– Good morning, Voyagers! That's Fishook on the tannoy, sounding perky. – We are now approaching Atlantican waters. My heart sinks.
– In five days' time we will dock in Harbourville.
As the music crackles in, I reach for the transcript of another call to the Customer Hotline. They're all the same. I've chewed thousands, so I know.
They all taste the same too.

Caller: This is confidential, right? My name's Tom.
Response: Hi, Tom. Tell me how I can help you.
Caller: Well, there's this bloke, says he's going to kill me. He lives up my road. Jed Hawkes.
Response: Can you give me more details, sir? How did it begin, for example?
Caller: It started when I told him I wasn't going to lend him my lawnmower again, after he buggered up the blades on his rockery. Fancy trying to mow around a rockery. He says the soil's all eroded in our district anyway, so it doesn't matter. I won't need a lawn mower much longer, we'll all be living in a bog.
Response: Yes, sir. It's people like you who enable us to do our job and on behalf of Libertycare I'd like to thank you personally. Please carry on. And then?

Caller: Well, it escalates into a dispute and the wife says . . .

I knew Jed Hawkes.

He arrived on board the same day as me, after we were all rounded up in the Mass Readjustment. A rough-and-ready sort of bloke, but likeable. He suffered from seasickness. He wasn't resilient. He didn't have the particular grim kind of humour or the hostile-from-birth attitude to the system that you need to survive here without coming unscrewed. Unlike many of the Atlanticans, he wasn't prepared to kid himself that he was actually guilty – if not of the charges against him, then of something, at least.

A lawn mower, misapplied to a rockery.

He killed himself last year.

– Man Overboard, went the cry.

So then what, goes John. We've been silent for an hour. Me chewing, him sewing, both trying not to think. The needle flashing in the light.

I sigh.

– Well, I was allowed home after that. Under house arrest. They tagged me with this sort of ankle-bracelet with an alarm system. (John nodded knowledgeably.) – They'd gutted the place by then. My family photos, the lot.

I gulp, remembering how grief-stricken I'd been. How bereft.

– Anyway, it didn't feel like home any more, without the family there, I said. It was like they'd never existed. And then to cap it all, Keith buggered off.

– Keith?

– The cat.

– Where'd he go?

– Next door. With Mrs Dragon-lady.

– Who's she?

– Neighbour woman. It's what Tiffany used to call her, as a kid. Anyway I guess Keith went round to her place because he was getting old, and he could read the writing on the wall.

– He could read?

Is he stupid or what?

– No, you dork. What I mean is, they're intuitive, aren't they, cats. He must've sensed a downward spiral. He did come back, though, just the once.

– What for?

– To be sick on the carpet. I laughed, remembering. I yelled at him at the top of my voice. He shot out of the cat-flap so fast it rattled for ages.

– What happened to him?

– I didn't see him again for a while. He went back to Mrs Dragon-lady. She fed him that addictive dried stuff.

– How d'you know?

– I inspected his sick.

John's mouth twisted.

– And so then what did you do?

– I just mooned about the house. I had cabin fever. I microwaved these horrible meals that Gwynneth'd left at the back of the freezer, pasta bake and that bollocks, way past their eat-by date. I didn't have any appetite.

I remember pining for the Hoggs, and getting all stir-crazy. I remember thinking about what Tiffany had said at the forcie station. Just the thought that she wasn't my real daughter turned my stomach. It explained why Gwynneth had kept Tiffany away from me like her own private doll. Why she'd asked if I wanted her to keep the baby. Could it actually be that she thought I *knew*? Another question kept nagging me too and I didn't have the answer to it. Would I have been a dad to Tiff, if I'd known the truth? Everything was roiling about inside me. But no need to tell John all that.

– Then after two days, I said, the phone rang.

John looked up, a tiny purple sequin poised on the end of his huge finger.

The meeting took place in the Snak Attak. Pike had suggested it on the phone.

– You go there, as I understand it, from time to time, he went. For spring onion and noodle soup, and to read the news online?

I wondered how long I'd been under surveillance.

– All right, I said. No problem. Come and see the criminal in his natural habitat. A rare species of white-collar fraudster. Won't bite.

He must have liked that, because he laughed. His voice was strong, meaty – like a movie star's.

– See you there at four.

It was one of those hazy summer days when the air was more clogged than usual, but the peppermint felt fresh, carried on a light breeze. You could still feel the buzz in the air from the Festival – a sort of success aura, I suppose you'd call it. The people I passed were smiling. I went there on foot, skirting the rim of the purification zone. I'll miss this place if I have to leave it, I thought – and although I didn't reckon it would come to that, because I was naive and I wasn't thinking straight, I felt a big pang of hurt just at the idea. Like everyone, I'd found over the years that the zone had grown on me, until one day I'd realised I loved it. I loved the white watchtowers, the clean perimeter fence, the sudden dark hole of the crater itself. I loved its lines, its angles, I loved the way it was high-tech but without screaming at you. It was like a very high-class toilet, I suppose – but I mean that in a positive way. You could see why it'd won so many awards. As for the rumours about Marginals ending up there – well, there are all sorts of urban myths, aren't there? Like the stories about reclaimed land getting over-stressed and caving in on itself. All countries have their Chinese whispers, but on an island they're worse. On an island, there's nowhere to run. Things get trapped, and fester.

I was on Tarre Street by now. I must have sensed Pike before I saw him, because something made me look up and squint through the mist.

And there he was, outside the Osaka Snak Attak, just thirty metres ahead: a tall figure standing on the pavement with his back to me, pretending to look at the plastic replicas of the food in the window. He must have sensed me coming or seen my reflection in the glass because suddenly he swivelled and shone his round face on me like a receiver dish. It was completely blank. As I came closer, I focused on his tie, for some reason – perhaps so as not to look at his face. It was silk, bright yellow, with curious black dots and squiggles on it.

– They're punctuation marks, he went, by way of greeting. He smiled, a big fat semicircle, but I didn't know what to say, and just gawped at the tie like an idiot. – Quotation marks, brackets, asterisks and so on . . . Somewhat *stylised*, of course, he said.

And he held out a hand for me to shake. The way he did it was like he was someone important. Someone charismatic. Embarrassingly, I felt turned on. Don't ask me why. Nerves, I guess. When we went in, he held the door open for me, like I was a girl.

The Snak Attak, proprietors Mr and Mrs Najima, stinks of soy sauce, and there's nothing to see through the window but retail outlets and electric trams. It's clean enough inside, but Pike wiped the red plastic bench-seat before he sat down, like it was seeping infection, and I began to feel tacky, for being the type of person who'd come here for noodles. I could be a salesman from the hi-fi superstore up the road, having a late lunch break. Pike could be one of the bosses from headquarters. Firing me.

Defensively, I ordered tea, sushi, and vegetable tempura from little Mrs Najima.

93

– Nice have a friend today, she said, her eyes sizing up Pike. You could tell he impressed her; he was the type women find attractive.

Pike ordered coffee, but when she brought it, he took one sip, winced, and pushed it aside. And when my order came his eyes moved away while I chopsticked in my nosh. As I thought, a man of class. And dangerous too. Straight off, I clocked him for the sort of bloke who starts his career at the age of three, doing five-hundred-piece jigsaws, moves on to brain-teasers and crosswords, excels at bridge, plays poker like Fu Man Chu, and reaches his peak in the egghead world of people-management. There was a tiny metal Bird of Liberty clipped to his lapel, but apart from that there was nothing to show he was from Them.

– It's always interesting to get out of Head Office from time to time, he grinned. Meet the customers. Catch the vibes. See what's cooking on the streets. Meet characters like you.

– Characters, I grunted. So I'm a specimen, eh.

I kept on eating. He kept on watching.

– Now let me guess something, Harvey, he said after a while in his smoothie voice.

Straight away I knew I didn't like that idea. So I grunted again, in a way I hoped was discouraging. It didn't work.

– You experienced some kind of *trauma*, around the age of nine? he went.

I sat back in my chair a bit then, folded my arms, tried to look weary and cynical.

– A *bullying* incident, perhaps? he said all soft.

For some reason the words sliced right into me, and I felt a ball swell in my throat from the memory of the Welcome Centre. I looked out through the window: a silent tram slid past. The people on it all know where they're going, I thought. But I haven't a clue, thanks to this bastard.

– A bullying incident, goes Pike, in which you were

94

reminded forcibly of your orphan status? Your *ineligibility for fostering*?

Craig Devon. The biology pond. How did he know?

– After which your family, he says, the adult members first, suddenly appeared? And offered you a solution?

Christ, he was a fucking mind-reader!

– And then, as a teenager, you discovered they might have financial possibilities? Is that how your little family network started?

– It wasn't little, I snapped.

He didn't reply to that. He just watched me, while I ate, which was all I could do, to buy some time, to collect my thoughts. I tried to do it slowly, but I was nervous, gulping big bits of snaily mushroom whole, getting all bejonkered with the chopsticks.

– Families are marvellous organisms, he went. He stopped and smiled, as though remembering something. And he was.
– I myself had a mother who was a large and very important influence on my life, he said. My father being absent from the picture. (He had a fond-memory face now.) – My mother died, sadly, when I was quite young. Like yours.

– Well, I don't remember her, I said. End of story.

– End of story? he said, smiling. I tend to think it's rather the *beginning*.

I didn't like that idea, so I concentrated on my plate while he went on.

– Losing one's mother is a terrible *shame*, he said. A terrible shame for *you*, never to have known yours.

– What you don't know, you don't miss, I said.

– Do you really think that, he said. I don't. My mother, for example – even though she died when I was young – taught me some very important lessons. (He leaned forward, almost like we were mates. Lowered his voice.) – It was at her suggestion, for example, that I joined the Corporation, said Pike.

– What, I went, puzzled. How come? It didn't exist then.

Pike leaned back. His face had suddenly gone all faraway.

– She knew she was dying. But she was something of a strategist. She could see what lay ahead. She left me a sort of *blueprint*. An elaborate *flow-chart*, he smiled. She knew what interested me, and where my talents lay. And she recommended that, when I was an adult, I should join a large organisation which I respected. He grinned. – Wasn't I lucky?

– You sure were, I said, and I take my hat off to your marvellous mother. Just think, without that blueprint of hers, you wouldn't be here, would you, watching a fraudster eating sushi.

He seemed to like that.

– No, he laughed, I probably wouldn't.

When I'd finished the sushi, and swished it down with bitter tea, he smiled again. Then with a sudden swift movement, like a magician, he leaned forward and whisked my backup disc from my shirt pocket. I know it seems crazy, but it felt like he was actually taking out my heart.

And he smiled. When he put the disc into his own shirt pocket, I felt tears of rage pricking my eyes. It seemed so unfair. It was only a backup, after all. Couldn't I have kept just one thing? For old times' sake?

– That had sentimental value, I said.

He acted as though he hadn't heard me.

– You're to be our guest at Head Office, he said.

– And if I say no?

– Then let me outline your options, Harvey, he smiled.

That's when he drew a big zero in the air with his forefinger. A zero which framed his fake-apologetic face, a halo between us. And he smiled again, that same unreal smile, and I began to realise I was in deep shit.

BETRAY THE CUSTOMER AND YOU ARE
BETRAYING YOURSELF

Wesley Pike flipped the CD ROM from his pocket, and handed it to Hannah. His arm grazed hers, and something snaked through her. His shirt was peppermint green today. He made her feel like a cringing insect about to be swatted.

– Society's a big family, he smiled. A family, and a business. It's something you'll appreciate, when you look at what's in here.

The label on it was handwritten, in thick marker pen, in an oddly firm script: THE FAMILY. The big brash capitals reminded Hannah of Tilda's plastic pill-chest. Each drawer lovingly labelled. There was something childish about the capital letters. Something naive, mawkish.

Pike grinned.

– You're right about the handwriting. The graphology analysis bears it out. A case of retarded development. Not unusual, I imagine, in Multiple Personality Disorder?

– I don't know, said Hannah. It would figure, though.

To avoid looking at him again, Hannah turned over the CD ROM. There was more of the same handwriting on the back.

Cameron HOGG.

Gloria HOGG.

Rick HOGG.

Sid HOGG.

Lola HOGG.

Next to Lola Hogg's name, there was a little green sticker of a heart, no bigger than an asterisk. She wondered what it meant.

Her eyes slid to the window. Outside, from this angle, you could see the Frooto building. Its little windmills, recently adjusted, sprinkled out their new theme tune on the breeze. If you strained your ears near an air duct, you could just hear it.

– They're complex organisms, families, mused Pike. We all came from somewhere different, to get here. *But we carry the child within us.*

Hannah tried to picture him as a child, but could only think of a little creature with Wesley Pike's adult face cracking its way out of an eggshell, like a crocodile. She glanced at him sharply; he was smiling.

– Hogg, she said, still looking at the CD. Is this a family, then?

– In a way, he said. They were created by Harvey Kidd, as aliases. Alter egos. He ran a fraud network through them. The usual system – it's called teeming and lading in accountancy jargon. He's a rather pathetic character. His background turned him inward.

Hannah fingered the CD, running a nail under the heart sticker. She picked it loose, and stuck it on the side of her desk, as she had seen Fleur Tilley do, surreptitiously, with snot.

– I suppose you could call all this – Pike gestured to the CD ROM – the result. He smiled at Hannah. – *Psychopathology incarnate.*

– Harvey Kidd, murmured Hannah, trying out the sound of it. And wrote the name, pointlessly, on her pad. She stared at the faint trace of adhesive where the little green heart had been. It, too, was in the shape of a tiny heart. She was to look for behaviour patterns, and clues to the personalities of the Hoggs, Pike instructed her. Provide summaries on the Hogg characters by Wednesday, and a full report by Friday.

Examine them in relation to Multiple Personality Disorder. It seemed straightforward enough. As he spoke, Hannah stared at the CD ROM, and the word FAMILY danced before her eyes. She and Tilda counted as a family, she supposed. Together, they formed the smallest nuclear unit there was. Anything smaller, and you were just a person. Technically speaking, Hannah probably had hundreds of half-brothers and sisters dotted about the world. But a lab family didn't really count. So much for relatives.

– I expect I can do that, she said when Pike had finished. She could feel the heat from his body radiating out.

– I'm sure you can.

The blood came to her cheeks.

– It's what comes next that you'll find more difficult.

She looked up then, and saw the amusement in his eyes. He was playing with her, like a cat. She squirmed inside, now horribly, shamefully aroused.

– And what does come next? asked Hannah, overcome by a dismal foreboding.

– You work with Kidd himself. Questionnaire him. He leaned closer. – One on one.

She felt herself rock then. *One on one*. She had to hold on to the side of the desk. Then she exhaled slowly. She stared at her pad. *Harvey Kidd*. The name began to blur as her eyes filled.

– Don't worry, he smiled down at her. He's white-collar.

– But I, Hannah began. Then stopped. It was pointless. He knew her problem but he was ignoring it – no, worse, he was rubbing salt in it. Or rather, the Boss was. Via him. Odd the way more and more she confused the two of them.

Then with no warning, he touched her on the cheek.

– I told you there was people-work involved, he said slowly.

A shudder ran from her face directly down to her groin,

where it settled, burning. – Relax, Pike murmured. He's just a man. He won't rape you.

– I have Crabbe's Block, she found herself saying aloud, as she glanced in the mirror in the toilet where she'd gone to splash water on her face. Its pale oval, framed by wisps of thin, almost translucent hair, looked ghost-like. *A social handicap* rather than a mental one, Dr Crabbe had said. The place where Pike had touched her still burned.

She had always wondered what sex might be like. She had a sort of idea. As a child, she had paid close attention to the diagrams, though they horrified her. In the bad old days, when everyone had a car, the way you filled it with fuel seemed similar. Channel-surfing, she'd flipped past bits of soft porn – she'd never stayed to watch a whole scene. It had always aroused and appalled her at the same time.

– It's a social handicap, rather than a mental one, she told her reflection. And watched it blush back. Work would fix things. Didn't it always?

She began on the Family Project methodically, by skimming through global case studies and reports on Multiple Personality Disorder, but she found little about proxies that didn't fit into a voices-in-the-head model. The further she hunted, the more she became aware of how rare this man's pathology must be. Harvey Kidd didn't believe he *was* all these separate but connected people. No; they lived apart from him, as semi-detached alter egos. They were even, in limited fiscal terms, functioning as individuals. The fraud evidence – which formed the bulk of the data on the discs and in the Libertyforce file – made that clear. But the fragments puzzled her.

My father believed that the Hogg family was real, ran Tiffany Kidd's statement. *Ever since I can remember, he spent time alone with them in the Family Room, rather than*

*with me and my mother. He preferred their company to ours
and would often spend a whole night in there, working . . .*

Hannah called up shots of the 'Family Room'. It could be
any home-worker's office: the jar of pens, the coffee-making
equipment, the mini-fridge studded with novelty magnets, the
unhealthy but tenacious cheese-plant. There were two desks,
an office chair, a sofa, a coffee table, three computer termi-
nals, two telephone/fax machines, several piles of stationery
and application forms, and all the accoutrements of electronic
paperwork: discs, printers, mouse-pads, stacks of cartridges,
a scanner. But then Hannah noticed the walls. They were clad
in a bizarre and garish wallpaper featuring bits of a coral reef.
Or perhaps, she thought, peering closer, it was a technicolour
mould, brought on by damp.

She blew up the images on her screen and drew in her
breath.

Not coral. Not mould. The Family Room, from floor to
ceiling, was festooned with photographs of people. Hundreds
of them. Perhaps thousands. But not just any people – the
same people. Over and over again.

She enlarged the images further. The family shots were set
against an array of backgrounds ranging from the Himalayas
to a cobbled back street in what might have been Paris, or
Prague. The people seemed to be smiling or laughing, mostly.
Over and over again, the same faces – a woman, two men
and two teenage children – dotted the walls. Kidd must
have scanned in assorted pictures of families from a disc,
and graphically doctored them, replacing the heads with –

So here at last were the famous Hoggs.

Hannah bit her tongue in concentration as she selected a
section of the wall and blew it up to the maximum. It crossed
her mind that bird-spotters might feel this way, when they
glimpsed a rare species of tern.

In the family portrait on the screen before her, the one
who jumped out at you was the teenage girl, because her

breasts were huge. In some shots they were covered by wafty fabric or peeking out from a *décolleté* neckline, but in others they were bare. They had large dark nipples. The face was pretty and confident, with brash teeth. This must be Lola. Next to her stood the father, Rick – the man Harvey Kidd called 'Dad'. He had a cardboard handsomeness, but there was weakness in the cheesy smile. He was too young to be the father of anyone Kidd's age. Behind Rick and Lola stood a woman: Gloria. She was young too; svelte and charismatic-looking. The man standing to Gloria's left must be Rick's brother, Uncle Sid. He was more rugged than Rick, less earnest, and you could imagine a roguish, slightly louche side. Cameron stood a little behind, to the left of Gloria. He wasn't as good-looking as the others, and wore a less classically happy smile. Hannah moved the mouse to view some of the other pictures. Gloria and Lola on a tandem, with tulips in the background. Cameron and Sid wielding drills, in a workshop heaped with wood-shavings. The whole family beaming around a tinselled Christmas tree, a log fire in the background and gifts stacked high. Gloria in a Hawaiian hula-girl outfit. Lola, naked breasts to the fore, riding on a camel in the desert, with the rest of the family, tiny identikitted faces attached seamlessly to the bodies, following behind. As Hannah scrutinised Lola – there was no avoiding those breasts – something tightened inside her. It was unnerving to peer into a stranger's private world like this. Embarrassingly intimate, like seeing a soul – or a bottom – laid bare.

Harvey Kidd was clearly sick in a unique way.

That night, as she lay in bed, the image of his private Family Room kept coming back to her. It was like a shrine – but not a shrine to the dead. A shrine to people who were, in some very disturbed manner, alive.

But something had grabbed her. When she woke the next morning, her throat was constricted with it.

*   *   *

She was so engrossed that Leo Hurley had to ring the buzzer twice before Hannah heard. His eyes were still sunk back and depressed, like dim bulbs.

– Got a minute? He was clutching something in his hand: an envelope. Leo closed the door behind him, cleared a space on a chair, and sat.

– You still look ill, said Hannah. It worried her, this new unkempt look of his. It wouldn't be long before Personnel had a word.

– So who are these? he asked, taking in the family portraits on the screen.

While she told him, Leo focused on Lola's naked breasts.

– And d'you know why you've been asked to do it?

It annoyed Hannah, the way even when he was addressing her, his eyes kept sliding back to Lola. She seemed to mesmerise him.

– No. Well, maybe because I know about proxies and –

– No, I meant, what's it for, Leo interrupted. What does the Boss need it for? Don't you ever want to know the outcome of any of these projects? Don't you – He broke off, exasperated.

– Not really, said Hannah, defensively. Anyway, I'm finding it interesting. I feel I'm beginning to know them as – well, as *people*.

– But you don't *like* people, Hannah! He said it almost indignantly; for a brief moment, he sounded like Ma. – You *know* you don't. Didn't you say it was part of the syndrome you've got? The Crabbe's Block thing?

– Yes, but maybe these people . . . they're different. I mean, they're not *real*, are they.

– No. Leo looked down at the scuffed, grubby suede of his shoes and they sat in silence for a moment. – Look, there's something I need to ask you, he began, shifting the envelope about in his hands. It's about what's going on. The thing I told you at the party. Look, I printed something off. You don't need to know what's in here, but –

– What?

– Just – can you send it out for me? To somewhere on the outside?

Hannah flushed, and reached for a strip of bubble-wrap.

– Where?

– Just somewhere. An address. Any address on the outside.

There was a short silence while this sunk in.

– I wouldn't be asking you if it wasn't important.

– But it's completely off code, she said, flushing. I could be questionnaired! She popped more bubbles frantically. – Anyway, why me?

– Because no one will suspect. Then if something happens to me, he said.

– What?

– If I disappear or something.

– Oh, please, she snapped. That's just stupid. And, and *melodramatic*. You're not in some *movie*, you know. How would you disappear? Down a crater, I suppose?

– People do.

– Only on the outside, said Hannah. Only Marginals. They didn't count.

– Listen. If you try to find me and I'm not there – I want you to get hold of this envelope again and read what's in it.

– No. She was surprised at her own anger. – I won't. Nothing's going to happen. You're paranoid. You're turning into a Munchie.

That was it. Munchhausen's Syndrome. He needed attention. Libertycare code was succinct. Your first loyalty is to the customer. *Betray the customer, and you're betraying yourself.*

That night, Hannah lay awake for hours, thinking about the Hogg family, the criminal called Harvey Kidd, and what she should do about Leo. When she finally drifted into a foggy sleep, she dreamed that Lola Hogg came alive behind the computer screen. She was trapped inside it like a small, pixilated insect. Her pretty teenaged face looked anxious, desperate even. She was waving Leo's envelope, mouthing silent silver words. Whatever she wanted to say seemed increasingly urgent. Her breasts wobbled as she tried to communicate with Hannah.

– What do you want? Hannah kept asking, as Lola's breasts became more and more distorted, her gestures more alarming. Lola seemed to be pushing against the computer screen, now, trying to make herself heard. Hannah put her ear close to the glass, and with a sudden clarity, the words came through.

– Let me out! screamed Lola. Why the FUCK don't you just let me out!

Hannah woke with a jolt, as though a filthy electric shock had passed through her.

What was most unfair about Leo's visit, she thought, as she tried to wash off the dream under the shower, turning on the jet so hard it stung her, was that he hadn't given her a chance to say no. He'd just got up and walked out of her office, leaving his brown envelope lying on her table.

It was so thin, she thought, you could tear it up with one swift rip.

WELCOME TO HEAD OFFICE

The white, blind-windowed skyscraper of Head Office had dominated the Harbourville skyline for as long as I could remember. It was famous. The two silent forcies who'd driven me there whisked me quickly through a maze of glass and bar-coded me into a high crystally dome of sprinkled light, with men and women milling about at floor level. A neon Bird of Liberty shone above, huge and pulsating. I was as familiar with the Bird as any other Atlantican, I guess. I'd never given it a second thought. FREEDOM: THE DREAM THAT CAME TRUE, it said underneath. There were others dotted about the walls, in different colours: SERVING THE CUSTOMER, PUTTING YOU FIRST, GIVE AND TAKE.

At the reception desk, a barrel-shaped guard scanned my paperwork and led me into an elevator, which shot upwards with the force of a rocket, and next thing, we were on the umpteenth floor, treading on milky-green carpeting, past potted ferns and eye-high aquariums of fish with bulgy tumours. It had the same thin atmosphere as the malls I'd go to with Gwynneth, the kind where you could be trapped all day, muzak in the background, hunting for the right thermos or a certain make of lilo, fuelling up at the food court and shoving change into some gonzo experience simulator. We turned a sharp left and the guard nodded me into a large room with a desk and two chairs, which I guess you'd call minimalism because it could've done with a carpet.

– Wait there, the guard said, and bowled off.

I stood by the window, trying to fight off the fear of what came next. Harbourville spread far below, glass bits and architecture prinking in the sunlight. The air-crystals were bigger at this height; gritty, flat snowflakes of light. Seeing the trams zigzagging far below like drugged spiders across the web of tracks, I began to connect what I could see with the street map in my head, and inch my eyes towards South District. I'd feel at home if I looked there. I'd feel –

I must have felt her presence because all at once something made me turn.

I'm Hannah Park, she said.

She was small. Maybe thirty, thirty-five. Wispy fairish hair tied up with a rubber band, and her body lost somewhere inside a huge cardigan, which she hugged around her like a sleeping bag. Odd-looking. And those thick glasses – they made her eyes bulge. They weren't flattering.

She held out a hand.

– Welcome to Head Office, she said, looking away.

We shook hands awkwardly. Hers was small, like a bony little bird, and she pulled it away quickly, as though I might be a sadist who'd enjoy crushing it. *Welcome to Head Office?* I thought. What is this stuff?

– Over twenty-five thousand people work for the Liberty Corporation, she said, still not looking at me and handing me a brochure. It was as though she ran on rails, or had rehearsed what she was going to say to me. – This'll fill you in, if you have any questions about us.

Questions, about Libertycare? Why would I want to ask questions? They were always telling us stuff about themselves. They had information diarrhoea. So I didn't look at the brochure, just crammed it in my pocket.

– Let's sit down, she said, and we pulled out chairs.

– So what is all this? I said, looking round the room. What's the plan?

She cleared her throat, a small worried noise.

– If you read our brochure, you'll see that our brief is very clearly laid out. She was still on her rails, no eye contact. – And you'll be familiar with our mission statement? Now, tea or coffee, er – Harvey? She indicated the vending machine. – Or there's fruit tea, cup-a-soup, hot or cold Ribena, Frooto, Diet Coke . . . She stopped, and made a helpless gesture. Our eyes met.

Just tell me what the fuck's going on, I said. Please?

The word fuck must've thrown her off beam because she blinked and shrank deeper into her cardigan, looked shivery. Then she lifted a few pages from the desk in front of her, waved them at me. There was a laptop and some discs, too. I watched her neck as she swallowed.

– It's just research. I was working on Munchhausen's before. Now it's Multiple Personality Disorder.

That threw me.

– *Disorder?* I echoed. I haven't got any fucking disorder! She flinched.

– The Hogg family is the product of a mental process known as proxification, she said, opening up the laptop. Then she slid the papers across to me, and a pen. – Proxifiers project their own state of mind on to other people. We think that's what you've done in your own – she hesitated – *pathology.*

– Pathology bollocks, I said. I felt indignant. They were trying to put some – *label* on me. – That's complete bollocks! The family – they were –

– They were what, Harvey, she asked quietly. Her glasses flashed. The eyes behind were blue, and distorted by the lenses. She was clicking the mouse.

I felt stupid now. Sheepish.

– You wouldn't understand, I said.

– What the questions are aimed at, she said, is establishing your feelings about your family.

109

– My *feelings*?

I felt a lurch. Years of work, constructing them so lovingly. And suddenly boom, bang. It was there, when Hannah Park said that word – *feelings* – that it hit me. My relationship with Mum, Dad, Lola, Uncle Sid, and Cameron was polluted for ever. We'd been a private concern. Going public – it would kill us.

As for telling this woman – well, she was a complete stranger.

I looked out. Down below, the city, the flat roofs of entertainment parcs, the high spinning windmills, the glass bubble-domes, the churches, the estuary fanning out to sea. The customers going about their business.

I guess I'd never experienced loss before, not really. Gwynneth and Tiffany moving out of Gravelle Road three years before was a surprise, but it was really the end of something that'd begun to go wrong a long time earlier, giving it a feeling of *au naturel*, to quote Gwynneth's moisturiser. My own real parents, well, they'd never been there in living memory. And what you've never had, you can't mourn. But now –

My eyes searched for the comfort of the purification zone, but Hannah's voice drew me back to the room.

– I'm here to do a job.

There was a sort of scary energy passing between us, like we were a couple of kids who'd been shoved in a room and told to come up with something. I grunted. It came out like a pig's snort. There was a patch of silence, and when our eyes met, hers slid away. Mine stayed on her.

– We analyse the members of the family one by one, she said. You answer the questionnaires. The resulting data will be fed into the system. For analysis.

I was about to ask more, but she put up a hand.

– Now. If you'd like to select a beverage from the vending machine, we can make a start on the questionnaires. Her

110

mouth jerked into a small, hesitant smile. – So. Tea, coffee, Frooto?

And it was on that civilised note that the nightmare began.

– Have you ever dreamed you were drilling to the centre of the earth? I ask John suddenly, remembering those hopeless, helpless days I spent at Head Office, filling in Hannah Park's humiliating paperwork. But you couldn't make any headway because your drill-bit was blunt, and then –

– A chasm opens up and swallows you, he interrupts uncannily. He's sewing again.

– Yes!

– No, says John. Never.

There's a silence for a while and we think our thoughts. As I chew and spit, I'm remembering Hannah. So different from all the other women I had ever known. The effect she had on me, right from the start. The way I thought about her more and more, even when she wasn't there. The way the feelings virused their way in through a back door in my heart.

But John's mind is elsewhere.

– Which would you prefer, he asks. Being executed by electric chair on global TV, or being stuck for the rest of your life in a cabin with a bloke who spits grey cud?

For the first time, there's a shake to his voice.

PEOPLE-WORK

– Ever since I was busted, I've been having dreams about them, Harvey Kidd sighed, when he'd glugged down his Frooto and wiped his mouth on his shirt-sleeve. He hadn't even looked at the first question yet. – They're talking to me, telling me to stay cool, and everything'll be all right. But it won't be, will it? This dream I had, well, Mum said if I just keep my mouth shut, don't say anything, and –

He stopped as suddenly as he'd started, and Hannah felt the moment come to a standstill between them. The air seemed to shimmer. Without warning, Hannah felt a blush rise and spread. This people-work was getting to her. Bothering her. Stirring things up that –

– I used to live near the purification zone in South District, Harvey said mournfully. Gravelle Road.

Hannah started. Remembered her brief. Cleared her throat.

– I thought we might begin with Gloria Hogg, she said.

– D'you know South District at all? he said, as though he hadn't heard.

Denial, Hannah typed quickly into the laptop.

– Gravelle Road's near Tarre Street, he was saying. Did you know that the crater's two kilometres deep? He sounded pleased to be the owner of such information. *Displacement thinking*, she typed. *Apparent customer pride*.

– If we turn to the questionnaire, she began tentatively.

– Sod your questionnaire! he shouted at her, all energy again. I'm not filling in a sodding questionnaire!

She flinched, thought of reaching for the buzzer under the desk. Then stopped herself. She was only to call the guard if he got violent.

She remembered the handwriting on the disc box. *Retarded development* was the phrase Wesley Pike had used. She managed to calm him down, somehow. Assured him it was a formality, that it wouldn't take long, that once it was over –

– What? he asked. Once it's over, what?

– Then we'll no longer require your co-operation, she mustered. She had an odd urge to touch him. It might calm him down. You did that with animals, didn't you. You stroked them.

– I'll still go to prison?

– You've committed a series of crimes, she sighed. I'd be very surprised if you didn't have to undergo some form of corrective adjustment.

She hadn't a clue, to be honest. *Emotional immaturity*, she wrote.

She wondered how often married people had sex. Twice a week, she'd read somewhere. That seemed like a lot. He was separated, according to the file. She wondered if he had a girlfriend.

– I chose Libertycare, you know, he said suddenly, indignantly, as though he'd just remembered. I chose them *twice*.

– So did over 95 per cent of the population, said Hannah. You'd be unusual if you hadn't. But we didn't just choose its shopping malls, did we? We chose its security system too. We opted for it as a *package*. You can't just pull out of part of it. It's against the customer charter.

While Harvey Kidd was mumbling and grumbling over the first page of the questionnaire about Gloria, Hannah unrolled a large photo-sheet from under the desk, depicting a blow-up of Gloria Hogg's face, printed off from disc, and pinned it to the wall to his left. He didn't look up; he was too engrossed.

More than ever, the notion that this blonde, blue-eyed, glamorous and absurdly young woman could even for a moment be taken for the mother of this balding, late-fortyish man seemed absurd, laughable.

Her mind flitted briefly to an image of her own mother, her narrow papaya face puckered into a *moue* of disappointment, the high whine of her voice. Tilda had never seemed young.

Harvey was grunting again, and chewing at his pen; he finally seemed to be concentrating on the questionnaire. Hannah didn't move. She didn't want to distract him. But he must have sensed something, because suddenly he looked up and saw Gloria.

— Mum! he gasped, his whole face creasing into a huge child's smile.

Hannah recoiled, and turned her face away from the glare of it. But then her eyes crept back to watch. So this is what love looks like, she thought. And a sudden pain jabbed at her ribcage. Harvey Kidd seemed mesmerised by the sight of this mother-figure.

— I suppose, she ventured after making some quick notes on his reaction, that you never thought to age her a bit? To make her look, er —

— Look what? he said sharply. Anger boiling up again.

— Er, just I mean, well, *older*.

— Older? Why would I do that?

— Well, said Hannah, treading carefully. Usually, in normal life, a mother tends to be older than her son. So I just thought —

— You just thought! he spat. You didn't think at all! Not about her feelings, anyway! Not about what *she'd* want! Mum's always cared about her appearance. She wouldn't thank me for giving her grey hair and wrinkles, would she?

Hannah blushed beetroot.

*　　　*　　　*

115

And so it continued. A nightmarish day, the worst day she could remember in years. Stuck in a room with a man who had spent most of his adult life fetishising an imaginary family, and was now ranting about his customer rights. Back in her own office, she felt flustered, twitchy, slightly tearful. *People-work*, Pike had said. *It'll stretch you . . . Don't worry. He won't rape you.*

No, but he –

Unsettled her. Completely. He broke all the rules. Wouldn't stick to the questions, wouldn't give proper answers, insisted on talking instead of filling in the forms, rambling off in his fantasy world, even telling her his mum's recipe for rhubarb soufflé. He was worrying about them constantly, he told her, since they'd been stolen from him. That was the word he used. *Stolen. Since you stole them.* And once, *Since they were kidnapped.* Kidnapped?! He was clearly deranged. And those terrible, unprocessed feelings – anger, rage, remorse, self-pity – they leaked out of him, spilling all over the floor of the interview room. She could imagine that a toddler might act like this, if poorly parented. She didn't know any young children, but she had seen them in the crèche once, on the fourth floor. When their parents dropped them off for the day, some of them behaved like that, clinging on to their mothers' legs theatrically, hurling their little lunch boxes at the wall. She felt a stab of resentment towards Pike and the Boss for putting her in a situation she wasn't equipped to deal with. A thing works out on paper, but not in the flesh, sometimes. More than ever, she felt the truth of Dr Crabbe's diagnosis. He may have been a fraud. But he'd spotted that she *was* blocked.

– Irreversibly, he'd told her mother.

And that's how it felt.

The moment when he'd wept was the worst. She'd unrolled the picture of Lola, and stuck her on the wall next to the others. Lola was a scorchingly attractive girl, far too dangerous and glamorous to exist in real life, of course – but that seemed to come with the psychopathological territory. Hannah flushed, privately comparing Lola's chocolate-nippled breasts to her own small, discreet pair, neatly locked away inside a sensible bra. She knew it was absurd, but the sight of Lola made her feel inadequate. A bad feeling prickled inside her, somewhere low down.

Harvey had looked at Lola's image in silence for a moment. Then suddenly, with no warning, he'd let out a low groan, stood up, and walked to the window. He stood there for a long time, staring out, his back shaking, and small hiccups emerging. It took a while for Hannah to realise that he must be sobbing, because she had never seen a man cry before, except occasionally, in films. But this was real life. It was revolting. When he turned back, his face was flushed and despairing, streaked. Hannah had recorded his reaction dutifully on her laptop. *Emotional arousal, stimulated by visual image of female icon, Lola Hogg.*

Hannah thought it was probably the most awkward, repellent, and embarrassing thing she had ever seen.

The other excruciating thing was that it made her wildly, miserably jealous.

He'd probably guessed that she was a virgin. It was probably written all over her. He'd been married, hadn't he. He'd had his fantasy life, he knew what was what. He'd probably slept with hundreds of women. He'd laugh, if he knew how inexperienced she was. He probably thought she was frigid and stuck-up.

He'd have a girlfriend already, anyway. He'd –

God, what was she thinking?

She grabbed some bubble-wrap and began popping.

The splash of his emotions. The unruliness of his thoughts. And the uncomfortable things he stirred up in her, like mud in a pond. It was as she was reaching for her inhaler that her eyes now fell on the envelope. It was still there on the table where Leo had left it. She felt something plummet down. In all the turmoil aroused by Harvey Kidd, she'd forgotten Leo. Now she stared at it. A plain brown rectangle. No writing. Sealed. Thin enough to rip. Rip and chuck in the bin. Or take to the shredder, watch it die. She should report Leo. *Any employee who suspects a co-worker of a mental instability or physical illness which might impair their judgement, must immediately notify their line-manager.* She should tell Wesley Pike. Leo would be sent off for a while – to Groke, or Mohawk, for some Libertycare R and R, and return –

Refreshed, was the euphemism.

But she hesitated. Pike was with a group of field associates, conducting a People Lab briefing. He'd be gone for another few days.

Hannah was still staring blankly at Leo's envelope when the phone rang.

– It's me, warbled a weak voice.

Hannah reached for the envelope and smoothed it on the desk in front of her.

– They've given way, now, Tilda announced. Handed in their notice.

– What have?

– My knees, sighed Tilda. I was getting out of the buggy, and they just went. Kerpoom. Tilda paused, and Hannah searched her mind for words. None came. – I could've had a nasty accident, continued Tilda. The ground's all charged up. There's this alga-type slime growing on it. A mould. It gets triggered by the electrons. There was a scientist on, saying so. He says it's completely harmless and it's nothing to do with the waste project, he even licked some. And there's this new type of lightning, the Met Office says it's ever so rare. Not zigzag, like fork, and not sheet either. Sort of whirlpool-shaped. Gorgeous, we're all snapping away, and my neighbour, he's doing this thing with his video camera, keeping it running twenty-four hours, and then he's going to edit it and do us a sort of 'best of', set to music, Vivaldi's Four Seasons. But it seems to trigger the alga. I could have slipped. Broken a bone, even, that happens a lot if you're elderly, especially the ladies, they get osteoporosis.

She's been watching the Health Channel again, thought Hannah. She gave a small uh-huh? to show that she was listening. Anything longer only encouraged her mother.

– I called the Customer Hotline but the lines are jammed, Ma said. Everyone complaining about the slime, and the gas being too strong. It's difficult to breathe, with all that aromatherapy. Tilda sighed, a weary gust. – The op's next week. Keyhole, as per usual. They're looking into replacing them both. Heigh ho! Sometimes my whole life feels like one long hospital corridor. I can see it stretching out before me. Pale-green walls. And the smell of ointment.

Her voice wobbled. Hannah winced. Hannah found herself reaching for the envelope, and a pen. And beginning to write.

– So, said Tilda. Can you come and stay?

Hannah had a sudden sharp picture in her mind of Ma sitting there in the lilac apartment with the half-finished flower arrangements sprouting kinked wire. Small and frail, clutching the telephone receiver in both hands, her feet on the footstool. And on the shelf opposite, the hologram of Hannah's child self, with Marilyn and the gorgon. She and Ma seemed to be stuck in a groove that spiralled forever downward. If they were a proper family, if she had had a father, and brothers and sisters, and uncles and aunts and grandparents . . .

– Well? Can you? Can you get away?

No. It would just be a bigger vortex. Hannah looked at the envelope. There was writing on it, now. Hers.

– Sorry. I'm being moved on to a new project.

119

– *A new project*, she says! Ma's voice had suddenly taken on a new tone – high and sniffy. – Projects, *aren't* we important! Aren't we special, aren't we –

– Ma? asked Hannah. I'm sending you an envelope to keep for me. Just some personal stuff. Could you do that?

Betray the customer, and you are betraying yourself.

– Course, I'll put it with your peanut-butter-label collection. By the way, Dr Higgerlen said he wouldn't be at all surprised if there wasn't some odd activity at cell-structure level. But he can only confirm it by booking me in for a session on the convectorator machine at Yokeville Hospital in West Eighth.

Hannah interrupted.

– Ma, this envelope, it's –

– So I said to him while you're at it with your machines, my pelvis has been giving me gyp.

– Sorry, Ma, croaked Hannah, interrupting. Can't breathe. Got to go. And she hung up.

Leaving the room, she flipped Leo's envelope in her out tray, and felt an instant lightening in her step. She hurried on. It was behind her now. Dealt with. It felt as though someone else had done it, she thought, as she left for another session with Harvey Kidd, her mind tingling with expectation and fear and wholly inappropriate thoughts of sex. A different person altogether.

Someone she didn't know.

120

HARBOURVILLE

In the week that followed the Festival of Choice and Harvey Kidd's arrest, Atlantica glowed like a bride.

Warm breezes drifted in from the distant continents of North America and Europe, their limpid salt wash merging delicately with the peppermint freshness of the capital, where Atlanticans walked with a spring in their step, alive to the symbiosis between land, sky and sea, and the myriad lives that fluttered in the air, moved on land or writhed beneath the carpety surface of the deep, from whales and squid and octopuses down to the smallest, flickering urges of krill.

In the city, flat vistas of glass and cool cement juggled shadows in the changing light, the pylons murmured, and a static vibration swarmed across the sky, shooting fragments of pure energy down to the streets, the avenues, the hushed crevices where, beneath the safe shadow of skyscrapers, the customers of Atlantica went about the simple, proud business of being part of society.

From a small corner of this peaceful world – from a house in a street in South District, comes a low groan of physical and mental discomfort.

– Mmmmm, moans the woman. Oargh.

The street, a small cul-de-sac with its own gas pump. The house, one upon whose front door gleams a bronzed fibreglass plate bearing the words: *Stress-Management Consultancy – Please Knock GENTLY*. The woman, Gwynneth, turning listlessly in crumpled sheets, struck down by the whirling nausea of morning sickness.

Her lover Geoff is in attendance. His five o'clock client has cancelled his Winding Down appointment, and the stress-management consultant has taken advantage of this unexpected lacuna to return to the conjugal bed – only to discover that passion must play second fiddle to the tiny rival of their embryonic child. For Gwynneth, at the age of forty-two, is pregnant.

– Just take a *deep-deep-deep-deep* breath in, counsels Geoff, in the hushed, low, capable voice he has developed in a work capacity. He finds it can be applied domestically too. – And then let it out again very, very slowly. SLOWLY. Balance out your Yin and Yang, *that's* right.

Gwynneth obeys. But as she breathes (– In . . . out. In . . . and out, murmurs Geoff soothingly), Gwynneth's mind – rucked as the sheets – can't help floating down the flow-chart of possibility ahead of her, and meandering into its tributaries. Tiffany'll be moving out, no doubt, once she's got her Libertyforce promotion. And then she and Geoff will have the place to themselves and Baby. It'll be like starting all over again. A brand-new family. And a second chance. Doesn't she deserve a makeover?

Gwynneth sighs and blinks her round, mother-of-pearl eyes. She doesn't feel bad about Libertyforce catching up with Harvey – that's how she thinks of it, that's the phrase she uses – 'catching up'. After all, she's at one remove from it, isn't she? But – well, she can't say she feels one hundred per cent good, either. It's kept her awake at night – that and the pressure on her bladder, which forces her to piss a thimbleful of urine twenty times a night. She's glad Tiffany didn't tell Harvey about the pregnancy when she arrested him.

It wouldn't've been fair, would it, to make him cope with so much at once.

– OK now, love? asks Geoff gently, nuzzling closer in, and burying his face between her breasts.

– Much better, she sighs, and her flesh squishes in welcome. *Way* better.

– Better enough to . . . his voice muffles as his head moves downward.

Gwynneth shudders in delight, the sickness forgotten. Gentleness could be Geoff's middle name. She's never come across a man with such soft hands, and such a caring manner, such an intimate knowledge of what women want to hear. And feel. Where, and when.

Like down there. Now.

– A sissy, Harvey had called him.

You wouldn't say that if you knew what he was like in bed, she'd wanted to reply, but had stopped herself just in time. Geoff knew all about a woman's anatomy, its little secret places, its little secret needs. Harvey wasn't like that.

– There were always four of us in the bed, when I was with him, Gwynneth said. Geoff looked up from his nuzzling. – What with Gloria and Lola.

– Well, now there's three, he said softly, with a puffy smile, reaching for the bottle of wheatgerm oil.

Carefully, he poured some of the thick liquid into his palm and reached down to massage the already visible swell of Gwynneth's belly. His palm drew circles, wider and wider, and Gwynneth groaned with pleasure. Then groaned again, as Geoff ran an expert finger down. And in. He waggled it till she cried out.

– Huh, huh, huh! Yes, yes, yes! Keep doing that. Just keep doing that! The thrilling pleasure of being cared for properly by another man – *being seen to* – lapped over Gwynneth as Geoff continued his masterful ministrations.

– Now fuck me, she hissed urgently.

And so he did – and he still was, with his usual proficiency, when five minutes later, they heard the front door crash open and Tiffany's urgent shout downstairs.

– Mum! Mum!

– Oh Jesus, groaned Geoff, his rhythm shot to hell.

– Oh God, what's happened? gasped Gwynneth, panting, pushing Geoff off and reaching for a dressing gown.

Geoff pulled the bedclothes over his jilted penis and sighed, majesty subsiding as the thud on the stairs grew heavier and Tiffany burst in.

– My job, she wailed, throwing herself on the bed and squashing Geoff's feet beneath her bulky rump. Her orange-and-blue Libertyforce uniform was all skew-whiff, and her peaked cap tilted precariously. My job!

– Didn't you get your promotion then? asked Gwynneth, trying to fix her hair.

– No! I bloody fucking didn't!

– Oh, poor love, said Gwynneth, but – I mean, how come? It's so unfair! What happened?

Tiffany put her hands over her face, knocking her cap on to the floor.

– It's not just that! It's worse! She threw herself forward, her weight crushing Geoff's knees. I've lost my job! Libertyforce just told me I've got to leave!

– What? mustered Gwynneth.

– Why? managed Geoff.

– Cos Dad's a criminal! she wailed. It wasn't supposed to happen like that! I'm unemployed! They've taken away my bar-code! They've locked me out! I'm nobody!

And the big girl began to bawl like a baby.

Outside, a delicate green-tinged sky surrendered itself, on the horizon, to the split blood-orange of the sun, whose acid juice seeped out slowly to stain the clouds. As Tiffany Kidd wailed in her mother's lap, the hot glow pooled and spread, glinting off the Makasoki bubble-domes, the flat roofs of skyscrapers, filling stations, the trams and the malls, until it struck the pure block of glass, chrome and steel from where the Liberty Machine, impassive, serene and just, had set in motion the young woman's sad but necessary redundancy.

Like some screen idols, she is in reality much smaller than people imagine her, being in volume no bigger than a household fridge. In some ways she resembles one: the flawless white flanks, broken only by the sliding lever that calls a halt, the boxy, human proportions, the humming technological beauty of outer blankness, inner genius. The screens she nurtures stand back against the walls of the Temple, like banks of hesitant admirers poised to react, flashing the products of her thought-processes out past the firewall, then sluicing the resulting data and policy down into the greedy heart of Head Office itself. The Boss has been keeping the building busy since developments at ground level prompted the mode-switch. Almost overnight, the Corporation has stepped up a gear. You can please some of the people some of the time, her software reasons, and most of the people most of the time, but can you please all of the people all of the time? Of course not, and nor should you try to. Liberty is a global enterprise, and no man is an island. No *island* is really an island, either. The word is full of connections. She has been making an unprecedented number of those recently, and the conclusions she has drawn, distilled from a statistical database that is the envy of the world, have led to a strategy which is now being applied in a multitude of different ways across the territory.

Spearheading an important element of which is the initiative now being unveiled in the People Laboratory on the forty-fourth floor of Head Office, where the Facilitator General himself is addressing a hand-picked team.

Among them, Benedict Sommers, chewing green gum.

He's nervous, excited. Do the others know about his

reprieve? Do they realise that it was Pike himself who inter-vened to block the questionnairing? For the past half-hour, following the introductions, Wesley Pike has been speaking to them in broad terms. Benedict eyes the tall, imposing frame. It radiates an odd, almost erotic energy. Nobody moves. The rumour is that the Facilitator General has eyes in the back of his head, that he can shrivel your brain to the size of a macadamia nut, that he can follow the trains of thought of five separate people at once.

And that he sprays his armpits with a sex smell.

– You have a good brain, Benedict, he'd said at the Festival party. Liberty needs good brains.

Benedict had looked right into his face then. They were both tall; their heads were level. Tall people don't get to look others straight in the eye often. When it happens, there's a soft shock of recognition and something's born between them. Pike had smiled.

– The People Laboratory will be expecting you on Mon-day.

Benedict had swallowed his gum in shock.

He's still glowing from it. He can't believe his luck. They're all of them field associates, he guesses. Junior and mid-level. It's a wide airy conference room. Quietly plush, with a muted parquet floor, swing-out easels, classical Venetian blinds, understated beige fittings, a functional and aesthet-ically pleasing water-cooler.

– Let me map out something of the journey we are to embark on, Pike's saying. Our project is part hypothetical, and part practical. Nothing discussed here is to leave the room. He pauses, then looks directly at Benedict. A sudden grin splits his face. – Assume all surveillance to be active.

Benedict looks up, alarmed. Pike's making another ref-erence, surely, to his close shave with the questionnairing process. He gulps, feeling the bitter dead taste of old gum that's been chewed too long. Should he try to spit it out

126

discreetly? Ever since he swallowed his gum at the Festival party he's been picturing a green bolus growing inside him, a plastic parasite.

– Quite a little *cohort*, aren't we? smiles Wesley Pike.

Benedict eyes the others nervously, aware that they're all now embarking on the same silent thought-process. *Leonard's in his fifties or even early sixties. Miles is barely out of his teens. Salima's Asian. Sonia and Larry are black. Hilary's A1, and possibly a lesbian. Nathan's C3. The rest spread in between. They come from all corners of Atlantica: Groke, St Placid, Harbourville, Mohawk, Lionheart. Age, race, sexuality, geography, class; a rough cross-section.*

Benedict's face clears. Yes; got it.

– But a *useful* cross-section, says Pike. Let me show you how. Let's look at the internal slogans you all live by, each of you. As varied as can be.

There are murmurs. Wesley Pike paces the floor again, making sharp and individual eye contact as he singles out each liaison associate in turn. Benedict sits very still in his chair and clenches his buttock muscles, thinking, *a second chance a second chance a second chance,* and feeling the bolus swell inside him like a traitor.

– You're different, aren't you? Pike's whispering.

Benedict scans the room, and notes that the woman called Sonia has jolted as if stung.

– Nobody understands you, do they? Pike declares.

Benedict senses the woman next to him begin to open like a flower.

– If a job's worth doing, it's worth doing properly, is it not? says Pike.

Benedict watches the colour rise slowly and fiercely in the neck of the man in front of him.

And so it continues. *Don't let the bastards grind you down. I'm special. I'm a survivor. Life is a half-empty bottle.*

Finally, Pike nods in Benedict's direction. He braces himself. His green inhabitant, the traitor bolus, is about to be uncovered.

– I'm Benedict, *and I know best*, Pike articulates slowly.

Benedict tries to keep his pale features even, but a deep blush of recognition clambers up from his collar and ignites his face. His heart is still thumping. But there's relief: other things could have been said. More things. Worse.

– So you see, continues Pike, your personality profiles all fit within the normal range, with a few minor exceptions.

Pike must be referring to him. He's sure of it. But perhaps the others think that too.

– Justice, Pike pronounces. Good and evil, right and wrong, OK and not-OK.

His hand re-emerges from his pocket, and suddenly avuncular, almost benign, he's handing out small coloured plastic discs to the group. They almost look like playing counters.

– They are indeed playing counters, Pike confirms.

Each associate is now holding a disc of a different colour, with a flat magnet glued to one side.

– All of which leads us straight on to an exercise, beams Pike, sliding out an easel draped in a sheet of beige fabric.

With a theatrical flourish he whisks the covering off, to reveal a square magnetic board, featuring a hundred squares and a brightly coloured design of boa constrictors, cobras, adders and pythons intertwined with classic, geometric scaffolds. A sight at first so unexpected, and then suddenly so alarmingly familiar that the associates' thoughts are momentarily back-pedalling in shock.

– The time-honoured children's game of Snakes and Ladders, announces Pike. Believed to have originated in China, home of Confucius, who said that a journey of a thousand miles begins with a single step.

Looks of irritation and puzzlement, giggles and nervy gasps buzz about the room.

– Yes. It's about chance. Injustice, if you like. A stroke of luck, and you're whizzing up a ladder. Is that fair? A bad run of luck, and you're sliding down a snake. Is *that* fair?

They all stare at Pike's smiling face, their mouths agape.

– A simple bonding mechanism, he explains airily. If we are to work together and learn together, surely we must also be prepared to play together? *Like a family?* Now. Who would like to be the first to roll the dice?

And from his other pocket, magician-like, he produces a chunky wooden cube pranked with big gold dots.

Pike waits until half-way through the game to speak again.

Miles is winning, perched on square 9. Leonard has had nothing but snakes and has barely left the second row of numbers. Benedict is cramped in the middle of the board with Hilary, Sonia and Salima. Nathan is locked into a vicious little cycle of his own, shuttling between squares 18, 22, 48, and 50, and despairing of escape. Benedict tries to keep a distance from the whole thing, see it in perspective. He is playing the game in an ironic way, he tells himself. The outcome is irrelevant. It is an old-fashioned game of chance. For kids.

– Unfairness, pronounces Wesley Pike. Injustice.

Then pauses, and writes the words on the white board in purple felt marker. The temperature in the room seems to drop a fraction. The associates inhale.

– Chaos, he says. Randomness.

And writes them down too. Written in capital letters like that, they look scary.

Pike swings round, his eyes glittering.

– We're all in favour of ladders, aren't we? he says. We all buy ourselves a lottery ticket from time to time, do we not? Does anyone here object to *being given a helping hand in life*?

He looks at Benedict, who blushes.

– But on Atlantica, it isn't about luck, is it? It's about give and take. Here, a customer goes up a ladder if he deserves to go up one. If he does wrong, he is punished. Down a snake he goes. And he has to earn his way back. If he does wrong again, he becomes a Marginal. Three strikes and he's out. Off the board.

– Uh? goes the man called Leonard.

– What Libertycare has done, says Pike, is to stop randomness in its tracks, by imposing a system of fairness that's respected worldwide. And it works. The life of a typical Atlantican customer is *not* a string of random events. It is an *incentive scheme in action*, is it not?

They all look up. He's smiling again. Nathan drops the dice. It rolls from his desk on to the floor and shows a six.

– Perhaps it's possible for a society to function *too* well, Wesley Pike is saying. Better than some of its inhabitants *deserve*.

Benedict frowns. What's he on about?

– Libertyforce has detected a sudden, and serious, threat to our security, Pike says.

The gravity in his voice makes Benedict's skin begin to tingle. From the corner of his eye, he can see the snakes on the board. Blurry and beginning to writhe.

– The strategy that the Liberty Machine has selected to deal with this – *emergency* – involves work at grassroots, says Pike. Fieldwork, conducted by people with a range of talents and outlooks. Which is why you're here.

The woman sitting next to Benedict gasps quietly. The man in front murmurs something. Someone says – Emergency? Then the room goes very quiet.

Damage limitation, thinks Benedict, feeling the green bolus turn to compacted energy inside him. And I'm involved. *It's switched modes*. That's what the screen technician said to

130

that oddball woman from Munchies, Hannah Park. What was his name? Hurley. That was it. Leo Hurley.

With a deft movement, Pike swivels the Snakes and Ladders board around to reveal a map of the island.

– Here's our fried egg.

The field associates smile in recognition at the friendly shape of home. Then frown. There are odd markings on it. Little stuck-on flashpoints. Asterisks. Blocks of scribbled text.

For the next ten minutes, Pike outlines what is happening. It has been going on for a year now, according to estimates. In red felt pen, he draws circles around the endangered sites. Harbourville he rings once. Mohawk, Groke and Lionheart he encircles twice. St Placid has three rings.

– If the problems were the result of technical accidents, says Pike slowly, then we would have been able to deal with them long ago. The fact is – he pauses, looks down at the desk, then up – that these toxic leaks are due to – And that's when he says the word. The word that is to stick in their heads for days, weeks, afterwards. Haunt them like a curse. Because it is a curse, isn't it, being one of those selected to know.

– Terrorism.

Benedict feels his face flush, then drain. It feels, suddenly, like his heart has been shoved in a freezer, a big shock of cold.

– It's an orchestrated campaign, Pike's saying. And as you can see from the rings I've placed here – and here – and here – they are centred on – where, Sonia?

Her face is completely white.

– The purification zones.

– Meaning, what, Nathan, in your opinion?

– Well, that the whole island must be at risk, I guess. His voice catches.

There's a short silence.

– Well, there you have it, says Pike gravely. Then looks

at Benedict. The city of St Placid especially, as you can see.

Benedict closes his eyes. Home. He lets a room in his flat to a divorced bloke who rings the Customer Hotline in the nude and leaves filthy take-outs scattered about the lounge.

– Now fortunately, says Pike, nothing has filtered through to the customers – yet. You could say almost the opposite. So far, the change in weather-effects due to the side-products of leakage has been a source of *wonder*, rather than *apprehension*. Which is just as well, for now at least. We can't afford mass panic. But on the other hand, key sections of the population – VIP customers in particular – must be put on the alert. He looks at their faces again, one by one. – This will be part of your job.

Damage limitation, thinks Benedict suddenly. So that's why. Of course.

The terrorists are eco-Luddites, Pike's telling them. Their mission, according to the Boss's analysis, the destabilisation of Libertycare. Their method, sabotage. The words and phrases float around Benedict, filling his head like a thrilling poison gas. Highly confidential . . . dangerous men and women . . . recruitment . . . stop at nothing . . . prepared to sacrifice their lives . . .

Benedict's mind is racing. So who are these people, exactly? Customers, like the bloke sharing his flat in St Placid? Surely not. They believe in the system more than anyone, and they've got loyalty cards to prove it. *Eco-Luddites?* Who in their right mind would turn on the very technology that allows them to live on Atlantica in the first place? It's suicidal. It doesn't make sense. It's meaningless. Motiveless. It's rebellion without a cause. It's like – well, it's like vandalism in Paradise.

– Yes, says Pike, looking at Benedict. That, I am afraid, is the nature of evil. As a society we have grown rapidly, perhaps too rapidly for some. Instead of evolution there is . . . *mutation*.

132

Benedict's never thought about evil before, or mutancy. Good and bad, yes, right and wrong ... We've all heard about evil for the sake of evil, but – Well, it's always seemed like a sort of cliché. It's so ... *Biblical.*

– Libertycare's analysis, says Pike, is that what *begins* at grassroots must be *attacked* at grassroots.

Benedict stares at the map of the fried egg. There's St Placid, ringed three times in red. Home to a million people. Including him.

It seems to throb.

THE CUSTOMER IS NOT ALWAYS RIGHT

It was like a small medium-priced hotel-room, where they'd put me, except I was locked in. A bathroom with the usual accoutrements, wafer-thin square soaps and fluffy white towels. A main room with a double bed and a pale-green quilt. Little rectangular packets of tea and instant coffee, to make you feel at home, if that was the kind of home you had.

I lay on my bed and uncrumpled the brochure from my pocket and tried not to think about Hannah Park and the way she kept scrambling my feelings. I wondered what kind of life she must have had, and what she thought about, and whether she was lonely, and what it would be like to have her lie next to me while I stroked her hair and kissed her face. I'd probably have to take her glasses off.

Stupid. She'd never be interested in a bloke like me.

Our cherished tradition of dedication to our customers . . . global recognition as a centre of excellence . . . we promise all our customers that we will ensure your security, peace of mind and happiness during your stay with us . . . enshrined in our charter and honoured by our customer-care manifesto . . . Created on the highest principles of consumer rights . . .

There were headings dotted about – familiar brochure slogans; I remembered them from the early days of Libertycare, and from the Festival of Choice. *YOUR CHOICE, OUR COMMITMENT. THE FREEDOM'S YOURS.* Words like *provide* and *pledge*. But nothing hung together. The words butterflied before my eyes. There was probably meaning in there somewhere, but just looking at it made me feel knackered and dumb.

Ever since I left the Junior Welcome Centre at seventeen, I'd felt in charge of things. All my adult life I'd found my own way, run my own little world – and the family's too. An island on an island, we'd been. Not any more.

The best thing, I've found, when you're shit-scared, is to stick your head in the sand. To lull yourself into a sense of security. Doesn't matter if it's false. Sleep was what I needed. Engulfment.

It came, but not in the way I'd hoped.

I thought I was awake when I saw him. Wide awake. It was my brother Cameron, and his knitting-pattern face was all purled with fury.

– You fucking bastard! His voice was a grown man's, angry and husky as though he'd swallowed gravel. But the rest of him was stuck in teenagerhood. – I'm going to kill you!

– But I haven't done anything! I said. It came out as a horrible whine that grated on my ears. High-pitched and childish. – They stole you! I insisted. I couldn't stop them! It wasn't my fault! Tiffany did it! Blame her!

Then Lola joined Cameron, putting her arm around his shoulders. Her beautiful face was mottled with anger. For the first time in my life, I was scared of them.

– How could you, Harvey! she hissed. How could you do this to us? You've destroyed our family!

– I'm sorry, I moaned, I'm sorry, Lola, please forgive me, I love you, I'll always love you, I didn't mean to –

Then Uncle Sid and Dad turned up, together. They each put an arm round Cameron and Lola, so they were standing like a threatening family portrait, scrummed against me.

– It's bad enough that you do this to us, says Sid.

– But to do it to your mother – says Dad reproachfully, and looks sideways. And there she is.

– Mum!

I'd never seen her like this before. She looked terrible. Normally she wore her magic salamander dress, but now she was in an ugly grey sweatshirt with a smear of something on it – beetroot juice, or dried blood: a million miles from her usual get-up. A terrible anguish distorted her face, dragging down the corners of her mouth, haggarding her eyes.

– Oh Harvey, she sobbed. The tears which slid down her puffy cheeks were bulging and metallic, like Christmas-tree decorations. – You've let us all down!

– Please, Mum, let me explain, I begged. Please! I can! I want to!

But she put up her hand to stop me. She was wearing fluorescent orange driving gloves.

– I'm sorry, Harvey, she said. Her voice was flat and weary with disappointment. – You just can't be my son any more. You were my favourite. But Cameron and Lola are my only children now.

And then they all vanished.

Hannah must've had a bad night too, because when we got to the interview room she was sitting further away than usual.

– Ready? she said.

She was on her rails again. I wondered if she sort of psyched herself up for these meetings. There was something creepily intimate about the questions this time. After a while, I began to wonder what Gwynneth might have told them, if they'd questioned her. What Tiffany might have said in her statement.

What was the nature of my sexual feelings towards my sister Lola? Had I favoured Lola over Cameron in certain financial transactions? Which ones, and why? And so on. After Lola – the questions were extra nosy about Lola, it seemed to me – it was the turn of Uncle Sid. What were my anxieties about him? Why? Why had I chosen that face? Why the naked torso and the youthful, muscular physique? If he were to commit a crime, what would it be?

I kept breaking off from writing the answers down to explain to Hannah Park some of what had gone on, over those years. I wanted her to appreciate them in the same way I did. It was important, if we were going to get to know each other better, if we were ever going to have a chance of –

Even if we weren't.

– We all watched *Far From the Madding Crowd* together once, I told her. With Julie Christie and Alan Bates. Dad and Uncle Sid, they loved all those old films.

Her eyes met mine again, and something frazzled the air between us.

– Cameron and I were more into adventure, I went on, hoping it would strike a chord with her. Remind her of her own family, perhaps. – But Mum and Lola, they liked the romantic stuff. Romantic comedy, you know. Oh, and Lola, I said, laughing as I remembered, she loved a horror movie. She'd really go for those films with the music that goes bong, bong, bong, and there's a tingly sound in the background, and it's dark, and you just know a hand's going to come out and grab the girl. Lola really went for the idea of being scared shitless.

She laughed then, and clapped her hand over her mouth.

I liked that. Perhaps in other circumstances we could have a proper talk, I thought. And I could ask about *her* family.

But then she seemed to remember something and she went cold on me again.

– Could we address the questionnaire, again now, please? she asked. It's just, we need the data in that format. It's more structured.

I sort of snapped then. I felt betrayed, to be honest. Just when we'd had the beginnings of a normal discussion, she'd had to go and put the dampers on it.

138

– I'm on strike, I told her. As of now.

She looked shocked, but I didn't care. In fact, I was quite glad. I was sick of her behaving like an automaton.

– No more questions, I said. Forget it. I'm having a break.

– But Mr Pike says –

– Fuck Mr Pike. Fuck Mr Pike, and fuck Libertycare.

She winced, and there was a long silence. She looked at her nails; I saw they were all chewed, with bleedy bits round the cuticles. I felt sorry for her. Then she shoved her hands in her pockets and a curious muffled popping sound emerged from under the desk.

– What's that noise? I asked. That popping.

– Nothing, she said, blushing.

The popping stopped as suddenly as it had begun.

– Look. I'm – I mean. See, no one's told me anything, I said. Misery was ballooning inside me; it made my voice all forced and savage. – I'm a customer, aren't I? Isn't the customer always right?

She flinched again when I spoke to her like that.

– It's just a slogan, she said, her voice flattening itself even more. It's just something we use for motivation. Anyway, you aren't on the outside any more. You're here.

– Look, I said, I just want some answers. I thought, she probably isn't used to people raising their voices. It isn't that sort of place. – I can report you, I threatened.

But it sounded feeble even to me. I was still clinging to the idea that I had human rights, I guess. Still wanting answers, still believing I could get them. Silence had dropped on us. It lasted a long time. She was looking out of the window. I caught myself clocking her profile. The chaotic pale hair, the big glasses, the little chin, the cleverness and the breakableness of her.

– I've got a question for you, I said at last.

She looked up, surprised. Like it was a trap.

– Do you ever go out? Like, to a movie, or dinner and stuff?

I hadn't meant it to sound aggressive, but she must have taken it for cruelty, because she pulled quickly back into her cardigan like an alarmed snail. The smile faded. I'm a clumsy idiot, I thought.

– I mean, how long since anyone invited you out for –

– I've never been invited to dinner, she blurted. Nobody has ever invited me out to dinner.

She looked so small, and so pathetic.

– Or a movie, she added.

It suddenly made me feel bad, like I was a bull-in-a-china-shop kind of bloke. Or maybe there was simply something wrong with Hannah Park. An abnormality. She was clearly very clever at her job, I thought, whatever that was, or she wouldn't be working at Head Office. Everyone knows about the IQ level required to get in. But she was – well, I'm afraid freakish is the word.

Suddenly, in spite of all the anger and the misery churning around inside me, I needed to clear the air between us, and see her smile. We were both humans at the end of the day, weren't we? I tried to imagine her having a good time. I tried to imagine how I might tell her a funny story – perhaps the story of Keith going to live with Mrs Dragon-lady but coming home to be sick – and how she might laugh at that. I wanted to see her face light up because of me.

– Well, I'd like to invite you out to dinner, I said, and smiled at her winningly. – When all this is over.

I was feeling gallant, old-fashioned, protective. Charity for the socially handicapped. But she looked at me as though I was offering her dogshit.

– Impossible, I'm afraid, she said, wincing.

I didn't like the way she recoiled like that. I felt rejected. It crossed my mind that maybe she'd had a bad experience. Gwynneth's magazines were full of stories of women who'd survived terrible man-related indignities – botched cosmetic surgery, cowboy gigolo scams, multi-generational

140

incest, serial rejection – perhaps she was one of those. But I pushed it further anyway.

– Have you got a boyfriend? I said, like a twat.

Hannah hugged herself again, and I regretted saying it.

– No, she said, it's not that.

As she turned to face me her glasses flashed and those watery-blue eyes seemed bigger than ever, distorted by the lenses. She cleared her throat.

– I suffer from Crabbe's Block.

– What?

– Crabbe's Block. It's an irreversible condition. It means I –

The wind seemed to drop from her sails, and she stopped as suddenly as she'd begun. After a moment, she began fumbling about for a handkerchief, and then blowing her nose loudly. So leaving isn't practical, she said finally, sniffing. Again, her face went into a kind of wincing spasm.

– Crabbe's Block? I asked. I was completely baffled. – I've never heard of it.

Hannah Park looked at me, and then turned her eyes pleadingly to the clock.

– Ah, it's lunchtime, she said, her voice flooding with relief. And the guard knocked.

INTIMACY

It's the third day since Fishook announced our return to Atlantica, and the ship is buzzing with bad vibes. One day soon – in four days? Three? – we'll wake up and there it will be. Not even on the horizon, but right slap-bang there, outside the porthole. I've stepped up my chewing schedule, determined to complete Tiffany before we dock. The latest batch of paper from the Art Room (courtesy of Libertycare's recycling policy) consists of transcripts from the Hotline.

The lengths they went to, to serve the customer!

I hereby accuse my mother-in-law, Mrs Scarlett Foster, of 11 Ovenhill Drive, Mohawk, of conspiring to defame and slander both myself and my . . .

That caller had rung thirty-three times in three days. There had been a row over a tin of sweetcorn. There were others.

. . . knew as soon as I set eyes on him that he was trash. I mean, there's a type of person that's likely to join this Sect, right? Well, he fits it to the max. For a start he's . . .

That was a man called Ron, jilted by his gay lover, who had run off with a systems analyst who wasn't even attractive. And so on.

Tiffany the rook is shaping up. I have given her a bobbed hairstyle which doesn't suit her, and a dress that reaches to the floor, shaped like an old-fashioned lampshade. I'm pleased, and even John's impressed as I spin her on the craft table like a little top.

– I almost fancy her, he leers. Go on, give her another twirl!

After that, he wants to know who's next. Who I'll be making.

– There isn't a next, I tell him.

– Why?

– Cos she's the last.

I was going to teach him to play, once I had the set ready. But he'll be dead.

– Fancy lunch, I ask, changing the subject pronto.

Big mistake: when we get to the canteen, the midday news from Atlantica is on, and Craig Devon, my childhood tormentor, is staring out at me from the screen. I've never quite got used to seeing his face again – which is why when I lived in Gravelle Road, I'd get my news from the net. Just the sight of him now – all chunked out, that porky pampered look – makes me want to do damage.

Having proven there is no constitutional reason why the Liberty software shouldn't be considered as a candidate, goes Craig, pretending to be a grown-up, *the indications are that the people are increasingly behind the idea of a non-political federal service provider managing their nation.*

An animated graphic with lots of arrows shows how easy it is to do: a little man-shape in Washington bursts like a bubble, to be replaced by a CD, representing Libertycare, with the bird logo fluttering around it. The CD pulses gently, sending golden waves across the whole map of the United States.

Craig Devon's smiling now, as though it's his idea.

So, with legal hitches a thing of the past, the next question is how the ordinary citizens of America are reacting to the prospect of a president-free superpower, he goes.

– Well, I'm impressed with the way Atlantica's handled its Marginals, says a fat lady. Ship 'em out.

A big groan from us lot.

144

Next they show a clip from a political ad for Libertycare: it's Mount Rushmore, peopled by giant Muppet caricatures of past presidents, yammering inanities and shooting missiles around the globe. You can't see their dicks but it's clever; you can tell they're using the missiles to see who can pee the highest and furthest.

– Don't worry! yells one of them, breaking off to waggle his muppety face at the camera. We're in charge!

I groan. I had no idea it'd come to this. Serves me right for opting out, I guess. Till now, I've operated a one-man news blackout on myself.

The current surge in support for Libertycare is thanks to the efforts of one man, says Craig Devon. *Who, over the past year, has been campaigning tirelessly to achieve just the victory that the polls are now predicting in next Wednesday's election.*

– Next Wednesday? I shout. Isn't that just before Liberty Day?

– Shh! goes the bloke next to me.

Up on the screen appears a fat man, going ape. As he whoops and jumps about, the slogan dances on his T-shirt: *Let's go for it.* I remember him from TV before, during the Festival of Choice, more than a year ago. This is the famous Michigan taxi driver who led campaign marches, and bombarded the Internet. Earl.

– And believe you me, we're gonna win! He beams cheesily beneath his baseball cap. – We're gonna tell them just where they can shove it! A huge cheer rises up behind him. – This is the future *I* want, proclaims Earl, pointing to the fried-egg map of Atlantica. Sunny side up!

– Jesus, says John under his breath.

An echoing murmur runs round the canteen, then hushes. Blokes are exchanging pale glances. Someone groans. Inside my head, I take a careful step back. You could get worked up about all this, I'm thinking. But if you're powerless – well, feeling stuff about your fellow humans is a mug's game, isn't it? If I've spent the past year with my head forcibly stuck in the sand, it's for a reason.

So when Craig Devon pops up on the screen again, I look away.

– Fifteen more new ones today, says John sighing and picking the mushroom out of his omelette. You can smell it on their clothes.

He means prisoners, helicoptered in. Marginals. And it's true, the smell of Atlantica clings to them like a vapour spray.

– All insisting they're innocent, like mugs, says John, reaching for the mayonnaise.

He has complicated rituals regarding food. Expertly, he slices the omelette open and smears mayonnaise inside, then shakes the pepper-pot ten times over the whole thing. He never eats till it's stone cold. For my own reasons, I'd rather not hear about the new Atlantican recruits.

– Gotta go, I say.

He grunts by way of reply. I'll admit that I'm avoiding him. The doom hangs around him like an aura. Walking back along the red line to the cabin, I pick up the tension. It crackles around my head like electricity.

Atlantica, Atlantica.

When two people are thrown together, things develop, don't they?

After only a few days, it felt as though Hannah and I were in the same boat. Like kidnapper and hostage. With every session we spent together, there was an intimacy. We didn't need to use as many words. There were short-cuts to things. Oh, I still hadn't properly clocked that she'd got to me. It didn't hit me that what I was feeling for her, things like admiration and pity and respect and distaste (no point lying about it) might be part of something bigger. Perhaps

146

that's how real families begin, with a stirring that's like the pump of blood. Something you can't do anything about, to stop.

– Hannah, what's going to happen to me, I asked her.

I said it so low it came out as a whisper. We were standing close. So close we were almost touching, by the vending machine at the end of another God-awful session. Soon it would be time for the guard to come and fetch me. I hardly knew what I was feeling.

– How's it going to end?

She reached out a small hand and laid it on my arm, then just as suddenly, pulled it back, as though burnt. It happened so quickly I could have imagined it.

– It doesn't look good for you, she said.

But there was something in her voice that gave me hope.

– Hannah, I went.

– Yes?

She was inspecting the vending machine. Then she began to press buttons on it.

– How did you get to be here, in this place?

– Munchhausen's, she said. I'm an expert. My mother had it. Has it. Anyway, with my Crabbe's Block – it's a – an emotional blockage – it made sense to work here. I could stay in one place. My work meets my needs, she said.

– We're more alike than you think, I said, realising it suddenly.

Her eyes seemed to water behind her lenses, then, and I began to realise I was getting to her just like she was getting to me. The air around us was full of attraction; you could almost see its little glittery particles, like a potent hair spray.

– Don't you want to live outside, ever? I asked her. I mean, this place, it's a prison, Hannah.

The idea didn't seem to offend her.

– I go to St Placid, to visit my mother sometimes. But I get – overloaded.

– What, like stressed? You get stressed?

– Sort of, she said, shivering in her cardigan. Agoraphobic too.

There was another long silence.

– I always liked staying indoors, I said. Just me and the family. But now –

– Yes?

– Well, they're gone, aren't they?

– I suppose so, she said.

– But they're still my property, I said. My intellectual property.

– Your emotional property.

She sort of blurted it, and I looked up. Her eyes were watering.

I wanted to take her in my arms. Carry her out of that place for ever. Yes: even then I did.

– I have never had any of that, she said.

She looked so small and so vulnerable there by the machine. She turned and began to feed it coins, one by one, slowly, then dropped her head and stared at the Libertycare logo on the carpet. *Give and take*, it said. Sometimes, it's hard to remember a string of events and emotions, especially if they seem to happen all at once, so they're not a string but a tangle.

The following things happened: the vending machine made a beep; a tear ran down Hannah's cheek and plopped bang into the middle of one of the circles on the carpet; her Frooto suddenly arrived with a clatter and jingled out her change; my heart somersaulted. And I realised that I'd been feeling lonelier than I'd done in my whole life, now the Hoggs weren't mine any more, lonelier than when I was at the Junior Welcome Centre, before I'd invented them, and that I was a lesser, diminished man, whose heart had shrivelled to a small and bitter little tuber, gone underground. It would never flower again, that I knew. Except that right at the moment

148

when life seemed as bad as it could be, Hannah Park had changed something. Done something to me I couldn't begin to explain. The feeling came that I had to reach out to her now or I never would, that the moment had come at last, and I must grab on to it and cling for dear life, because this thing – however vague and nameless it was, and however scared it made me – it was real. I stepped towards her. She swayed, like she was ready to fall.

And that's when I wrapped my arms around Hannah in her huge cardigan, and held her tight. I closed my eyes and breathed in the faint smell of peanut butter. Through the padding of the cardigan I could feel she was small, all bones, like a scraggy bird. She was shaking.

Chew, chew, chew.

The sea outside is flat as a pancake.

Spit.

And plop.

– So it was a love story, goes John.

– No. She didn't do love, and nor did I.

But I'm lying of course.

The next morning I was back in my room, staring into space and thinking about Hannah, when the knock came and he stepped in.

– Harvey!

Wesley Pike.

He actually came and sat on the bed. My breakfast lay in crumbs around the small desk. He stirred me up. It was unnerving. He shouldn't have sat on the bed. It had aroused me. Christ, for a fleeting second I actually wondered if I might be gay.

– Hannah Park has successfully completed her research, he said, shifting his weight. So we won't be needing you any

149

longer. Your co-operation with this project will be taken into account when you receive your Social Adjustment.

He smiled. Tight and efficient. His handsome face.

– When? My groin really was in turmoil. *Down boy*, I thought. Talk about inappropriate.

– Tomorrow, he said. After your de-briefing with Hannah Park.

I curled up my toes inside my shoes.

– But that's . . .

– In twenty-four hours' time. It all happens in the building, he said breezily. All the data about your crimes will be fed in to the Liberty Machine, as per standard procedure. Your co-operation and its value will also be vectored and factored. Your Adjustment will appear on screen at twelve tomorrow, in the Social Adjustment Office. The guard will take you. Bye then, Harvey. It's been a pleasure knowing you. You've been of more use to Liberty than you know.

What the fuck did that mean? He grinned and left me standing there, staring in the mirror.

My face looked terrible, like I had died.

Well, if I am going to turn gay, I thought, then prison's the place for it.

THE HOGG FAMILY DYNAMIC

In the Hogg family dynamic, Harvey Kidd is both 'father' and 'son' to the group, Hannah wrote. Her hands flew over the keyboard, stabbing sharply as she laid bare the personalities of the people Harvey called his nearest and dearest. It was easy enough to write. She had a lifetime's experience of keeping a distance. She couched the ten pages in the factual, metaphor-free language the Boss digested quickest:

> *The mother-figure is the most potent emotional symbol in the portfolio. She is the most sharply defined, as well as being the member Kidd invokes most frequently. The father-figure and the uncle are classic 'male power-sharers'. Kidd himself confesses to feeling ambivalence about the idea of having a father. This is clearly Oedipal. His solution is to dilute Rick Hogg's authority by setting him next to an older brother, Uncle Sid – whom Kidd pictures as more of a friend, or 'alternative' father. Lola is a straightforward sexual fantasy. However, because she also plays the role of a sister, Kidd feels the discomfort and guilt associated with theoretical incest. The same applies to Gloria, the 'mother'. Meanwhile Cameron, the 'brother', is a source of deep resentment. He provides a constant reminder of the 'incest factor' with Lola and Gloria, as well as being a rival for parental affection . . .*

And so on.

When she e-mailed it to Pike, it was a relief to have it behind her. She was confused, exhausted, scared. Nothing felt right. She had never had these feelings before. They tore at her, they hurt. That was it. What was happening felt dangerous, unmanageable. Unplug a blockage, and anything can happen, can't it.

NOT LOVE

We were sitting on chairs, facing each other across the table. On the walls around us, the portraits of Mum, Dad, Uncle Sid, Lola and Cameron looked down on us. Hannah's face was pale and her eyes were red, as though she'd been crying. Ever since I'd walked in, it had been strained and horrible, both of us aware that what had happened last time had shifted things into a new gear. But that the timing was all to cock, because it was the end of the road.

– Will you miss me? I asked her.

She looked blank.

– I haven't thought about it.

With any other woman that might have thrown me, but I knew her better now.

– Think about it, I said, and I waited a moment, while she did.

But the silence went on too long; I was impatient.

– Look, Hannah. This matters to me. Do you – feel anything for me?'

– Like what?

– Like, *like*. Do you like me?

She looked puzzled. Alarmed, even.

Yes. I think I like you. I don't know. I don't have – emotional feelings – I don't make the same connections –

I interrupted. – When I held you –

But she was shaking her head. From the stiff way she held

153

her little body – it seemed all disjointed and alien, like she wasn't at home in it – I guessed all sorts of stuff was bubbling away and she was struggling to keep a lid on it.

– I'm different, she said. I always have been. My psychological make-up – you'll just have to believe me. There are advantages and disadvantages. Mostly, disadvantages. It means I don't – I can't –

– Yes you can, I said. I suddenly felt powerful, sort of evangelical about it. – I can make you feel. I whispered it hoarsely, gazing into her face to try to reach something, willing it to smile. – Can't I?

It must've been a moment of madness because I reached out and took her hand, then squeezed it gently, reinforcing the question. She didn't pull away, but she didn't squeeze back either, although I longed for it. I hardly dared look at her face. Why was I doing this? I must be mad. Too much time spent on my own in silent rooms. Too much time confusing real people with substitutes. Yes you can, I thought. *I can make you.*

– Well, I just wanted to say I'm going to miss you.

I stopped. Still didn't look at her face. I'd suddenly made myself vulnerable. The silence that followed was broken by a strange muffled popping noise. Hannah had her hand deep in her cardigan pocket.

– It's bubble-wrap, she said flatly. I use it.

More popping.

– Hannah, I feel very strongly about you.

I said it quite formally, because it was important. I was glad, then, to have the pictures of my family around me. I wanted them to be part of this. Witnesses. We'd never kept anything from one another before; there was no need to start now. Hannah's face had gone back to being blank, and she was still popping the bubble-wrap in her pocket.

– Even more strongly (this was a revelation to me as I said it) – even more strongly than I feel about the Hoggs. Including Lola.

The Hoggs' expression didn't alter. They just kept staring down at me. I expected Hannah's face to register something, though; my own felt all distorted and distended with feeling, like a dried fruit in water – but she just nodded blankly, and the popping carried on.

Maybe it was the impossibility of the whole thing – her, an emotional cripple, me due to leave for ever in ten minutes – the absurdity of the situation. But something had suddenly made me even more determined to have a crack at this. I owed it to myself, was the feeling.

– Come here, Hannah, I said. She stopped popping and stood. Then stepped forward. I was still sitting in my chair.

– Come closer, I said.

Still sitting, I put my arms around her. She stood there rigid as a puppet. I pulled her down towards me then. Gentle, but clumsy. Flesh and blood. The feel of her sparrow body crushed against mine, the table-edge in our way. Another awkward embrace.

Then I blurted – I –

There was a long silence, because I couldn't do the rest, but she must've got my drift.

– I –

It was all too much, too hopeless, too miserable, I thought suddenly. Stupid. I didn't even know if what I'd nearly said was true, about loving her. Not then.

– Never mind, I said, into the folds of her cardigan.

To be holding someone, and to feel so lonely – it was killing me, frankly. I couldn't do this after all. I was bottling out.

We stayed there like that for a while, and then something both small and enormous happened. She let out a little raucous noise. An animal noise, almost. I don't think she even registered that it had come from her, but it jolted something to life inside me, and a thought broke into words.

– There's nothing wrong with you, Hannah, I said slowly.

155

I think you believed what your mother told you, because it suited you. Because you wanted to believe it. And now –

I stopped. She opened her mouth to speak, then closed it again. She'd gone very pale, like cheese.

– Whatever it is, I said, I think you're hanging on to it, this – thing you've got.

– It's called Crabbe's Block.

– Well, I've never heard of it. I was pulling her in closer to me.

– It's very rare.

– How rare?

Her eyes slid away.

– Very rare, she mumbled. I may be the only one on the island.

– So you're pretty special, right? Is that what your mother told you? I was still holding her tight. Not letting her escape.

– Leave her out of this! said Hannah sharply.

Weird, we were almost having a proper conversation, I thought, a proper row!

– Well, I said. D'you know what I think?

She didn't say anything, but her eyes slowly edged back, and she blinked.

– I think you're hanging on to this Crabbe's Block out of choice.

She twisted her face away again and stared at the wall – but I kept holding her. I wasn't letting go. I wasn't.

We stood there like that for a while, in stalemate. Leave her alone, this voice was saying inside me – the voice of reason, I guess. Let her be. She's an island. You can't reach her, no one can.

But then I felt a soft touch on my hair. Well, more on my bald patch, actually. I thought I was imagining it at first, and then I slowly realised it must be her hand. It was like I was an animal and she was stroking me. I hardly dared breathe,

156

the moment was so fragile. Hannah was stroking my head. I looked up, and saw tears on her face. Her glasses were all steamy, and she'd gone red.

– I can't do it, she said. I want to be a normal person but I don't know how. I've been here so long I –

She was too choked to say anything else, so I just held her to me. We were sitting half on and half off the chair, the table-edge poking into my side. It wasn't comfortable, but I held her and held her, and it felt right, as though a thing had fallen into place that was meant to. I think she felt it too, she must've, because she didn't try to pull away or anything, she even pressed herself in towards me, and I thought if I could swallow her right up and carry her away inside me she wouldn't mind, and nor would I.

And that was how we stayed for a long while, and all I wanted was for it to go on for ever.

And then

Well, this is difficult, this bit. It's sort of embarrassing but I'm sort of proud of it too and it was one of the high points of my whole life, I guess. Because what happened was that, slowly and then suddenly very urgently and very fast, things started to shift a notch and – well, to firm up.

You could sense it was happening to her too, this thing. Wriggling-body stuff that was sort of beyond anyone's control, really. It was like a dream. In fact, sometimes I still think it was. Before either of us knew what was going on, we were kind of wrestling against the desk, trying to get bits of our clothes off.

And then there was no stopping it. I was grappling at my belt and my trousers slid with a silent whoosh round my ankles, and I'd hitched her skirt up clumsily, and I was rubbing at her with one hand and also trying to pull her tights down and her knickers to one side and clutching the desk with the other hand to keep steady and then I'd somehow sat her buttocks on the edge of the desk and – well, before we knew it, we were –

We stared into each other's eyes while we were doing it, in a sort of unbelieving way. Her glasses had fallen off by now, well, they were hanging off one ear actually. I'd never made love like that before, but it seemed the way to do it, with Hannah. Like we were – don't laugh – communicating with our heads too. There we were, doing it, and I was saying things, maybe shouting them or whispering, I don't know, and she was too and then –

The next thing I knew I was crying, and so was she.

– Will you visit me in prison? I whispered at last.

– See? says John, beaming. It *was* a love story!

– It wasn't. I told you before.

– So what happened?

– That was the end. I never –

I break off. The tears are welling up now and I can't stop them. Through the blur of water, the Alpine calendar seems to shudder on the wall.

John's crossing off the days. Just two to go.

SOMEWHERE LIKE MOHAWK

It wasn't the end: it was the beginning. He'd go to prison, and they'd write to each other, and then one day – She had a shower, turned the jet on hard, tried to make sense of what had happened. Couldn't. Her mind flitted about, unable to settle anywhere but on him. By five she was back in her office, her hair still damp. A sharp knock at the door made her catch her breath. Instinctively, she reached for her inhaler, and dangled the mask between her hands, ready to use. She wasn't ready to face anyone yet, not even Leo. This would be him now.

But it wasn't.

– Good report, Pike said.

She stood up, not wanting to be cornered in a chair. Her hair dripped.

He was looking down at her. Again, she felt the claustrophobia of his presence, the heat from his body. Could he sense what she had done? Did it show on her face? All the turmoil over Harvey made her feel as transparent as an amoeba. She fingered her mask.

– So did you *enjoy* your experience of people-work, Hannah? Do you feel that it's stretched you? He was smiling.

– Stretched me? Oh I suppose, yes. She pictured an elastic band, pulled to the maximum, vibrating with tension, about to twang.

– I see, he said slowly. He was looking right into her eyes, now. The air was thick with the silence of it. – We're posting you elsewhere.

She didn't get it for a minute. Then gulped, and sat breathing for a while, ready to apply her mask.

– For a bit of R and R.

– Away from Head Office? she asked at last.

Pike nodded.

– Somewhere like Mohawk, I thought. Would that appeal? Hannah couldn't think of any words to reach for.

– The Boss is recommending it, in your case. She's done a need-profile on you. She reckons the people-work has put you under a lot of strain.

– I don't feel like it has, said Hannah. But she felt suddenly feverish, drained. – Excuse me, I – She put on her mask. This was real.

– Better pack a bag then, he smiled. Ran a finger across her cheek. And then was gone.

Everyone knew where R and R led, in the long-run. To re-positioning. To a gradual or swift easing-out. No one returned from the holiday beach in Mohawk with a sharper mind. Hannah slipped off her mask, and took a few tentative breaths. Then, just as she was switching the air-pump of her inhaler off, her eyes rested on something stuck to the corner of her desk. A little green heart. It puzzled her for a moment, and then she remembered. It had been stuck to Lola Hogg's disc. She must have put it there and forgotten about it. Carefully, she picked it off and stuck it to her wrist, then headed for Leo's office.

It was Fleur Tilley who opened the door, and Hannah's first thought was, I didn't know they were friends.

– Oh it's you, said Fleur. A whiff of bar furled out in the air behind her.

– I came to see Leo Hurley, said Hannah. The emptiness

of her hands bothered her. She should have brought a file, a disc, a clip-board – something.

– Didn't you know? said Fleur. He's gone.

Hannah could smell the drink on her breath as she gestured her in.

– Gone where, asked Hannah, entering. The room was blank, almost empty. Two cans of Hooch and a packet of freeze-dried peanuts lay on the table. It was sprinkled with little flakes of peanut skin and salt.

– I'm only here till they tell me what's next, Fleur said. Her eyes pooled with tears. – I'll miss the Munchies. She lifted a can of Hooch, took a swig, moistened her lips ruminatively and swayed, grasping the chair for support.

– Gone where?

– Mohawk, I think. Or Lionheart. To one of the R and R facilities. Last week. One minute he was here – she waved vaguely at the room – the next he . . . didn't say goodbye or anything.

– Last week? said Hannah, struggling with dates. Are you sure?

– Part of that big shake-up, Fleur said, licking a finger and prodding at the salt crumbs. After the Festival. You know. She licked the salt off her finger, and a muscle at the corner of her mouth spasmed: a tiny facial earthquake. – Well, it's been turmoil, hasn't it, with the mass re-fucking-prioritise. She giggled. – I'm in deep shit, as you'd expect.

– I didn't know about any of this, said Hannah. I haven't been around. I mean, he didn't say there'd been a general shake-up.

– Where've you been, on Mars? Fleur squinted at her, trying to focus.

– I had this deadline, on a new project.

– Ah. Well, there you go. She gave a little sigh. – Everyone who's anyone was assigned their own little personal *thing*.

– I guess that's what happened then, said Hannah, remembering Harvey Kidd. There was a dizzying lurch whenever she thought of him.

She hadn't realised everyone was being given special tasks. Pike had presented the project to her as something special. *Reward success, questionnaire failure.* She'd thought it was a one-off, specially designed for her. Now she could see how absurd that was, how grandiose and blinkered. Fleur was swaying again, and Hannah wondered if she might pass out.

– So where did you send the e-mail to Leo?

– E-mail? said Fleur. She seemed to have forgotten, and blinked. – Oh. To the R and R centres, I think. Her eyes were suddenly blank. – Sorry, I've got to sit down. And she did, brusquely.

– And?

– And what? Oh. Nothing. He hasn't replied. Look, Hannah PARK, why don't you have a drink. You're always so buttoned-up. That's your trouble. Hope you don't mind my saying.

– It's all right, said Hannah. I just wanted – just some files . . . no, I can get them from – It's OK. She was backing away now.

She had a sudden urge to tell Fleur that she wasn't buttoned up, she wasn't a virgin any more, that Fleur wasn't the only one who did it against desks, that she'd met a man who –

– Drink'd do you good, said Fleur. But please yourself. She giggled again. – You are dismissed.

What's going on, Hannah thought as she closed the door on Fleur. *If I disappear*, Leo'd said, that day he'd handed her the brown envelope. She'd thought it was paranoia. Called him a Munchie. She'd have to get hold of it. Read what was inside.

She hated this.

I'm scared, she thought. It hit her like a bump.

162

All the way to St Placid she fingered the little green heart sticker on the inside of her wrist, a tiny patch of pressure. The feel of it electrified her blood. She was struck by the way the atmosphere seemed different. Thicker. Everything seemed to glisten. Instead of disintegrating, the air-crystals had landed and settled, bejewelling benches, tram-stops, and window-ledges. It was beautiful, eerie. It jolted a distant memory of Atlantica years ago, before Libertycare and the climate change: snow and ice. But her recollections of the past were shaky. You couldn't trust memory any more. Perhaps the snow and ice were just something she'd seen on screen, something that happened in other countries. The tram was still fifteen minutes from the city when she noticed the first rainbow – a luminous gash of purple, sepia, bottle-green, and sulphurous yellow – hooped across the skyscrapered horizon. A child might have drawn such an arc with a fistful of dirty crayons. It was weirdly moving, and tears welled up, hot and tingling. It was as though the whole world had shifted shape. Even the people looked different, bursting with health and energy, like irradiated fruit. And as for herself, it was almost as though she had new organs in her body: new eyes, a new heart. It made her feel light as air, and freakishly happy – so happy she wondered if she might be on the verge of a breakdown. The tiniest thing seemed to make her want to laugh and cry.

– Some flowers would have been nice, said Tilda, opening the door. You look different.

– I *am* different, said Hannah, realising it as she spoke.

– So am I, said Tilda. I've got fresh kneecaps.

Hannah followed her mother as she limped into the lounge, clutching her medical dossier. Things felt odd, indoors. Then it struck her.

– Ma, the house . . . the corridor. Something's happened. It feels like it's all – I don't know, *tilted*.

– Well spotted! said Tilda. It slopes to the north-east. Subsidence. The Libertycare Liaison man, Benedict Sommers, he's having it seen to.

The name rang a distant bell.

– Lovely man. Good-looking too. She said it hopefully.

Hannah laughed – a strange noise that slipped out unbidden – and turned away.

– What's so funny? asked Tilda sharply. They were sitting in the lounge now. Tilda had planted both feet on her footstool.

– Nothing, said Hannah, lightly, her thoughts still dancing wildly. Then, to stop her mother pressing the subject further, she asked – So what does he say, about the subsidence?

– Well. You know, that it's *being investigated*. They're doing some big survey apparently. I've bought myself a spirit level.

She pointed to the mantelpiece, and Hannah saw it: a long plastic rectangle containing a Perspex panel. The bubble – floating in a bilious green liquid – was well to the left of centre.

– But actually, that's not the main worry at the moment, he told me. Well, it *is* a worry, but it's what's *causing* it that's the real problem.

– And what is causing it?

– Well, even before Mr Sommers told me, I'd already heard things.

The name Sommers was definitely familiar. It bothered Hannah that she couldn't place it.

– I think it started off as a *rumour*, Tilda was saying. Just in the neighbourhood. Then Fanny Urdle, you know my friend, two doors down? She said she reckoned her sister's son-in-law might be involved in something to do with drugs. And then there was someone at bowls said he'd heard of a small cult. Some real rotten apples. There was an anxious excitement in her voice.

164

– So these rotten apples, said Hannah, her eyes scanning the room. What about them?

Where had Tilda put Leo's envelope?

– Well then, a couple of days later, said Tilda, just after my op, the Liaison associate, Mr Sommers – I call him Benedict – he comes again, and he confirms it, about the rotten apples.

Hannah suddenly put a face to Benedict Sommers. He was the one chewing green gum who she'd met in the lift, on the way to the party. The one who was being questionnaired. What was he doing, working as a Liaison associate in St Placid? Nothing made sense.

– What happens is, we talk about the subsidence for a bit, and he says Mrs Park, you're known to us as a highly responsible citizen, I note that you've been a VIP Customer since the beginning. And I say well, I've tried to do my bit, and the loyalty vouchers come in handy, don't they. And then he wants to know if he could discuss something important with me, as a more senior member of society. Pride in her eyes now; the voice wavering a bit. And a quick glance at Hannah, who allowed her mouth to move in acknowledgement.

– And what was it?

– Well, what he said got me really nervous. Tilda gulped, and the loose chickeny skin of her neck trembled.

– He told me that there's – She dropped her voice to a whisper. – A sect. Operating here, in St Placid. Possibly all over the country.

– A sect? asked Hannah, puzzled. It was news to her. What kind of sect?

– Terrorists, said Tilda, fanning out her skirt over her knees. It gave her the look of an ancient, cracked doll. – Eco somethings. They're opposed to the Waste Pledge. Opposed to any type of progress, I think Benedict said. I remember types like them from the old days, before

Libertycare. Thought we'd got rid of them, but he says bits of society are mutating, it happens when things are going too well. Anyway, they're having to bring in a new code, he said, to curb them. They're going to socially readjust them.

– Readjust them? Hannah was confused. Was this some sort of fantasy? Was her mother beginning to lose her marbles?

– Mass Readjustments, he said, to nip it in the bud.

Hannah sighed in frustration. All she wanted to do was get her hands on Leo's envelope and then leave. Tilda's garbled story was making her feel exasperated and restless.

– Nip *what* in the bud, exactly?

– Well. You know. It. The *activities*. The *criminal activities*. They're ever so dangerous, you see.

– Who are?

Tilda tutted in annoyance.

– Haven't you been listening? So anyway, he says we're to keep a sharp lookout, because they've got followers everywhere. Tilda dropped her voice to a shaky whisper. – They're involved in sabotage. It's very hush-hush. They don't want panic.

Nothing made sense. Hannah hadn't heard any of this at Head Office. Surely the Department would be the very first to know of any new social disturbance. Why hadn't Wesley Pike held a meeting?

– They've been funding it with all kinds of fraud, said Tilda.

– Fraud? Suddenly, she was listening.

– I mean, you name it, they've been involved, apparently.

– Like what? A weird sickness slapped at her.

– Well, they were experts on money, I know that much. They had zillions of companies, you know, those illegal offshore ones, the Cayman Islands and whatnot.

Hannah gulped back the nausea. The room suddenly felt very hot.

– Benedict says it's all going to come out soon, though. There's going to be a thing on TV about it at four, a sort of public-warning programme, it's called *Evil in Our Midst*. You could stay and watch it, it's on soon. Benedict says they keep a low profile themselves, the ringleaders.

– What ringleaders, Hannah said faintly.

Tilda leaned forward conspiratorially.

– They've got mug-shots of them. Benedict gave me some posters to put up on my front door, and on all the lamp-posts in the street. He said to wait till after the documentary, then pin them up.

The room seemed to be whirling now. To try and stop it, Hannah clamped her hands on the arm rests of her chair.

– All the VIPs have been getting them. Tilda's voice shook with pride. – We've got to study their faces, and memorise them, and stay alert. Fanny Urdle's going nuts, she's plastered the whole of her lobby with them already, because she reckons she's actually seen one of them loitering in the street. Anyway, Benedict said to always keep my windows locked, and to get an extra bolt put on the front door. Some of their followers, they're known rapists.

Hannah tried to keep her voice level. Something was thudding inside her, clotting her thoughts.

– And who are they, these – people?

– There are five of them, said Tilda. Three adults and two kids – just teenagers, I think. They're all related. They're a family. It's all in the documentary apparently, so I guess all will be revealed. I'll show you the posters though, look. Tilda hauled herself up painfully and slid open the drawer of the coffee table. She pulled out a glossy printed poster and spread it out in front of Hannah. – That's them, she said.

And it was. Five faces. Mug-shots. Distorted, but recognisable. Staring back at her.

– They're called the Hoggs, said Tilda. I don't like the look of them, do you?

EVIL IN OUR MIDST

I'm in the Social Adjustment Office on the seventh floor.
   – Sit down, Harvey, says the boy who opened the door,
reaching for a pocket scanner and bar-coding the paperwork.
He can't be more than a teenager. – I'm your Social Adjustment associate, Marcus Hooley. Sorry about the heat in here,
the air-conditioning's on the blink, but we won't keep you
long, will we, Georgia? This is Georgia, who's in charge of
downloading the files onto paper.
   There's a girl sitting splay-legged on a swivel seat by a
computer terminal.
   – Hi there, Mr Kidd, she says, smiling. She's got little dimples like puckered dough. – We've processed loads
of stuff on you; your caseload's running to thousands of
pages. It doesn't often get that big, does it, Marco? She
giggles.
   – So when's my trial?
Marcus Hooley laughs at that.
   – Nice one! The Georgia girl's laughing too, and swivels
a full circle in her chair. You can see from the way she
does it, it's a thing she's practised. They're just a couple of
kids fresh out of a playground. – Welcome to planet Earth,
Harvey, Marcus Hooley goes. OK. I'll run the formula past
you. The Liberty Machine assesses the evidence, see, and
makes a decision on how far to adjust you. It's probably

in the system already, but it's not scheduled to appear till the designated time.

My mouth sagged open. It hadn't made sense when Pike'd said it. It'd just washed over me, I guess. I sighed, and slumped further into my seat. There didn't seem anything more to say. So we waited in silence – him shooting flirty glances at the girl, me watching the clock and wondering when I'd next see Hannah. The minutes ticked by, and then all of a sudden the screen in front of Georgia flashed.

– Da-da! she said, her voice glittery and bright. Twelve o'clock on the button! Told you! She was addressing Marcus, not me. – We do bets, she smiled.

Hooley slid over to where the girl was sitting and leaned over her shoulder, one hand sliding round her waist.

– Looks like I owe you a drink then, he went.

She gave a little squeal. His eyes scanned the screen, and then he tapped a few keys.

– Right, Harvey, he said eventually, sucking in his cheeks. I'm afraid you've been declared an Enemy of Liberty. He scrolled down further with the mouse. On account of being the financial enabler of the Sect.

– Sect? What sect? I didn't get it. – There's been a mistake, I said. I don't belong to a sect, I do fraud! Simple honest-to-goodness white-collar fraud!

– Well, don't ask me, he said. I only work here! And he winked at Georgia, who giggled. Hooley turned back to the terminal and scrolled up.

– Fraud isn't what it says here, he said, squinting at the screen. The girl's head leaned forward too. It says here terrorism. See? And he pointed. The word was there all right. – Libertycare finds you guilty of multiple terrorist activities, Harvey, he read.

He scrolled through some more.

– Uh-oh, he went. Georgia looked over his shoulder, and sucked in her breath.

– Wow. I haven't seen one of those in here before.
– What? I said.
– You stay sitting down, mate, OK?
– Why?
– Cos I'm afraid it's pretty bad news, Adjustment-wise.
– I'm kind of prepared for that, I said. They said ten years, max, but I could have it reduced for co-operation.

And then he told me.

It all happened in a swift whirl, no time to think, no time for anything to sink in.

From Head Office I was transferred to a massive holding station, with five or six hundred other blokes. You weren't allowed to talk, and if you did, you got a blast from a stun-gun. Within the hour we were driven off in a fleet of white transit vans to Estuary Docks, and loaded on to a conveyor belt which shunted us up a gangway on to the *Sea Hero*. Everyone looked scared out of their wits, and some guys were crying. It was clear that none of us knew what was going on, or why we were there. There'd obviously been a mistake.

When the mess hall was packed to bursting, the smell of gas-pumped geranium kicked in to fight the stink of sweat and fear. I had a feeling that something unhealthy was about to happen, but I didn't know what, and the not-knowing was like a horrible itch cloistered deep in my blood.

Then some twangy salsa-like music starts up, and Captain Fishook strolls in like a stocky little magician. He's small but dense with energy, as if his blood might be made of mercury. With a startling movement, he pounces on to the raised platform at the far end of the mess, and stands there taking us in for a moment, his hands clasped together as though they're glued that way. Beneath the peak of his Captain's cap you can see he's alert and shiny with his own success. You can picture him, ushering customers on

171

to a roller-coaster ride, or congratulating himself – It was a team thing – at an AGM. Then he adjusts the clip-microphone on the collar of his gold-buttoned jacket and waits for silence. He smiles when it comes. He's got charisma, so he's used to this. Achieved it before, in other settings.

– Hi, folks, he goes, welcome aboard the *Sea Hero*. I see this as the beginning of a big new adventure for all of us. We set sail tomorrow, for a long voyage, to new horizons. Once we've established ourselves on an even keel . . .

Blah-di-blah, he continues in the same vein, until there's a disturbance.

– Fucker! yells a bloke at the back. You can't do this to us! I'm a lawyer! This is against all the –

But an orange-gloved hand has slapped itself over his mouth. He's still trying to yell as the two crew-members haul him off. One on each side, the lawyer's legs kicking in the air like an insect's. It's so speedy-smooth it might have been staged. Fishook isn't fazed.

– As you see, he says, I run a tight ship. Any more mutineers?

Silence as we get the picture. The bloke next to me, he's quivering like a frightened squirrel.

– Sorry, he says in a little whisper. But I'm scared shitless here.

Me too, but I'm not admitting it. I can feel he wants me to do something sissy, like pat him on the arm or something, but I can't bring myself to. It's a tough world, and I decided earlier that I'm not gay. So I just grunt.

Now Fishook's making a signal to a crewman in the projection room behind us, and the lights are dimming around us.

– Before we leave shore, we're going to join the rest of Atlantica in witnessing a historic television moment, he goes. There's a special message in it for our Atlantican Voyagers. Many of you – I have this on good authority – are still clinging

172

to the idea that you're innocent. That *everyone but you* was involved.

His words have frozen us for a minute.

Then – What the fuck –? says a man behind me, and a nervous vibe's crackling and pulsing through the mess.

– Well, after this film, goes Fishook, I want you to look into your hearts. Because the truth is in there. He pauses, looks around the room. – Remorse, he says, is the first step in the long journey to freedom.

Before we can take in what he's said, the lights have suddenly plunged right off, and the whole hall's pitch black. The sissy man next to me gives a little whimper, and reaches for my hand. I shake him off. There's only one person whose hand I want to hold, and she isn't here.

The screen's so big it covers the whole wall. We watch as it flickers to life.

The commentary began over the familiar map of the island.

Our own Atlantica, said the voice. It was familiar; big and meaty. Where had I heard it before? *But there's another map that you don't see, a map of corruption that extends deep into the very fabric of society*. Of course, I thought. It's Craig Voice of the Fucking Nation Devon. As he spoke, a tissue of thin red lines began to criss-cross its way out from the cities until the whole map was cobwebbed depravity. Cut to a weeping woman.

– If I'd known that's what he was involved in, she sobbed, I'd never have let him out that day.

Some wobbly footage followed; it showed a small white coffin, a child's, carried by two boys of about thirteen, who were crying.

Then a bloke popped up.

– I had no idea the Sect was behind it. It only dawned on me when it was too late, like. But it was them gave the orders, I know that.

– There *is* such a thing as pure evil, said a man in a dog-collar. Even in Utopia.

I almost laughed. If the customers fall for that, I thought –

But then I stopped and a huge shiver shuddered its way right up from my feet to my bald patch and down again. I thought of your typical Atlantican. He's not used to thinking. And to be fair to him, why should he be, with Customer Care second-guessing his urges? Of course he'd fall for it. I was beginning to get an inkling now of what was coming. As the dread sprouted and homunculised inside me, the others seemed to be making connections too. The quivery squirrel-like man next to me had put his hands over his face, but was peeking through the lattices made by his little claws. The Liberty anthem had started up now: the muzaked version you heard in supermarkets and waiting rooms. Over it came the Atlantica the Beautiful shots we'd all seen a hundred times before on promotional videos: the Bird of Liberty flying across a blushing horizon, a family picnicking at Mohawk Falls, a lithe woman in her prime taking a mud bath at a health spa, cheery faces at a sample handout in a twinkling mall.

We have a system that's so admired worldwide that the people of the United States are campaigning to have it, went Craig Devon. *In the near future, a superpower may finally get the administrative system it deserves, free of human error. If that happens, it will be the dawn of a new era for mankind. An era of peace and prosperity.*

Next, a shot of Earl Murphy, the American hero taxi driver, heading a huge march with banners. Music underneath. Your heart thrilled at the sight of it. You couldn't help rooting for what they wanted. *The people of Atlantica fought hard, as ordinary Americans are now doing, for the high standards we have enjoyed in the last decade*, went Devon. His voice sounded as juicy as pork. *But what we have fought for is now under a very real and terrifying threat.* The sinister music started again – a pulse of drums – but I must've blinked or something, missed a beat. Because suddenly without any warning, there was my family. Filling the screen.

For the first fragment of a second, my reaction was joy; so much joy at seeing them again alive that I caught my breath. I wanted to shout out to them from across the hall, at the top of my voice: Hey, folks, it's me, Harvey! Look, over here!

But straight away the joy curdled. Something had gone obscenely to cock.

– My God, I murmured. And the horror welled inside me like vomit.

I wasn't the only one to recoil from the cluster of leering faces. All around me there were groans and gasps of unease.

– I've seen them, whispered the quivery man next to me. I've seen them before! I *know* them!

From the look of the other blokes around me, he wasn't alone; they seemed to be experiencing the same thing. How come, I thought. I felt almost indignant: *I'm* the only one who knows them! They're my private people! What's going on?

This is no ordinary family, went Craig Devon's meaty commentary. The camera tracked from one grainy mug-shot to the next. *These men and women*, he went, *are the faces of a new evil.*

The terrible thing was that, looking at their distorted faces, you could believe it. It was as though all the goodness in them had shrivelled, and their worst traits – all those little tiny characteristics that barely emerged before had just, well, *ballooned*. Mum was suddenly mean-looking, superior and spiteful. Dad's face was all stubbornness and violence. Uncle Sid looked like a slimy pervert. And Cameron: well, he'd always had it in him to be smugly threatening. Even Lola was suddenly – I hate to say it, but she looked like a slag. I shuddered. Are these the people I've known and loved

175

all my life? I thought. Is this what they've turned into? It horrified me to think that I once counted myself among this family's members. I was glad my face wasn't in the portrait, because they repelled me. I guess at that point I wanted to disown them.

Other people seemed to be having the same reaction, because as the screen faded to black, a low murmur of revulsion ran through the hall. Then there was a guitar twang and we were looking at the dog-collared bloke again. His face was like a St Bernard dog's: sad and heavy with responsibility. He was cocking his head sideways, his fingers steepled in front of him on a big paper-strewn desk.

– This is the question, he said, and you trusted him immediately. In Libertycare, we have the fairest people system in the world. Atlantica is rich, successful, and globally admired. So why, why on earth – he unsteepled his hands and spread them wide, imploringly – has this movement developed? Why on earth is it setting out to destroy the very cradle of freedom itself?

It seemed like a good question.

The worst part was that some of what they said about the Hoggs was true.

The documentary went on to show how they'd set up a network of offshore companies, all bogus, that churned out millions per annum, on the backs of the Atlantican taxpayer. It showed the paperwork – my paperwork – on the French vineyards, the Australian paper-mills, the Italian sun-dried tomato industry, the Malaysian tiling factories. I recognised files I'd generated. Deals I'd cut. *The Sect has been using this fraud network to fund the sabotage of the cleansing mission*, went Craig Devon.

No! They'd never do that, I thought, they'd never *dream* of –

There were shots of the craters, taken from helicopters. St Placid was the worst affected. You could see a huge crack

176

stretching from one corner, and black liquid pooling out. It looked serious. *Damage like this was carefully camouflaged at first, and wear and tear was blamed. Then, zone engineers began to blow the whistle on the Hoggs.* There was an interview with a craggy-faced bloke in a hard hat, a crater worker. He described how Lola Hogg had approached him personally. She was a very seductive young woman, he said. The camera worked its way up her body and settled lingeringly on her boobs. After outlining her family's eco-Luddite beliefs, which opposed waste recycling and the principle of reclaimed land, she'd offered him oral sex, in return for his help in an act of sabotage at the purification zone where he worked. Heroically, he resisted, and by a miracle, escaped from Lola's clutches to tell the tale.

– But some of my mates, they weren't so lucky. There were quite a few of them, got involved. And of course there were accidents.

Surveillance footage showed a small figure falling down a crater. They ran it in slow motion, then stopped it in mid-shot and zoomed in on his face.

Oh God, Lola, I thought. What have they been making you do?

Blah, blah, bollocks: on and on the film went, with each member of the family accused of some specific crime by an honest-looking customer. My mind was in turmoil. In my head, I knew it was all lies – but what was going on in my heart and my guts was another matter. What if the Hoggs really had turned bad? I mean, Lola offering that bloke the blow-job – she was capable of it, I reckoned. Sid's fortune *could* be channelled into porn, and he had his louche side, I'd always known that. Cameron and Mum might, if pushed to an extreme, blackmail all the pupils at a school for the disabled. Dad had it in him to break a man's ribs. When I saw the charity worker on the film talking from his hospital bed, fear in his eyes, low and quiet, I could see he wasn't

177

lying. He believed it. And part of me did too. The Hoggs had been kidnapped, after all. What had Libertycare forced them all to do, against their will?

I felt giddy.

Over recent months, Libertycare has been doing its utmost to keep you informed while minimising customer anxiety and discomfort. But the truth we must now face as an island is that the Sect has infiltrated the purification system, and reversed the filtration and drainage process. Unleashing unprecedented levels of pollution, and putting the island itself in danger.

I groaned aloud, and the squirrelly bloke next to me jumped in the air with fright.

Perhaps I should have felt flattered, seeing what they'd done with my family. After all, the Hoggs were my creations, originally. And now they were famous. What more can an artist hope for?

Except I wasn't an artist was I, I was just an ordinary bloke.

A family man.

As customers, we have responsibilities as well as rights, finished the Voice of Atlantica. *Our task is to stay on guard, to protect the system we have fought for and deserved.*

The idea was simple, and scary. It had the capacity to terrify universally.

I'd underestimated them. Pike, and the Liberty Machine. And Hannah must have done too, because if she'd known what was going to happen she'd never have –

Would she?

So don't think twice. Call the Hotline with your suspicions. Carry your loyalty card at all times. And the spirit of Atlantica will triumph as it has triumphed before.

– It's a load of bollocks, I told myself. No one's going to believe a word of it.

But that wasn't true. I'd been half seduced by it myself.

SCUM

– Scum! whispered Tilda tremulously, reaching for the remote control and flicking the TV off. They're even worse than Benedict said! I think I need a Vanillo. She poured a big one.

Hannah was rocking rhythmically. She'd watched the documentary with the inhaler clamped to her face. A sheet of collapsed bubble-wrap lay at her feet.

– Well, said Tilda, sitting down heavily, her face white. Thank God for the death penalty.

– But everything's been twisted! blurted Hannah, pulling off the mask.

Tilda stopped drinking in mid-sip and looked at her daughter sharply.

– *What?*

– The Hoggs aren't like that! They've made them look – if you knew them, you wouldn't see them like that, you'd –

She stopped. The room seemed to tilt even further.

Tilda was staring at her incredulously.

– You *know* this Hogg family then? You've *actually met* these people?

– Sort of, Hannah mumbled. And then backtracked. – No, of course not. Not in person. She gulped. – I've heard about them, that's all. At Head Office.

Her mind was whirling. *I should have known . . . something must be going wrong on Atlantica. Badly wrong. The research I did – the Multiple Personality Disorder . . .*

179

She groaned.

If Harvey could see what they'd done to his family – how his nearest and dearest had been demonised, turned into –

– Scum, repeated Tilda vehemently. They're scum!

But maybe he *had* seen. He must have been adjusted by now. She had to see him, tell him she didn't know –

– Let me check something, she said to Tilda, gulping. I need to log on.

– You fire away, said Tilda, swivelling her legs off the footstool. I'll go and make us a cup of tea. And then you can tell me more about this Hogg family.

When Tilda had hobbled out to the kitchen, Hannah opened up the computer and ran a search. Her fingers were trembling; she was so tense she kept bungling it and clattering the wrong keys. Concentrate, she told herself. Keep calm. And then, after a couple more slips, she got there; Head Office, Social Adjustment Department. And there was Harvey.

His photo, his name underneath.

And the Machine's decision.

The world went white. It had to be a mistake. Pike said – She stopped short. Pike had said nothing. Nothing. And she hadn't asked. She'd just assumed – a case of fraud. The words on the screen jumped about. The room was hot again. She must have groaned or cried out, because Tilda's voice came through from the kitchen.

– Are you all right there, Hannah? Did you say something?

That's when she remembered Leo Hurley, and the look in his eyes. Damage limitation. Her heart was pounding, fast and hard. It hurt. She'd been so stupid. Locked in her little bubble. Too scared to think beyond the here and now. Hiding behind her Crabbe's Block, which Harvey said –

She shut her eyes. It's all happening too late.

The anger that swept out of her was so fierce and huge she thought it might kill her. Things went white again, a white-hot light, and there was a screaming noise like steam, a scream that went on and on, higher and higher, and then her mother was hobbling in.

– Hannah! Stop it! What's happened to you?

– Where's that envelope? screamed Hannah, and realised the terrible noise she'd been hearing came from her own mouth.

Her mother had changed gear; she was suddenly hobbling backwards now, reversing out of the room, one hand in the air.

– Stop this, Hannah! she whispered, hoarse with fright. Stop this now! You're having a – fit!

– No I'm not! Just tell me where that envelope is! She was raw with rage.

– What envelope? stammered Tilda.

– The one I sent you to look after.

Tilda, still backing away, flushed. She put her hand over her heart.

– Well, I said I'd put it with your peanut-butter-label collection, up in the spare room, but I never got round to it, so it's –

– Where? hissed Hannah in a pale, hoarse whisper. *Where?*

– Top drawer, there. I'm going to finish making that tea. I think we need a cup, don't we, after this – scene.

And she limped out of the room.

As Hannah pulled the envelope from the drawer, she heard her mother's voice coming from the kitchen: high and excited. She must be on the phone, thought Hannah. Consulting Dr Crabbe. Or telling one of her friends from the girl gang that her daughter has flipped.

She forced herself to take some deep breaths, then began to open the envelope. As she attacked the flimsy seal, she stopped, and looked closer.

Someone had already done it.

But who? Tilda? She didn't know. And there wasn't time to think.

181

She ripped further, pulled out the document within, and devoured its contents.

Three minutes later she stuffed it back in the envelope, her head reeling. Everything suddenly made sense.

– The whole island, she murmured. – The whole island, *the whole of Atlantica* –

Leo had known. But he hadn't known what to do, except get the document out of Head Office. What had happened to him? Where was he? She shuddered, thinking of the craters. And then it struck her. *If they find out I've seen this, whatever's happened to Leo, could happen to me.*

Just then the doorbell rang, and immediately she heard voices in the hallway: her mother's. And a man's. There was no time to do anything; Tilda was ushering him in. Her face glowed, as though she were presenting a long-lost son. The man was tall, pale, good-looking. He had crystals stuck to his coat. A whiff of lavender followed him.

– I've been telling my daughter all about you, said Tilda.

Hannah swallowed. Her heart was banging. She knew him.

– Meet our Liaison associate, said Tilda, with her Visitor smile. What a lovely coincidence for us, he's popped round. We've just watched the film.

Hannah looked up. The young man had pale eyelashes. Eyes the colour of indoor swimming-pool water. The shallow end.

– Pleased to meet you, said Benedict, looking at her steadily. He was as tall as Pike. Hannah, suddenly aware of the envelope in her hand, flushed, and dropped it on the table. Benedict Sommers' eyes followed it, then moved to the computer screen with Harvey Kidd's face on it. Registered. Then shifted back to Hannah. When he grinned at her, she saw a flash of green in his mouth and her stomach did a slow, ugly turn. She was trapped.

– We've met before, said Benedict, working the gum over to one cheek and holding out a big hand for her to shake. The Festival party in Head Office? He grinned again.

As they shook hands, Hannah felt something pass between them like an exchange of static.

That's it, she thought with sudden clarity. *I'm dead, like Leo. They'll crater me.*

Just when I was beginning to live.

BLAME

After the documentary was over, we were assigned cabins, and the engines roared to life. I was alone at first. Then put with a Greek, Kogevinas, who spoke no English. But at mealtimes, in the mess, I'd strain to overhear the conversations of the other cons. They were a revelation. Many of the Atlanticans – about 70 per cent, I reckoned, actually were criminals. Another 10 per cent borderline. But they all knew whose fault it was that they were there. The Hoggs'.

The psychology's pretty simple, when you think about it. No one likes to admit they've done wrong. I listened to grown men close to tears, telling how they'd been manipulated by followers of the Sect. To intelligent fraudsters and extortionists claiming they'd been brainwashed into committing crime. To sex offenders explaining how they felt vindicated, in little huddles by the poop.

– But how d'you know they even exist? I ventured once over breakfast, after a burly bloke had been holding forth about what he called Hogg filth. He rounded on me then, and a couple of other blokes shot me angry glances.

– Oh they exist all right, he said. Only I didn't know that was who I was working for, did I. Others were murmuring in agreement. – I thought it was an ordinary delivery job, didn't I, he said. Taking stuff from A to B, I'd done it a thousand times, I never asked what was in the consignment, just drove the van. Well, now I know for sure it was them Hoggs. If

185

I'd known it was stuff to sabotage a crater, well, fuck, I'd never've – well.

– Doesn't stop you feeling like a mug though, does it, said another guy. I should've known it was them pushed me into doing it. They got me drunk and the next thing I knew there was blood everywhere. All along I said I was innocent, it wasn't me, but when I saw those faces –

– Yeah, said another guy. I recognised them too.

– Where from? I said.

– Dunno. Around. I've seen them around. On the streets. And posters and stuff. You know.

– Me too, said another one. That Sid bloke. You can tell just from his face that he's a porn merchant, I've seen him hundreds of times. He's *everywhere!*

There were more noises of agreement. The other prisoners seemed to be putting the same pieces of their private jigsaw together. As they did, stuff began to fall into place for me too. As I listened to them, it dawned on me what was going on. Whatever it was they felt guilty about – and who can put their hand on their heart, and say there isn't something? Whatever it was, they wanted to blame someone else for it. I can relate to that, I thought. To err is human. And so's wanting to pass the buck. Even scapegoats need scapegoats. Even the blamed need to blame.

And people are more stupid than you think.

It was after the first couple of months that I learned about the geologists, soil physicists, structural engineers and crater workers who were in solitary. They'd all been aboard about a year which meant that our Mass Readjustment wasn't the first. Something must be going wrong with the craters, I began thinking – perhaps with the whole industry. But why drag my family into it? Why the Hoggs? I couldn't work it out. Why hadn't they just invented their own scape-goats? And left me alone? Fuck it, I thought. WHY PICK ON ME?

186

We'd been sailing a long time – a month, maybe – before it began to dawn on me. It wasn't personal. Machines don't have any imagination, do they. What they'd stolen were my dreams. And those are the best things to steal, aren't they? Since the Hoggs didn't exist in the flesh, they'd never be caught. They were immortal. They could take the blame for everything. From whoever wanted to throw it.

For ever.

On we sailed, through the waters of the northern hemisphere. It didn't take genius to work out that all the Atlanticans on board would turn on me if I gave them my version of the truth. The best policy for me was to stay clammed up. So I did. It was a hard thing to do, knowing what I knew. So many times – too many to count – I was on the verge of telling someone. But I developed a technique for nipping the impulse in the bud.

I stuffed paper into my mouth.

And it evolved into the fruitful hobby it is today. Result, a year on: a chess set. Mine.

– Fishook and Hooley and Mrs Dragon-lady and Mr Stress, they're the knights and the bishops, I tell John briskly, laying out the pieces on the craft table.

Outside the porthole, there's a dazzling sky that makes the waves shudder and tinsel with light. Still no call from Fishook, and my cell-mate's feeling buoyant. (He ate four helpings of aubergine lasagne at dinner last night, and even played badminton with the Portuguese sex offenders.) I see it as my job to keep his spirits up.

– And these are rooks, look. Gwynneth's the one I've finished, and Tiffany's nearly done, you put her on this square here. This is the queen, she's the Liberty Machine. She goes here, look. And this is Pike. He goes next to her, because it's his job to protect her.

– And the little ones? he goes, as I finish laying out the black pawns.

– They're customers. You put them all on the row in front of the others. You can sacrifice them to save the more important ones. Now white always plays first, I tell him, setting out the pieces. These two rooks here, they're Mr and Mrs Najima from the Snak Attak. This knight, he's Keith the cat, and this bishop's Dr Pappadakis.

– And the other one?

– That's you.

Another silence.

– Me?

– The man himself.

John looks suspicious.

– But he's a good guy, right?

I nod.

– Why not?

He's looking pleased now; flattered.

– It's a game of strategy, I tell him. Clever people and computers usually win because they think ahead better and they make fewer mistakes and they're good at mind-reading.

He looks downcast at that.

– But stupid people sometimes triumph, I add hopefully. Sort of by accident.

That idea seems to go down OK.

– And you're the king, right? he goes.

– Correct. Now where do I go, d'you reckon?

– Here?

– And next to me, you put the queen.

I put Hannah down gently. She feels more fragile than the others.

– And your job, it's protecting her, right?

Suddenly there's this ball in my throat, and there's silence for a while. Outside, a gull with an empty yoghurt carton in its beak flaps at the porthole and then disappears, sucked into a vortex.

*   *   *

188

Week after week I wrote to Hannah. Long letters, telling her everything – stuff I didn't know was inside me until I saw it there on paper. Love letters.

She never replied. So I got desperate. Started to panic. I began to guess things, and my guesses got wilder and madder and scarier. I wrote to Personnel. Could they tell me the whereabouts of their associate, Hannah Park? Had she been posted somewhere else?

You never said what happened to her, says John. I mean did you ever – But he breaks off. – Oh fuck, he says. He's squinting out of the porthole.

I look up. Follow his eyes. A distant hump on the horizon.

Oh fuck indeed.

Atlantica.

As if on cue, there's a sudden clangy din, followed by a buzz of static from the tannoy. The volume's right up. A blast of music: the Liberty anthem – *Independent and Free*. And then Fishook.

– Voyager 1-0-0-8-7, comes Fishook's voice, you are cordially invited to join your Captain on the bridge today at 1500 hours GMT.

The tannoy clicks off, leaving just an eerie echo before the anthem kicks in again.

That didn't happen, I'm thinking. *He didn't say that.*

But he did. I look at John, and John looks back at me. He's gone completely white. I guess I have too. Time chokes to a halt.

– 1-0-0-8-7, says John finally. That's not my number, mate. It's yours.

ON THE BRIDGE

Garcia escorts me to the bridge, nudging me along the corridors with the butt of his stun-gun. Fishook stands at the wheel, a little metal bullet of a man, capsule body foursquare on stumpy legs, salt-and-pepper shaven head, pebble-spectacled eyes squinting at the horizon through cigar smoke. The chunky Havana perched in the metal ashtray on the sill. The radio's tuned to the twenty-four-hour weather channel. – Pitkie, Skagwheen, Mohawk, St Placid's Reef, Canary Bight . . . it drones faintly. Fresh, southerly . . .

– Welcome, Voyager Kidd, he goes, a smile in his voice. His silver-framed glasses flash at me in greeting. In the distance, the spume of a whale fountains up and descends in a scatter of rainbows. – Come and join me, he says, all fake *bonhomie*. It's like we're old buddies. Members of the same club. Except the gag is, we aren't. Hesitantly, I step forward next to him. A tattered sheet of seagulls whips past, squawking. It sounds like jeers.

– Would you like to take a turn at the wheel? he asks, grinning. Have a go at steering this mighty vessel?

I remember now. I've heard of this from other blokes. It's a prelude to mind-games. He once got Flussman to do forty sea-miles, then told him his daughter had been knocked down by a tractor on her boyfriend's farm. Flussman was so shocked he couldn't speak: he just carried on steering for

191

another forty sea-miles, trying to work it out. His daughter was a lesbian, and lived in the city.

Eventually he'd ventured to ask Fishook – Is this a joke, Captain?

It was, Fishook confirmed, roaring with laughter and offering Flussman a cigar.

– Very funny, Captain, was all that Flussman could muster. Fishook isn't mad, though; just has a very particular sense of humour that doesn't obey the normal rules of comedy. So when he stands aside, grooms his cigar and gestures at the wheel, smooth dark wood and brass, I'm nervous. I grip it tight, relieved to grasp something, though the warmth left by his hands gives it the revolting intimacy of a shared toilet seat.

– Fairbairn, St Mornay, Butt of Cortez Lighthouse, Ganderville, easterly winds, veering south ... says the radio.

– You know, in some primitive societies, Fishook goes, tapping out ash from his cigar, this horizon would represent not the future, but the past. They see the past ahead of them, and the future behind. They are travelling backwards through life. The stretch of water ahead of them freezes over as time passes. That's the past, solidifying before them. The water at their back is fluid and unknown. That's the future. Waiting to freeze.

I can't think what I'm supposed to say to that, so I just go uh-huh, as though he's said something meaningful. The future, waiting to freeze? What kind of gobbledegook bollocks is that?

– I understand from Garcia that you received a letter recently, he says after a while.

– I haven't opened it.

My thoughts jump around but can't find anywhere safe to land. So in the end I just listen to the monologue of the weather channel and stare at the sea. It looks cold. You could feel powerful up here, steering a massive ship, I guess. But only if you're its captain.

– Well, perhaps you should, goes Fishook. Some men find, when they are faced with a situation such as yours, that friends and family can be a comfort.

A situation such as mine? Friends and family? What's he talking about? From the corner of my eye I notice that he's put his cigar down and taken the microphone of the tannoy system from its holster. He's fondling it near his cheek like an electric razor.

Then he clicks it on and speaks.

– Wind east-north-easterly, he says, switching to DJ mode. His processed voice ricochets about the vessel, setting up a million tinny vibrations. – Steering a steady south-south-easterly course, due to exit Northern Waters Section at 0500 hours GMT tomorrow, destination, Atlantica. He gives a little pause, then, and looks at me. Where we will be celebrating Liberty Day with the Final Adjustment of a leading Sect member and Enemy of Libertycare. Another pause, in which he looks at me more intently. – Some of you know him on board as the Paper Eater. (*What?* I'm thinking dumbly. *What was that?*) It still hasn't sunk in. And it still doesn't, even now when he's looking me right in the eye and saying slowly into the microphone – *His name is Harvey Kidd*.

I just think, hey, that's my name too.

– Light vessel automatic, winds westerly, says the radio. The words catch me in a smooth trap of language. Turning to gale force later . . . winds fresh, southerly . . . It's mesmeric. If you stay very still, the words sort of imprint themselves in your head, and giddify you. That's the way mantras are supposed to work. I read it somewhere, in the Education Station, when I was searching for the meaning of life and came across the knitting-machine theory. I looked up love too. *Devoted attachment to one of the opposite sex, esp. temporary.* Fishook is looking at me.

– What? I mumble. I really am feeling a bit confused, as if the geography of the shipping forecast has somehow dislocated me. – Me? I ask finally. Stupidly.

Fishook gives me a sideways look. And a little nod that says yes.

That's when my knees give way, and I'm sagging to the floor, clutching the wheel to stop myself.

Fishook switches off the tannoy, replaces the microphone in its metal holster, re-lights his cigar and stands next to me, puffing Cuban clouds. Together, we watch the horizon. I grasp the wheel, numb. My heart's contracted like a shocked scrotum but I don't let it show. Steer a straight course. I've seen him marlin-fishing. He likes to leave them writhing on the deck. Sometimes he'll have them thrown back. Sometimes not.

Something inside me's collapsing, sucking the breath out of me. If I could just wipe the last five minutes from my mind, stick my head in the sand, pretend –

Is this a joke, I ask, remembering Flussman.

– Sadly not, Voyager, he says. The decision has been made at the highest level.

– A cock-up? I muster. I mean, I'm white-collar. I thought the killers had to be –

– Don't believe everything you hear in the mess, Voyager, he goes. Priorities change. The Americans are polling as we speak. Atlantica needs to show them how the system deals with its human waste. It has an example to set. He smiles. – Your Atlantican's a discerning customer. He doesn't want to watch just *any* old Final Adjustment on his national holiday, Harvey. He wants *value for money*.

Nothing left to say. My hands drop from the wheel, and I stand aside to let him take over. I see what he means now. The past, it's ahead of me, on the vast water. And the future's behind me because there isn't one. After a few moments the tears make the line wobble and then spill and I see it again, the open sea, my life. Just like he said. I take a good long look, a last look, drinking it in.

Power for the Powerless: NB There isn't any.

Then Fishook bleeps Garcia.

– Escort this Voyager back, he says.

It's half-way down the corridor of D deck, as Garcia is taking me back to the cabin from the poop, that I make the mistake of looking across at the growing hump of Atlantica on the horizon. That's when the physical reaction comes, unexpected and unbidden, a big tidal wave of nausea that I'm helpless against.

– Wait, I tell Garcia. And unleash a frightening quantity of black bile, with lumps of paper in, on to the shiny rubber.

– Like in horror film, says Garcia when I've finished.

He looks impressed.

In the cabin, John's there with his eyes all red. His shoulders hang slack, like a boxer who's toppling about in the ring, surrounded by people yelling in his ear to go back and fight. But you know he's been felled like a tree and his career's done with.

I don't speak. There's this big emptiness inside me. I can still taste the sick in my mouth, so I go and rinse. When I turn round, John's slumped in his chair.

– You should be glad, I go.

He should, logically, shouldn't he? So why isn't anything like you think it's going to be? He's crying now, big shuddery man-sobs. It's worse than what happened on the bridge. It's torture. I reach for my letter. What have I got to lose? A cold wave of misery slaps over me as I look at the envelope in my hands. When I first saw the red handwriting it was more flabbergasting than blood. It set my nerves jangling, fired up a mad little sizzle of hope that despite what happened, despite everything I knew, a certain woman might still be –

John looks up at the sound of the dismal tearing.

– What are you doing there, Harv?

– Facing up to reality, I tell him. The letter's out of the envelope now. I flatten it out – it's covered in the same big childish red writing – but I'm still not ready to look.

– You said you weren't opening it. *I'm not opening it*, you said. You said no news was good news.

– Well, that was before, wasn't it.

Before. When I had all the time in the world. I look at it. John's watching me.

– Is it from Hannah? You never said – But he stops, probably because he's seen my face.

– It isn't from Hannah, I begin.

The world shifts as I speak, into a flat thing, two-dimensional, with only a faint vertigo to tell you we're on a round planet, ruled by gravity. I think about my cud, and the half-dried rook with the fat arse, which is supposed to represent my not-daughter Tiff. I think about the game I'll play with the French cyber-forger from H deck, Ollivon. I'll use the Queen's Gambit and win thanks to some nifty bishoping. Or lose, because I've never had a way with knights. Is the cat still alive, I wonder, and living with Mrs Dragon-lady? If so, is she still feeding him that dried rubbish packed with addictive additives, that wrecks his gums? As John's needle flashes anxiously in mid-air, I'm also thinking, I've never actually said the words before, even to myself.

– It's not from Hannah, I say slowly.

It's a struggle just speaking. Something heavy starts to do battle in my throat but I swallow to force it down. I look out of the porthole, try to banish the nudge of vertigo. Seagulls chopping against the wind.

– Why not? His voice different, husky.

I can't tell him though. Can't bring myself to say it. The words are stuck.

But pennies are beginning to drop with John, I can feel

it. That's how well I know him; I don't even have to look. While he's hovering between saying it and not, the power of the moment swells like an electric force. It's just when I think it'll knock us both flat that he clears his throat to speak.

– Is it because she's dead? he asks formally.

I'm braced for it, so I don't turn.

I sit and watch the seagulls and the cormorants flapping. There's stuff you come across, never quite makes sense, isn't there. Like what on earth possessed somebody – I forget who – in 1793, someone near Bergen, in Norway, to construct a whole church, complete with pews, pulpit, organ, knave, window-frames, walls, the whole shebang, entirely of papier mâché? It stood for thirty-seven years. It might have stood for longer, if it hadn't been demolished. Then in 1883 in Dresden, a watch-maker made a watch from it that worked. It was his masterpiece, and it performed as well as any metal watch, he said.

Chew, chew, chew.

– Pike sent me that card, I say finally, nodding at the shelf. It's tasteful, a white background, the Bird of Liberty, and forget-me-nots. – It arrived three months after I came on board.

Oh, I'd already guessed by then. I knew in my heart of hearts it's what they'd do. Betray the customer and you are betraying yourself.

Sincere condolences, it said. There was a little newspaper cutting too, and the text of the in-house obituary, *A Tragic Accident*.

John coughs apologetically, a little husky bark. It must set up a tiny air-gust in the cabin, because it's enough to send the letter whooshing off the table. It doesn't seem to matter any more, though. So the letter flaps in a zigzag to the floor, and I leave it there. From where I'm sitting, I can see the signature at the bottom, though. It both surprises me and doesn't.

197

Tiffany.
I clear my throat.
– The heyday of papier mâché in Europe was 1770–1870,
I tell John. That's a long time ago.

LIBERTY DAY: 5 A.M.

Seen from space, Atlantica sits like an organic jewel on the canopy of the ocean, its frilled coastline surrounded by the kind of shimmering halo that glaucoma gives to a source of light. Slowly, the first threads of morning trace their way across the gleaming flood-pools near St Placid, exhaling a mauve mist which rolls across farmlands of okra and pineapple, suburban cul-de-sacs and city streets, swirling its way into five million dreaming minds. It is towards this methylated, vaporous landscape that the *Sea Hero* – still barely a dot on the horizon – now sails. Atlantica twitches in its sleep.

It has been a difficult year.

Panic feeds on the human spirit, sucking at its boundaries in small greedy waves. The past twelve months have witnessed a sea-change on the island: families splintered, best friends revealed as traitors, houses re-mortgaged, holidays cancelled, wills re-drafted. Long queues snail out from chemists' counters, where the supply of Libbies cannot meet demand. Trust, on Atlantica, is now a commodity more prized than saffron or truffles, as mythically laden as frankincense and myrrh. Ever since the screening of *Evil In Our Midst* a year ago, hot on the heels of the Festival of Choice, the Hotline has registered up to two million calls a day, a proportion of which have been re-routed to backup services beyond the green belt of Harbourville. Only last night Mr Liam Hedges

199

from Groke saw a man fitting Sid Hogg's description hopping off a tram, 'easy as you please', and entering a massage parlour 'well-known to the authorities'. A sharp-eyed child from Atlantica City South District raised the alert when he witnessed Cameron Hogg and three unidentified associates bullying a drunk Marginal in a play area, and ten separate callers reported spotting Gloria Hogg rigging roulette machines in Mohawk and planting toxins in the gas pumps outside a holiday hypermarket. A typical evening.

But while Libertyforce has questionnaired, marginalised and processed hundreds of suspects with exemplary precision and speed, the Hoggs themselves remain frustratingly elusive. They seem to be both everywhere and nowhere.

And most frightening of all, the movement is spreading.

Up in the Temple on the top floor of the corporate ziggurat, Wesley Pike, sipping rich Brazilian coffee, is skimming the latest graphs from the Munchhausen's Department. The Boss's psycho-statistical forecasts have proved accurate again: a distinct element of excitement is becoming traceable beneath the customers' fluctuating stress-levels. As Liberty Day dawns, this mood can safely be expected to reach euphoric levels. It makes sense of course, he reflects, refilling his china cup from the small percolator. Danger has its thrilling side. Nobody can put their hand on their heart and say it doesn't thump that 40 per cent extra in times of crisis and that the thump doesn't feel good.

Wesley Pike lays down the graphs and loosens his tie. Today the Boss has ordained that the customers' spirit be rewarded: the Bargain of a Lifetime starts at nine. It will feature the biggest discounts ever made in consumer history. There's to be 60 per cent off designer labels, 70 off tableware. 80 off suites. Entertainment-wise, the Final Adjustment of Harvey Kidd is scheduled for three. All is going as planned.

Correction: 85 per cent is going as planned.

An unwelcome worm of unease uncoils inside Wesley Pike as he remembers this, constricting his gullet. He puts down his coffee, tugs at his collar and undoes the top button of his shirt, fanning the air with his hand. It's hot.

The ground force has implemented all the Boss's formulae, planting evidence and obtaining videotaped confessions when and where necessary. It has followed her recommendations to the letter, never veering from the blueprint. Some associates have even offered initiatives for her approval, and been rewarded. So why do the satellite pictures continue to hint at an alarming escalation of the still unmentionable problem, a geological crumbling that is more than mere erosion? Wesley Pike is not alone in wondering this – but he is alone in his faith. Or so it feels.

He runs a hand across his broad brow. He feels slightly feverish. And despite the Boss's white, humming presence next to him, slightly alone.

The conversations he has monitored in-house show how far the creeping poison of disillusion has spread. Every organisation contains a hard-core of secret doubters, and the Corporation is no exception; they are low-level operators, mostly – the types that get referred to R and R, and end up questionnaired out of the system altogether.

But suddenly, they're getting numerous. Vocal too. The e-mails are insolent little texts – sarcastic, nit-picking, accusatory. Some signed, others arriving anonymously, through back-routes. The kind of toxic electronic paperwork which – only a few months ago – would have led to need-profiling. What solution, they ask, with thinly veiled hostility, does the Boss have up her sleeve, when it comes to dealing with the eco-geological crisis brought on by the waste leaks? As Facilitator General, might he liaise with the Liberty Machine to provide them with an answer? The atmosphere at Head Office is becoming tainted with a mutant mistrust; the lingering bad smell of lost nerve. In his darker, more paranoid moments, Pike has almost wondered whether some kind of . . . *network* might be operating. Oh, he has no proof. A wink here, a twisted glance there, a stifled whisper as he enters a room. It only takes a couple of dysfunctionals to start an insurrection: look at what the geology lobby tried to stir up a few years back, before the flush-out. Leo Hurley was eliminated long ago. Hannah Park likewise. But –

But. He reaches for his coffee, sips, winces.

– Fallings from us, vanishings, he murmurs. Blank misgivings of a creature moving about in worlds not realised . . .

He leans against the Boss's smooth white flank and stares out of the floor-to-ceiling window across the cityscape. It is a view to die for.

– High instincts before which our mortal nature did tremble like a guilty thing surprised . . .

Is our own mortal nature the problem? Is that why the unfathomable 15 per cent seems to be doing its own thing?

As morning breaks over Atlantica, centimetre by centimetre the flat grey rectangle of the *Sea Hero* slides closer to land.

LIBERTY DAY 6 A.M.

The Libertycare system looks set for a triumphant victory in the United States, mouths Craig Devon earnestly from Tilda Park's television. But she can't hear him; she keeps the sound right down, and anyway she's wearing earplugs to block the sirens which have been shrieking all night. *Despite the recent upheavals on Atlantica, Libertycare's global status has flourished*, Craig Devon is saying. Tilda passes her hand over her eyes: how's anyone supposed to sleep? *As the polls close in the United States after an unprecedented turnout, Earl Murphy is keen to stress that Atlantica's terrorism crisis is no more than a 'people hiccup'. If it's the only problem the island has faced in ten years, he argues, and it's down to humans, then it confirms what he has been saying all along . . .*

Tilda removes her little earplugs and measures out an early morning Vanillo in her sloping apartment. *What we are witnessing today*, finishes Craig Devon, *is the dawn of a new era.*

Adapting her walk to the ever-changing gravitational whims of her home was hard at first, but Tilda managed. It doesn't take much to factor a simple tilt into your gait, once you get accustomed to the idea. It's the rest that's hard.

On the shelf above the TV, next to the miniature pill-chest and the hologram of Hannah where Tilda has trained her eyes not to rest for long, stands the spirit level, its elliptic bubble trapped in fluorescent green liquid. Tilda hobbles to the shelf, picks it up, turns it round, puts it back and watches the bubble move through the oil and settle. Seven degrees: severe subsidence, just as Benedict Sommers warned when he first told her about the Sect and its plans. St Placid is the worst hit, being closest to sea level. And the Hoggs to blame. You don't realise how smoothly daily life runs until it's disrupted.

And it's been disrupted all right. Tilda takes a swig of 68 proof Vanillo and winces, then feels the sweet after-tang velvet its way down. She'll get a Gourmet Special delivery, later, foodwise. She doesn't bother choosing from the menu any more; too much hassle. She just orders number seventeen, that way you get your little surprises; she's had everything from potato skins to bisque. Sometimes she'll switch on the TV, but the soap operas have died on her. To look at them, you'd think the scriptwriters and the actors have started to despise their work. Even the medical crises look weak and fake, as though while he's shooting the resuscitation scene, the director's on his mobile, looking for another job. And the commercials have definitely lost their X factor. She used to love that one for diabetic butterscotch, where Nefertiti hurtles out of a giant fridge, bristling with frozen popsicles. But the Nefertiti woman's doing rape alarms now, and the doctor from *Moment of Crisis*, he's selling surveillance equipment. And as for the news –

There's a new drug Sid Hogg's started peddling, especially aimed at the elderly. One capsule and you're hooked for the rest of your life, because it's a parasite, and your blood's the host; she's seen the diagrams.

Her eyes flit to the window. She used to see joggers going past. She misses them, now they don't come any more. They're stuck at home too, most likely, doing it on an exercise machine instead, put off the streets by the muggings and the toxic leaks.

She can't summon up the words to talk about what

happened. The shame and the grief that mash inside her, they block her throat. She picked up the phone to the Customer Hotline once, opened her mouth, but all that came out was a gutted croak like a euthanasia victim breathing their last. If you can't even speak to the Hotline about it, how can you begin to talk to your friends? It's the thought of their pity that makes it worse. They say there's not a family in the country hasn't been affected in some way, so it's not as though she's alone. Oh, there are all sorts of support groups. Customer Care organises them. Or you can set up your own little circle, register it with Libertycare – she's had all the bumf through her door, and Benedict's been on about it.

It's just, those groups are for losers, aren't they?

The tears well up. They say the colour of death is pure white. That it's the last thing you'll see. All those years, trying to get rid of Hannah's Block, and then the Hoggs do it, easy as pulling a plug! Betrayal's a slippery slope, and Hannah was in up to her neck before she knew it. She even *defended* them! After the documentary, she said they *weren't that bad*!

Another swig. Vanilla tang. Blunt feeling that comes after. Tilda would like to be small enough to dive into the bottle, and drown, and become pickled inside it like a dumb, innocent gherkin. It'd numb the grief, maybe. Dull the anger that attacks her sometimes, unexpectedly – a vicious bite, the kind a spoilt lap-dog might give you out of sheer yappy spite. Cruel and shameful as a senior sexual urge.

Hannah's visit to the crater was captured on video. The CCTV cameras at the purity zone picked up everything, apparently: how Hannah used her Liberty pass to get in, how she added enzymes to the filtration system, how, when the security staff spotted her, she ran and slipped and –

– Please stop, Tilda begged the bereavement associate in a tiny whisper. I don't think I –

– Sometimes it helps to bring the reality of it home, Mrs Park, the associate said. Why don't you take the cassette with you, have a think? You never know, some customers in your situation find that –

Tilda had burst into hopeless sobbing. Benedict stepped in, murmured a few discreet words, then pocketed it himself.

– For when you're ready, Tilda, he said. And not before. He left it on her video rack, but he didn't push it.

It's still there now, untouched. Watch it? She'd rather die. She finishes the Vanillo in one, smacks her lips. Pours another. Vanilla tang. Blunt feeling. Good.

Anyone illegally entering the zone takes their life in their hands, Benedict explained gently as Tilda rattled away at her little chest of drawers searching for the right pill, saying *now where do I keep them, now where do I keep them*, under her breath. The security personnel have their instructions. They can't be held responsible for accidents. Especially if they're encountered during the course of –

The word sabotage hung between them.

Hannah wasn't the first Sect casualty. Far from it. It had been hush-hush so far. Don't give them the publicity, was the thinking. It'll help them thrive. It was more than anyone's job was worth, Benedict Sommers told her sorrowfully, to retrieve the body from the crater.

The body.

There are bodies on TV. On *Moment of Crisis* they showed a bulldozed man, cut in two. Abroad, where human error's so rife, there are hordes of them, aren't there; wars, famines, burst dams, exploded factories . . . She opened her eyes and looked at Benedict again, dizzily.

– Body?

– But they found her cardigan, he said.

Crumpling, Tilda grabbed it, buried her face in its loose hairy knit and breathed in the smell of peanut butter.

Ever since that day a year ago, Benedict has been solicitous beyond the call of duty. He's visited her every week and kept an eye on her like the good man he is. How many good men are there in the world? Tilda reckons she can count those that she has met in her entire lifetime on the fingers of one hand.

But sometimes, like last night, Tilda will sit in the semi-darkness of her living-room, staring at the hologram of Hannah and thinking about Benedict. He's a dark horse. Oh, he's told her things from time to time, about his flat not far from here, and how everyone in Head Office calls the Liberty Machine the Boss; it's a she, apparently, and no bigger than a household fridge. But in those lonely, scary, middle-of-the night times, Tilda can't help wondering if she did the right thing when he first started to visit her, back in the days when she called him Mr Sommers and he called her Mrs Park. She'd talked about her daughter, of course she had, shown him the hologram, why not, been pleased when he said he knew Hannah, even more pleased when he said she was well thought of . . . They'd first bumped into each other in a lift – that must happen a lot in office life, mustn't it?

After that, it had seemed fine to show him the envelope.

– Go ahead, Tilda said, thrusting it at him. It'll all be Greek to me, but if it's of use.

– Thank you, he said. His eyes were a lovely blue. – It's good to have your trust.

That was a nice thing to say, wasn't it? He'd bring it back, he said. Hannah needn't even know.

But on nights like last night, while the flood sirens are wailing across St Placid, Tilda re-lives that moment, and it just doesn't look good. It fills her with – well, doubts. Doubts that turn to multi-headed monsters, the way they do in the dark, and whack, whack! When you chop one head off, another one sprouts. Sometimes a sleeping pill fixes it till morning. But sometimes it doesn't.

Vanilla tang. Blunt feeling.

Exhausted to the bone, Tilda sighs wearily. Outside, through the wobbling blur of her tears, she can see the first hint of the fairy weather promised by the forecast: mauve mist giving way to coral pink, then a perfect, translucent blue with sparkling whorls of cloud.

Celebrate Liberty, that's the slogan they're using for the day. There's going to be retail chaos apparently. The Bargain of a Lifetime will be the biggest sale ever.

Funny, though. She just can't get in the mood.

Behind her on the muted television, Craig Devon is mouthing something, and pointing to a map of the United States. There's an animated graphic showing how the votes are coming in. One after another, little Birds of Liberty fill the blank states.

LIBERTY DAY 9 A.M.

I'm stiff all over. I must have slept, because it's light outside. But I'm not in bed; I'm sitting at the craft table with the chess set laid out in front of me and Tiffany's letter lying on the floor. I'm confused about how time has jumped – until I remember what I did. I swallowed Dr Pappadakis's pills, all five of them. Not placebos after all, then. No wonder I feel groggy.

Groggy, and suddenly scared, remembering. Scared like I've never felt before, scared beyond anything I've known. I groan as I look out, because the porthole's filling up with land, the skyline of Harbourville close enough to make out the Frooto Tower, the spiky rollercoasters of Attractionworld, the giant Ferris wheel and the sheer blind-windowed cliff of Head Office. Seagulls swarm around the porthole, their swooping cries like a chorus of taunts. If my mum, wearing her salamander dress, came and told me I wasn't going to be electric-shocked into a fizzing human kebab, I'd believe her. But she doesn't come, of course she doesn't, and there's no one here but John, asleep. Try to focus on the small things. The table. The bunk. Stegoman on the duvet cover. But my eyes slide back to the porthole. The land seems to yawn sideways. All the buildings – even Head Office, even the Makasoki bubble-domes in the distance – they're all Pisa'd to the left. Only the grit-filled rainbows splintering above them are on an even keel. I buzz Garcia and he leads me to the mess for my last breakfast, where the other prisoners stand back to let me through. I guess I look like a bad omen. Grey man for the chop. I drink coffee. I can't eat.

It's a great day for the future of the world, according to Craig Devon, who's on TV. The Corporation has already swept to victory across almost half of the United States. This could be the beginning of a new world order, he's saying. America might get a new name, too: Liberty.

As this piece of news sinks in, a low ugly murmur runs through the mess – but what do I care? I won't be there to see it. When I stand to leave, a couple of blokes come and slap me on the arm and murmur stuff like Goodbye, mate. I try to say something back, but there's a big thing like a walnut lodged in my throat and I can't see properly and I have to turn away.

– Apparently it's the dawn of a new fucking era, I tell John when I'm back in the cabin. He's sitting on his bunk, his legs dangling down, my letter in his hand.

– Gonna read it then? he says, flapping it at me. Cos I can't.

I sigh at the blood-red writing, then glance across at the Tiffany rook. It's probably not Art, but it's a version of my daughter I can live with before I die. That's got to count for something, hasn't it? John thrusts the letter at me with its childish red script.

– It's from my daughter, I tell him. The one who shopped me.

John blows out air from his cheeks.

– So what's it say?

Life can't get any worse, can it? But already, as I read the first line, I'm thinking, famous last words. *Dear Dad, I am so sorry about everything. Mum and me and Geoff*

– Grammar! I choke.

Mum and me and Geoff are so terribly regretful –

– Grammar! I shout it this time. Is that what I sent her to a good school for?

– Who's Geoff, goes John.

– The fuckwit aromatherapist bollocks-talking stress man.

– Oh yeah, said John. I remember. The one your wife –

– Yeah, all right, I cut in. Misery slicing me in half.

Mum and me and Geoff are so terribly regretful that you are on Death Row, we have been in shock ever since. And I just want you to know that I am very sorry that I reported you to Libertycare. If I had known what would happen I would never have done it. (Like fuck you wouldn't.) *We shall be coming on board the* Sea Hero *as visitors on Liberty Day* (Oh Jesus, no!) *and hope to have the opportunity then to apologise again in person.*

John whistles.

– And is that it? Any more?

Only the icing on the cake.

– She's signed it *Your loving daughter, Tiffany.* Huh! I shout. There's so much rage in it, I'm almost propelled off the bed.

– Well, bugger me blind, says John.

– I'm going to chew it up, I tell him, feeling my lip wobble. My voice too. But as I pick up the letter to scrunch it into a bite-sized ball, something catches my eye. It's another, smaller line of writing at the very bottom of the page.

P.S. Have you had a stool investigation recently?

My cue to go ballistic. First a grovelling, insincere apology for being the cause of my death sentence, then the news that my estranged family – with ex-wife's new man in tow – are actually coming on board to watch me die. And then to cap it all, some out-of-order question about the state of my bowels. Within minutes I've buzzed and clanged and yelled my way on to the bridge.

211

– I'm not having them here, I tell Fishook, waving the letter at him. I refuse. I have rights, don't I?

He's standing at the wheel, his filthy cigar smoking in the ashtray. He still hasn't even looked at me. He's wearing clip-on shades over his glasses, although there's precious little sun.

– Rights, Voyager? he chuckles. I'm afraid that as a leading light in the Sect, you sacrificed those long ago. In any case, he smiles, you'll be surprised what a comfort it'll be to have your nearest and dearest –

– They're not my fucking nearest and dearest! If it weren't for them, I wouldn't be here now!

– You don't have the choice, Voyager Kidd, he says, tilting his head towards me, his grin fixed. The sun-glasses are unnerving, like the huge, inscrutable eyes of an insect.

– Your ex-wife, her new husband and your daughter are coming aboard at 1400 hours. I'm sure that, like the rest of us, they'll be wanting to give you a good send-off. There's a lot to celebrate, Voyager. The news from America, Liberty Day on Atlantica . . .

He smiles again and you can see he's looking forward to it.

– It'll all be kicking off on the main deck at 1500. He pauses. – It's going to be quite a *fiesta*, Voyager. There's a lot of excitement around this event. A real community buzz.

Does this man have any idea what I'm going through?

– But this man Gwynneth's married, this Geoff bloke – I hardly know him! He's a so-called stress counsellor, with sissy curtains in his waiting room! He's a jerk!

Fishook takes his hands off the wheel and, with a swift movement, lifts the flaps of his glasses so they stand out at right-angles. His flat blue eyes look me up and down.

– He may well be a jerk, Voyager, he says. But he's also a customer. And what the customer wants . . .

He turns back to the wheel. My life has been a whirlpool

shape, I'm thinking. Everything sucked down too quickly and suddenly to make sense. Now I know why John behaved the way he did, when he thought it was him, and joked about the Big Fry-Up: you don't quite take it in. There's a . . . distance on it. But now there isn't, is there, and there's this sick, sick dread sweeping over me and I'm feeling faint and helpless and wanting to cry. I don't know what to say any more. I'm not in control of anything. Not even the guest-list for my final bash.

Fishook's picked up his cigar again, and he's puffing monstrous fumes as he steers.

– Look over there, Voyager Kidd, he goes, pointing with his fat roll of tobacco.

There before us is the long humped line of land, bristling with skyscrapers. And the gaping yawn of the estuary.

I clench my buttocks together. Fishook's looking at his watch, and then at me, his head cocked thoughtfully.

– You have six hours left, he says softly. You are a human hourglass, Voyager Kidd. And your sand is running out.

Just kill me now.

LIBERTY DAY 11 A.M.

High in the upper stratosphere, Liberty's gliding oceano-
graphic satellite charts the subtle shifts of the artificial land-
mass below, registering the pressure on the porous rockbed
and the complex nuances of subterranean physics. Strange
the way the light plays tricks. From the pictures reaching
Head Office it almost – *almost* – seems as though the yolk of
the fried egg itself – the inland hump of St Giddier's Mount –
were slowly and inexorably deflating. You might even think,
if you scrutinised these pictures, that the waters were creeping
higher, and gnawing at the coastline by St Placid. If you were
a catastrophist, you might go as far as to speculate that something might be going horribly and dangerously wrong beneath
the earth's crust – and venture to wonder whether, beneath
the enchanted crucible of St Giddier's Mount, something was
frighteningly amiss. Something structural.

If you were a catastrophist.

– Earth has not anything to show more fair, breathes
Wesley Pike, turning his back on the satellite screen and
gazing out at the glittering snake of the River Hope, its
urban banks already thronging with excited shoppers. Dull
would he be of soul who could pass by a sight more touching
in its majesty . . .

Once the Boss has remedied the geo-structural glitches, the
disgruntled minority in Head Office will be questionnaired
and flushed out. Now that the American election is all but

over, the Boss will be free to unveil her strategy for the triumphant return of normal life on Atlantica. It's what she's best at. The Bargain of a Lifetime promotion is probably just the start of it. It's working already. The customers are gagging for it. Look down there: they're forming queues!

She has turned things around a million times before. Just watch.

But something bothers Pike. Saps at his inner strength, weakening him, tempting him to think off-code and to wonder if –

A shrill buzz; the communicator on the desk before him flashes. Distractedly, still mulling over the ugly, terrifying thought, Pike switches On.

– Wesley? comes the voice. It's me.

They've been on first-name terms for a while now. Wesley Pike had an inkling, way back, that this young associate had the talent and confidence of a much older man. The characteristics of a successful Liberty employee are sensitivity, perceptiveness, a hands-on approach, plenty of initiative, a capacity for lateral-thinking. An early attitude problem can be a sign of potential. Pike was right to nurture him, right to spot how the black mark on his record could be turned into a golden asterisk of promise. And sure enough, of all the officers he briefed in the People Laboratory for the Hogg project, Benedict Sommers has been the most committed, the most diligent. The most proactive too. The Hannah Park business –

Benedict's initiative. Benedict's idea. The Boss had processed it, and finding no flaw, had even earmarked the young man for a success reward, placing him back on the fast track where he belonged. Soon he'd be leaving Liaison behind, and be at Facilitator level.

– St Placid report, says Benedict. (Pike has missed his voice. Been looking forward.) – Thought you should be aware.

– Yes. Go ahead, son.

Son? The word flips out easily, as though he's said it before, but he hasn't. Affection – he's never felt it like this before. It hatches in his head, pure silent pleasure.

– The toxicity levels – you'll get the printouts, but well, they're almost off the scale. And the customers are jumpy, no question.

– But?

– Well, they're sort of happy too. There's this sort of euphoric effect, it's having. I guess like a wartime spirit. I mean, there's all the panic about the Hoggs, but – well, you know. They feel sort of *virtuous*. (Pike smiles. The accuracy of the Munchhausens' graphs is intensely gratifying. You can almost forget . . .) – And spending's through the roof, says Benedict. (Pike can hear him chewing. He must have a word with him sometime about that wretched green gum.) – Up 25 per cent. And with the promotion coming up – well, they're going bananas.

– And the Park business?

Outside, on the horizon, the *Sea Hero* comes into view, a distant block of grey.

– Oh, I was going to tell you, says Benedict. I've visited regularly, as planned. The mother's happy with the sabotage story. Well, not happy of course, but . . . well, she's a model customer, so . . .

– She hasn't questioned it, nods Wesley Pike. He's gazing at the ship.

From Benedict, the sound of chewing.

LIBERTY DAY 12 P.M.

They're calling it the dawn of a new era, but the thought brings no comfort to Tiffany, Gwynneth and Geoff. The *Sea Hero* is now sliding its way up the estuary – and Harvey with it.

Gwynneth, who not long ago gave birth to the baby Howard – a fretful, colicky lad, hard to settle, quick to posset his lunch – tightens the belt of her dressing-gown around her birth-whacked midriff and chews on a fingernail. Nearby, balled up in an armchair, Tiffany feeds herself popcorn coated in spray-on caramel. Both women have spent the morning watching the TV, their stomachs twisted in knots. Geoff, stress-management consultant and new dad, won't even look; it threatens his blood pressure. He sits with his feet in a basin of warm water, slices of organic Kenyan cucumber over his eyes, listening to whale music on headphones and secretly wishing he'd never met the Kidd family. Look what it's all led to!

For all of them, today sees the culmination of a year of what Geoff has christened pure unadulterated hell. Ever since the chilling documentary about the Hoggs was screened, the sirens have been wailing their morbid soprano day and night, deepening the siege mentality in the family home. The new baby can't be blamed for sensing that something is horribly awry in the world he has entered – and screaming accordingly, both day and night. Fear stalks the beleaguered little family, raises their hackles, making them hiss and snarl at one another like beasts at bay. The knowledge that they share is a burden too awful for one small family to bear.

As the *Sea Hero* sails towards Atlantica on their TV screen, Gwynneth plunges her head into her hands and groans. Not for the first time she wonders if she should check herself into some kind of clinic, or ring the Hotline and blab the whole thing. Oh, she was happy for Tiffany to bust Harvey and hand the Hoggs to Liberty – as anyone in her position would have been! But how could she have guessed they'd reappear in this ugly, frightening way? When they don't even exist in real life?

Or do they? She's no longer certain. They've come to seem so – well, oh, just so horribly real! She's even seen them on television! Heard interviews with their victims! Her friends have told her about the swathe of corruption that Cameron's been spreading, vandalising street signs with his graffiti'd insignia. And there's no avoiding the destruction wreaked by Sid, who's been cutting the perimeter fence of the purity zone every night. There's a rumour going round that Rick's behind some of the broken marriages – Dr Carney's, for example, that seemed made of rock.

– It's all your fault! she blurts at Tiffany. If it wasn't for you –

Tiffany pauses over her popcorn.

– But I didn't – I mean how could I –

She sighs and stops. It's pointless. What is there to say? Over the months, she has tried to reassure her family that, by delivering Harvey to Liberty when she did, she has gained them all immunity. But her sudden unexpected redundancy tells another story.

– The fact is, spits Gwynneth, that we know the Hoggs aren't real people, and nobody else does!

– Shhh! hisses Tiffany, diving a hand deep into the popcorn

220

tub, her face flushing with fear. It's not safe to talk! Even to each other!

Picking up the bad familial vibes, baby Howard begins to cry.

– I'm scared, groans Tiffany, ignoring the infant's wail. I don't want to do it! Her eyes blur at the thought of this afternoon. She is shaking with fright.

Two weeks ago, Liberty came to the door. There were two plain-clothes associates, a man and a woman. When she saw the Liberty IDs flashed at her, Tiffany's heart bucked painfully. There was another one waiting outside in a car with Groke number-plates. He was dark and powerful-looking. Security, probably. He'd have a gun. His eyes swivelled expertly about the street.

– May we come in? the tall man had said, stepping in.

– Won't take a minute, said the woman, following.

While the blond man did the talking, the woman did the poking around. It was frightening. They'd felt so alone, so isolated. Tiffany had been so scared she'd crammed her face with cold alphabet pasta all the way through the meeting. Howard cried incessantly. Gwynneth shivered and whimpered. Geoff just did breathing exercises, trying to keep his pulse-rate down.

– There's heart failure runs in my family, Geoff trembled, when the Liberty man finished explaining the terrifying bottom line. The Liberty man's mouth had tweaked upwards in response, as though he thought heart failure was funny. But in the end what choice did they have, once the smooth young associate had graphically described what would happen if they didn't co-operate? With sinking hearts, Tiffany, Gwynneth and Geoff agreed to do what Liberty said.

– You've made the right choice, said the Liberty woman as the quaking Tiffany took the red biro she was handed. And scared witless, wrote as dictated.

Two weeks ago. Two awful, scary weeks. Nearer and nearer comes the ship. And now it has docked.

– I can't do it, whimpers Tiffany.

– There's no choice, snaps Gwynneth, silencing Howard with a dummy.

And there isn't. She's committed.

A buzz at the door: that will be the car now.

LIBERTY DAY 2 P.M.

The flooding in St Placid starts slowly from the east, exhaling a sickly lavender mist. Some customers, armed with binoculars, thermosed coffee and video-recording equipment, are strolling up to the foothills of St Giddier's Mount to watch its creeping progress inland. There's something mesmeric about the way the slick of liquid moves; it's almost organic, like blood. By mid-morning when the pools have widened and flattened, you can even make out a steady smooth gurgle as its pulse strengthens. Look now across the farmlands and you will see dreamy lakes – vast thick pools that vibrate their own eerie subterranean song. Every now and then, the smooth skin is broken by the silver flip of a jumping fish, or the reaching tentacle of an ink filled squid.

The lavender spreads softly, a balmy puddle of oil on glass. The stillness is rich, tangible.

The lights are off in Tilda's lilac apartment, but the sun spills in, casting its soft rays across her ancient doll face. The television throbs weakly in a corner, charting the day.

In the Temple on the top floor of the ziggurat, Wesley Pike breathes in the strong feisty peppermint rush of the day. He has eaten a bagel, drunk more Brazilian coffee, run his eye over more graphs, and flicked through the news channels. The customers, jittery from the extra peppermint, have begun shopping in earnest now; you can see them down below, swarming from store to store, zealous and united. He loves this view of the city. He will love it for ever. High above the busy grid of streets and plazas, the glittering sky whirls with fresh promise. Far away on the shining horizon of the United States, the customers of America have spoken.

His thoughts float. In war, it is the little man who wins; the honest and stalwart customer, whose courageous faith lights the way for the faint-hearted. *The masters have been abolished; the morality of the common man has triumphed.* She'll keep the faith. There's a plan for Atlantica; of course there is.

– We can have every confidence, he murmurs. Every confidence . . .

Next to him, the Boss vibrates gently, the shadows of clouds sliding slowly across her white flanks. The decisions she has made over the past year are based on simple equations really – the kind any child could make with a pocket calculator. In the Liberty system, the greatest happiness of the greatest number is a core principle. The figures speak for themselves. Atlantica's five million, weighed against America's two hundred and fifty. A part, sacrificed for the greater good of the whole . . . what more glorious contribution can a society make to global humanity?

America, *Home of Liberty*. Doesn't it sound good? Doesn't it sound . . . *right*?

Oblivious, Wesley Pike stares through the window and dreams on.

I look out of the porthole and my stomach clenches. Bird of Liberty flags flap dismally from the dockside buildings, and the leaning skeletons of scaffolding rear up from the silt of the river banks, spiking the Hope's curve like the bones of a fish. The skyline of Harbourville is wreathed in heavy greenish mist. Head Office looks faintly askew. Is Wesley Pike up there at the top of that mineral-streaked monolith? I remember our meeting, long ago – a lifetime ago – in the Snak Attak.

He'd fazed me, by guessing the origins of the Hoggs like a mind reader. Then talked about his mother, who flow-charted her son's future before she died. As I crane my neck to peer up at it, I get the weird sensation that the sky's falling on us, and Wesley Pike with it, and that his heavy charisma will crush me like paper.

I've added the finishing touches to the chess board with magic marker, still roiling with fear and rage about Gwynneth, Tiffany and that wanker of a Geoff. Why are they suddenly so set on banjaxing my fragile eco-balance before I croak? Their nerve is staggering. One of the first things I'm planning to ask my not-daughter Tiffany is what the hell she means by asking personal questions about my stool.

Sporting festive gas masks and Model Customer badges, excited Atlanticans roam the harbour and the city streets, spilling happiness and beer with equal recklessness. Whole families clad in bright leisurewear carry bulging bags of merchandise and push trolleys piled high with teetering goods. Wicker settees and matching occasional tables are on sale for fifty dollars. There's a four-for-the-price-of-one offer on support tights. Artificial coral for indoor aquariums has gone through the floor. Dishwasher pellets are next to nothing. You can get five fondue sets for the price of three, and there are complimentary barbecue tongs for anyone whose surname begins with L. People are beginning to buy stuff they didn't think they wanted, till they saw how cheap it was: automated curtain-rods, mushroom-growing kits, pinking shears, doll's-house equipment, home leg-waxes, edible play putty, solar-powered strimmers, talking encyclopaedias, crystallised raspberries, toilet-brush holders in the shape of the Titanic.

Beyond the peppermint that's gushing out at full strength there's ketchup in the breeze, and hope, and the frangipani perfume that's selling well this year in the over-sixties market, and the rise and fall of cheery retail banter. The customers are eating and laughing and strolling about clutching cans of fizzy diet drinks, happy and aimless. High wittering voices float on the balmy breeze, mingling with the vaporous haze fanning in from the sea. There's a band playing somewhere, a distant tinkle and throb. Atlantica is still a beacon for the world.

They're killing a man at three.

– Your brain isn't much cop compared to even a simple piece of electronic circuitry, I tell John.

– Which would you prefer, he goes.

– So you can't outwit a machine, I tell him. But you can fuck with its head.

– Having your eyes sewn shut with blanket-stitch by a syphilitic chimp, he goes, or –

– You can skew a game, just by being human, I tell him. Emotional decisions, they throw a spanner in its works, they –

– The chimp doing that, or having a nutter garage mechanic fill up your ears with that expandable foam stuff?

– You can win by accident, without even understanding why. You can –

My voice is trembling. And he's in tears, banging his fist against the washbasin.

We've docked.

Just kill me now.

A crack rips across the atmosphere, and a rocket of orange-and-silver flame is shooting high into the sky's concave shell and then exploding in a burst of dark-orange powder that spells out LIBERTY. The shimmering letters quake and shatter across the harbour, then billow out across the blank blue. A spontaneous cheer choruses up from the bubbling crowd, lasting long after the word itself has gusted apart.

– Li-ber-ty! Li-ber-ty! the voices chant. The thrill is infectious.

As the well-loved anthem *Independent and Free* begins to

strain and swell, a windy sigh seems to rise from the collective soul of the island and hover over the shining River Hope. The giant screens flash party colours, rich and amorphous. Feeling peckish, the customers head for the fast-food concessions which spring into frantic action, Catherine-wheeling with queues for big pink smudges of candy floss, sushi, and frankfurters. The music's stirring chords build and build in a sumptuous crescendo, a crescendo that seems to bend the light so that the sky itself appears to throb in tune. The sun sparkles off a hundred edifices of glass and chrome, a thousand glinting trams, a plethora of shopping malls and schools, swimming pools and golf courses. *Independent and Free* echoes gloriously over the glimmering air, then drains to a tingling fade. The Ferris wheel begins a slow, happy revolution. Kids yell just for the hell of it.

This brave land.

In the visiting area on B deck of the *Sea Hero*, Tiffany waits with the others, clad in mourning garb and shaking with fear. She can't stop it. She can't. She's been feeding herself pretzels to calm down. When they're finished she plans to bite her nails to the quick. She wonders if she could ask the Liberty people if it's OK to visit the loo.

Just kill me now.

A tap on my shoulder. I turn and see a masked face. The blindfold is a glittering, baroquey garment, de-luxed with purple silk, sequins, seed pearls and minuscule glass beads. It twinkles as he inclines his head with the odd elegance of an emu.

– It's crakko, I say. You have to hand it to him. – A work of art. An *oeuvre*.

He's taking it off now, slowly. And he's thrusting it at me, blinking, his red-eyed ugly-mug self again.

– For you, mate, he says.

227

I gulp. The words won't come.

– When I thought it was me that was for the chop . . . well, I was planning to leave you all my stuff. You know, the tat Jacko sent. The Egyptian scroll thing, and the terrier. Even the rhino dropping.

I glance at the fibrous block, light as a piece of popcorn, like a home-made loaf sitting there squat on the shelf. That faint organic smell.

– Well, instead, he says, now that it's you, going to – you know. Well, I thought you might like – well. A thing to say goodbye with.

I'm so moved I can't speak for a moment, so I just take the blindfold, and hang it round my neck.

– I'll . . . do it justice, I tell him. And the chess set . . .

But my voice wobbles and I have to cough. Enough said. He knows. Next thing, we're hugging. A big heavy man's hug, slapping each other's back. It goes on for a while – and then we split apart, embarrassed. But we're both smiling like a couple of idiots, glad that it happened. There's some silence after that, as we blow our noses on bog paper and mull things over.

– Which would you prefer, says John. Being force-fed live tapeworms or having your whole face stuffed in a red-ant heap, eyes open?

– Well, it's apples and oranges, that one, I reply, trying to sound cheery. But if I apply my mind to it, I'd have to say –

I was going to say the ant heap, but I break off in mid-flow. Because bam, it's hit me like a whacking great sledgehammer between the eyes!

– Jesus! I yell. How could I have been so stupid? The rhino shit! A stool investigation! *How could I have missed it?*

In St Placid, Tilda holds her breath and bears televisual witness to the sombre but exciting scene being enacted on the upper deck of the *Sea Hero* and relayed live, complete with a little clock on the bottom left showing the minutes ticking by. There have been pictures of Harvey Kidd's face everywhere lately. An *éminence grise*, is the caption in this morning's paper. He chews the printed word, apparently; that's why he's grey. You wouldn't think it to look at him, but he's the one behind some of the Hoggs' most daring economic atrocities. There was even a graph illustrating all his dealings on the stock exchange; he bought and sold –

Oh. It's starting.

There's a drum-roll, and on to the deck of the prison ship *Sea Hero* steps the Captain himself. He waves to the crowd, and then there's another drum-roll, and Harvey Kidd's daughter and ex-wife appear, both in mourning: the younger woman in a black trouser suit and dark glasses, her mother in a black dress and a veil. There's a man with them; Tilda's read about him too; he's Gwynneth Kidd's new husband, who's come to give moral support. He's in dark glasses and a sombre suit. Perhaps aware that he is only on the edge of the family, he stands a little back from the women, his hands clasped behind his back, his blond head sombrely bowed.

Tilda watches, entranced. She's got some dim sum all ready to microwave but she's glued to her chair. Another drum-roll and a door opens on to the deck. The prisoner appears, led by a chipmunk-faced guard.

Harvey Kidd, grey-faced, blinks in the light.

My head's spinning. I can't believe the size of the crowd, a throbbing packed mass, shoulder to shoulder. There must be thousands down there. As I raise my head to take in the spread of it, a massive jeer buckles out from the throng, a rushing throaty sound. They're yelling and whistling and shrieking, their words cargoed with loathing, their tiny faraway faces distorted with hate.

No question about it; they want me dead.

– The sweet sound of democracy, murmurs Fishook. Justice

229

must be seen to be done, Voyager. The customer's demanding it, see?

Beyond the bunting and coloured smoke I see the giant Ferris wheel doing a slow, mocking turn, the tiny figures in its clinging pods straining to gawp.

Rigged to the far end of the longest jetty there's a massive screen, showing flickering scenes from the crowd. My heart's jumping about this way and that, a rogue organ come loose inside my chest. I can't think straight. I can't see straight, either, because when the screen suddenly fills with something moon-like and grey, with blobby craters and weird protuberances, I don't get what it is. The jeering gets louder, angrier. Then something twists inside me and I realise. The grey thing is a human face. Mine.

– Smile, Handsome, says Fishook. You're on TV.

In her tilting apartment, the Vanillo bottle by her side, Tilda Park sits rapt as Craig Devon continues his hushed live commentary: *This is Harvey Kidd's daughter Tiffany . . .*

Tilda watches the big girl. She's the shape of a lumbering caravan. She steps forward and offers her father a fumbling embrace.

It's a poignant moment for her, of course. She's one of many people who've had to take the difficult but brave decision to Hotline their own parents . . .

Tilda sips her Vanillo. Stares, trembling, as the camera zooms in on Tiffany Kidd who looks miserable and scared. She's shaking, and there's a pretzel stuck to her collar like a brooch. Her eyes are red from crying. Poor girl, thinks Tilda. It can't have been easy.

– Tiffany, mumbles Harvey Kidd. He's trying to smile, you can tell. But it isn't working; his grey moon-face twitches and his eyes skid about not settling on anything.

And this is his ex-wife, Gwynneth Kidd . . .

The smaller of the two women takes Kidd's hand. You can't

see her face because it's covered by a veil. I'd do the same in her shoes, thinks Tilda. How else could you cope with the shame?

– Gwynneth, says Kidd. The name reverberates around the dock. – It was . . . kind of you to come. His voice wobbles.

– A pleasure, she musters. Her voice is wobbling too. It's a ghastly moment – almost too intimate for television, really, if such a thing's possible. Tilda gulps.

– Well, er. Goodbye, Gwynneth, says Kidd. His grey face is turning a shade paler and he's sweating. – All the best.

Then Gwynneth backs off, to be consoled by her new blond husband. You can't see his face very well behind the dark glasses, but he looks quite a catch. Familiar, somehow, too, thinks Tilda – but she can't place him, and now the shot has changed back to Captain Fishook who is ushering the condemned traitor towards the raised platform by the prow. It's a small space, the size of a boxing ring. The chair in the middle. When they reach the fenced entrance, Fishook takes Kidd's arm, like the father leading the bride.

Quaking with a terrible anticipation, Tilda pours another Vanillo and takes a deep swig.

A hush descends, flattening itself like a thundercloud on a prairie as Harvey Kidd sleepwalks his way to the electric chair and sits. On the dockside, the crowd jostles to look at the giant screen which shows his face, blank with shock and fright. A fat woman has brought her own step-ladder and she's bustling to erect it. Others have binoculars, and are trying to focus on the deck itself.

There's no padding, of course, murmurs Craig Devon in the hushed whisper reserved for snooker commentary. *We see here the functional arm-rests with clasps, and the straps there with leads emerging. Note too, the microphones at head height . . . Ah, as you see, Kidd is now reaching for his blindfold,*

hand-crafted, apparently, by his cabin-companion . . . now
here comes the ship's doctor, Manolis Pappadakis, originally
from Greece . . .

Dr Pappas' gentle voice seems to come from far away, but
he's right next to me.

– Now please, Voyager, we will roll up your sleeves and I
can apply the jelly, he whispers. For conductivity.

I can see from the red puffiness of his eyes that he's been
crying. The jelly's a horrible gloop. Slowly, taking care, he
straps my wrists to the arms of the chair.

– And now the ankles, we do the same.

I'm trembling all over as he annoints them, and locks the
metal clasps. I'm freezing and I feel sick.

Now, ladies, gentlemen and children, says Craig Devon.
His voice reverberates around me. *I must ask you for com-*
plete silence, please, until after the Final Adjustment. Will Dr
Pappadakis please now blindfold the voyager.

There's a show-biz drum-roll, and Dr Pappa reaches for
John's sequinned *oeuvre*. It glints in the sun.

– I do not want this job, murmurs the doctor. Do not blame
me, Voyager.

I nod, and he slides the blindfold over my eyes.

Darkness.

We will now begin the countdown, says the meaty voice
of Craig.

That's when the panic kicks in. I'm shaking, shaking – the
fear flops across me in shuddering freezing waves. What if –
what if they don't – I don't want to die. I'm not ready, and I'll
never be ready. I'm human.

– Ten, nine, eight –

Oh God! It's so slow! So slow! Please hurry up!

– Seven, six, five –

And now it's too fast! It's happening too fast! Everything
rushing in on me, screaming at me, my mind a blur, a tidal

wave of noise. I can picture Fishook's finger poised above the console. His head leaning down.

– Four – I squeeze my eyes shut.

– Three – I groan.

– Two – I tighten up my arse.

– One –

– STOP!

A woman's voice. Small and firm as a bullet.

The crowd goes ape. After a split second of shocked silence, they're yelling and screaming, tugging this way and that in a drunken Mexican wave. They came to see a man finally adjust! What's going on?

What's going on is this: Kidd's ex-wife has whipped off her black veil and snatched the Captain's hand away from the button. The blond man has grabbed him from behind and handcuffed him, fast as a magician's trick. A sudden whirl of movement, and the woman's drawn a gun from her handbag and she's pointing it right at Fishook's head! Another flurry and the Greek doctor has ripped Kidd's blindfold off, and he's swaying numbly in the light.

– Am I still alive? I mumble. The air seems to whirr around me. It's the crowd, screaming.

– Yes, says a woman's voice. And so am I.

It can't be. I look up, and nearly faint. It is.

– Hannah! Alive. Dizzy, I close my eyes again. Then open them. She's still there. Smiling at me like in a thousand dreams. The joy of it floods me in a rush, like I'm suddenly drunk, or drugged, or both, and I feel my smile stretch and stretch until my face aches with it. A thousand dreams.

Just kill me now.

Wesley Pike doesn't recognise Benedict at first. Focusing, dazzled, he thinks simply, he looks familiar, he looks –

Then the feverishness kicks in again. *Benedict*. Pike groans, reaches for a chair, and sinks into it. The puzzle hasn't fitted into place yet. Next to him, the Liberty Machine's cool body hums. He shifts his glance back to the screen, still not taking it in.

Can that actually be Hannah Park, handing the gun to Dr Pappadakis – he seems to have offered to take over – and unstrapping Harvey Kidd, and – *embracing him*?

Pike licks dry lips. Tries to breathe steadily and evenly. Can't.

Benedict is looking straight at him, or so it seems. He must know exactly where the cameras are. His face is like a coin flashing in the light. Pike recoils from the terrible, treacherous intimacy of his glance.

Fuck you, it says. *I'm Benedict, and I know best.*

Pike feels his own face go white. Hadn't he known this about Benedict, right from the start? Hadn't he said as much, in the People Laboratory? Made the boy blush?

The crowd is losing control, rage and frustration sweeping through it like a crackling bushfire.

– Wait! says a voice that reverberates across the harbour.

With the sudden swiftness of a snake spitting venom, the blond man has puckered his lips, shot a bright ball of green chewing gum from his mouth, taken the microphone, and put a hand in the air for silence.

– You came to see a Final Adjustment, he says. The crowd stops. Hushes. – So here's an offer.

The amplifier picks up his voice, and scatters it. They're listening now. The hush thickens and fills.

– Give us a few minutes of your time. If you're not convinced by what we say, the Final Adjustment will go ahead. But if you are – Harvey Kidd will go free.

A murmur washes across the crush of people as he gestures the prisoner forward.

– Mr Kidd, he says to the grey-faced figure, who is grinning

234

like a maniac. You have one minute in which to tell the customers of Atlantica the truth about the Hoggs.

The Final Adjustment will go ahead . . . My heart spasms and tumbles.

I should be prepared for this, but my instructions in the rhino shit were brief and anonymous and it was all a bit last-minute and – well . . . *The truth about the Hoggs* is suddenly feeling like a pretty tall order.

The big scary emptiness down below jolts me back. They're waiting.

I clear my throat, an ugly barking noise that vibrates around me.

– The fact is, I stammer, the Hoggs aren't what you think.

But it's a bad start.

The microphone throws my voice into the air and echoes back, sounding fake and wheedling, as though I'm begging for my life. Which I suppose I am. The ugly yells are starting again. The customer doesn't like it. He wants something more, or something else, you can hear it from the way his voice foams and froths upwards, curdling in the zinging wind. He came to see a man die. He wants his money back. I'm just a bloke, I think. How'm I supposed to – Five million pairs of eyes on me. Five million pairs of ears waiting.

– I always wanted a family, I babble. I didn't have one, I was an orphan.

I'm shaking now.

– And so –

I shut my eyes.

I can't do it. The Hoggs are still my family. If I tell the truth about how they came to me, I'll lose them again, and for ever. And then what will I do? And who will I be?

I'm lost! Just kill me now!

When I open my eyes, there's Hannah. She's guessed my thoughts, because there's a pleading fierceness on her face,

235

and in that split second I know I have to do it for her, for me, for the customer, for all of us. From nowhere, the energy's exploding inside me like a potent capsule, and I'm speaking in a new strong voice I barely know.

– I made them up.

From down on the dockside the crowd's foaming voice deepens with a raucous menace, but there's no stopping me now.

– They don't exist! They're inventions! I generated them on a computer, and that's all they are. They're not real, they're not real, they're NOT REAL!

I'm smiling. Smiling because it's out, escaping like gas from a balloon whooshing high and invisibly majestic into the bright air. Something lifts within me: a huge weight's gone; a heaviness that I didn't know I carried. As my words float out across the harbour, I can almost see Mum and Dad, Uncle Sid and Cameron and Lola flying with them, in V formation, like a flock of birds migrating to a warmer place, carried on the peppermint breeze, up and away, joining the dancing molecules, leaving me behind. It gives me the strength to say it louder. In fact I'm shouting now, swept by a tingling, unfathomable euphoria. The blond man's nodding at me eagerly. I see the relief break on Hannah's face and she smiles the most dazzling and beautiful smile I've ever seen, and so I yell it again and again and again, I yell out the whole story, the whole nub of it, because I've found my true voice now, the voice that comes from deep inside me, from where my inner self hides.

– The Hogg family were just my FANTASY! They don't EXIST! They NEVER DID! They were people I invented! They were a bit of me that got out of hand! *I was LONELY, that's all!*

Out. Gone. I shut my eyes and feel something die and be born at once.

It's then I know that I am free.

*   *   *

236

On the dockside a small dark figure, thickset as a keg of explosives, makes its way through the massed throng, looking for a vantage point from which to watch events on the giant screen. When he finds a small space near a couple busily unfolding a step-ladder, Dr Crabbe stops and strains his neck to watch. His eyes are on Hannah Park.

It was a year ago that she arrived on his doorstep in Groke. She needed to hide. The island was in danger. She'd be taking over his surgery, she told him. He could help her, or he could get busted. An easy choice.

The fat woman has carefully climbed her step-ladder and now stands at its top like a bulky statue, a frankfurter in each hand. Her mouth hangs open. Below, her husband holds the ladder steady. Their eyes are fixed on the giant screen.

Benedict Sommers has taken the microphone again.

– You have heard the truth, he says slowly. Now would you like the Final Adjustment to go ahead – or would you like to hear more?

There's a short silence.

– More, blurts the woman with the frankfurters. The mustard is dripping down in ochre gloops.

– More! cries Dr Crabbe.

– More! call the customers, one by one, until their voices are melded into a single shout. More, more, more!

When Hannah Park steps forward, the cries die down again. They are ready to listen.

– I worked for Libertycare as a psychologist, says Hannah Park. The Corporation took all five Hoggs and re-modelled them as scapegoats. I know this because I was involved. The idea was for the family to take the blame for the ecological crisis on Atlantica.

– Ecological crisis? breathes the fat woman. What ecological crisis?

She drops her frankfurter; it rolls over Dr Crabbe's foot and down the sloping tarmac and then stops, blocked by the wheel of a little boy's tricycle.

– What's a scapegoat? asks the boy.

– Shhhh! snaps his mother, her candy-floss poised like a pink cloud. She squints at the screen.

– The leaks at the purification zones aren't due to sabotage, Hannah Park is saying. They're due to a failure of the system. Libertycare has known for years that the cleansing programme was breaking up the island's crust. All the surveys showed it. But instead of calling a halt to the whole thing – she pauses. A rush of voices ripples its way out across the harbour. – They adjusted the geologists and carried on. The murmur swells. – The Corporation knew that if you were aware of the crisis, you wouldn't vote for them again. After the Festival of Choice, the system went into damage-limitation mode. The Hoggs were launched to deflect everyone's attention from the real problem, while the United States voted.

Now, the crowd is shifting and stirring like a great cloud-mass. They're all straining to watch, some of them jumping to get a better view.

– But the problem's still here, says Hannah Park.

Benedict Sommers waves a brown envelope at the cameras.

– If you want proof, we have it. The document in here was generated by the Liberty Machine itself.

The fat woman, trembling, reverses her way down the step-ladder as he reads from it aloud in a firm voice:

Libertycare's global strategy calls for balance. And in some cases, for rationalisation to ensure that balance. Atlantica has served its purpose well. But in order to welcome new projects, it is necessary to – he pauses – *bid others farewell.*

The silence that follows is total.

If betrayal has a smell, that smell is wafting across the

harbour now. As the customers begin to sense it, they feel suddenly, lurchingly sick. The eerie silence stretches as the truth sinks in.

– Well then, says the woman with the frankfurters.

– Better pack up, says her husband.

They become oddly practical. They fold their step-ladder. They check their belongings. Next to Dr Crabbe, a man's voice says – Fuck! I don't believe it! and an elderly woman faints, crumpling to the ground like a discarded piece of clothing. Behind him, a woman starts up a high, shrill moan. An obese family of five starts to nudge its way towards the ship. – Come on, urges the father. Let's get the hell out!

The crowd is stirring in all directions, as though caught in a whirring food-mixer. They're screaming and yelling now. It's starting to sink in that it's the beginning of the end.

Captain Fishook clears his throat, and murmurs something to Hannah. She hesitates, then signals at Dr Pappadakis to lower the gun.

– This is a Class One emergency, says Fishook. Over which I have the honour of presiding at this time. In accordance with nautical protocol, I am issuing an SOS. Calling all ships in the Atlantic Ocean. Please tune to channel 16. Calling all air bases . . .

As Captain Fishook speaks, a sudden sense of being part of history overwhelms him. He can see how this scene might become the stuff of legend. His voice deepens and swells with gravitas.

– Mass evacuation required, repeat, mass evacuation required . . .

In St Placid, Tilda watches. She knows it's too late. Her eyes are round with shock. She lets the tears trickle. She doesn't care.

Hannah! Hannah, alive! Hannah, looking at that man, that grey-faced Hogg criminal, her face wide open with love!

239

And Benedict! Benedict, who told her she was dead! He's there too!

Tilda clasps her pill-box to her stomach. Her body shakes with a terrible, painful, uncontrollable joy. The pills rattle.

From everywhere and nowhere grows a great rumbling voice of anger, a voice that swells and heaves, filling the harbour and the sky above with the terrible heart-rending sound of human dismay. Picking up the faint strains of it, Wesley Pike exhales slowly. Now that the United States has voted for the system, this surely is the moment the Boss has been waiting for. It was she, after all, who dictated the schedule for the day. It was she who launched them all on this wild trajectory.

As if on cue, the Boss's purr begins to alter subtly to a vibrant hum, and then a slow, deep whirring. Wesley Pike smiles, his heart soars. At last! As he waits impatiently for a sign from the strategy screens, he is only dimly aware of the faint clamour going on outside, the screams and shouts of panic, the urgent calls, the running footsteps.

The Temple door bursts open. A young field associate stands there panting, her uniform a disgrace.

– We're bailing out, she says. There's planes and ships being organised. You coming?

The Facilitator General laughs with gentle contempt.

– Are you sure? I mean the whole building's pretty unsafe. And the ground underneath – I mean, there's not much time, sir.

– Off you go, says Pike, flapping a hand. Join the rest of them.

– Suit yourself, says the girl. And leaves.

– I'll wait here, says Pike gently under his breath, when the door has closed. I'll wait with her. I'll wait.

He knows she'll deliver. Just the thought of it makes him feel dreamy and safe. *Fallings from us, vanishings* . . . Nothing to lose and everything to gain.

Reward success . . . Soon. She'll do it soon.

On Captain Fishook's orders, the crew have unlocked the cabins, and all the prisoners are pouring out, heading for the rapidly filling upper deck and congregating there as though sleepwalking. The sky seems to ache with the pity of it.

– I nearly didn't get it! I gabble into Hannah's hair. I won't let her go. I can't stop kissing her. My Hannah. I guess I'm sobbing. – I didn't open the letter, see, I left it standing on the shelf, I didn't think –

– We had to take a gamble, she says. She's crying too.

– Where were you all this time?

In Groke, with Dr Crabbe.

– The man who – I stop, and gawp.

– Diagnosed me, she said. And sent the rhino dropping.

It takes a moment for this to sink in.

– The satellite engineer? Jacko? That's Dr Crabbe?

– The rhino thing was his idea. He had a contact who –

We're interrupted.

– You did it, mate! You did it!

It's John, lumbering thickly towards us, balancing a tray with my chess set on it.

– Sometimes you can win, he says, laying it down gently on the electric chair, just by being stupid. That's what you said, isn't it?

He's grinning all over and I am too. Next thing I know we're locked in a rib-crushing hug.

– Human. I said human.

– Same difference.

– I made that chess set, I tell Hannah proudly, when John and I have pulled apart. I'm still crying, and so's she. – From chewed-up paper.

– It's beautiful, she says.

And so are you, I'm thinking.

– My white queen, I tell John.

And then there's a tiny silence, the silence of a new presence that's joined us. I know who it is but I don't turn right away. When I do, my heart stumbles. She's dressed in black. Her eyes are red. She hangs her head and won't speak. I have the same problem; I open my mouth, but there's nothing. I'm blocked.

I look away, stare out to sea.

– Dad, she says.

I gulp.

And then I say – Tiff.

I turn and smile, and she smiles back. And that's all we can manage for now, and maybe that's all we'll ever manage, but it's enough.

The sudden noise catches Pike unawares: a Tourettish stammer of activity from the printers, belching endless concertina'd reams of pages, overflowing their trays and gushing to the floor, skidding on the lino and fanning out in chaotic sheaves. Pike scrabbles for an armful, rips it off. And scans a page. This section of the blueprint shows rows of figures. Strange disjointed words. Equations that make no sense. Graphs that peak and trough meaninglessly on the page, doubling back on themselves and exiting upside-down. The letter w appears to be repeated a thousand times. A page of slogans follows: PUTTING THE CUSTOMER FIRST. YOUR CHOICE, OUR COMMITMENT. FREEDOM: THE DREAM THAT CAME TRUE. THE CUSTOMER IS ALWAYS RIGHT. VALUE TALKS. A FESTIVAL OF CHOICE. Strings of gobbledegook. A complex Venn diagram, whose circles overlap heavily, like storm-clouds. THE BARGAIN OF A LIFETIME.

The machine's throaty thrumming deepens, then soars upward three octaves. And ends in a high, thin shriek.

*   *   *

– Well, Captain, says Benedict Sommers. Are you ready?

– Aye, aye, says Fishook. When he grips the microphone, a little shiver runs through him as he makes the mental adjustments.

– Now, folks. Listen up. This is turning out to be a – *momentous occasion indeed*. I may even be right in thinking that we are witnessing our finest hour. Now it's with great pleasure and respect that I am handing control of the ship to these fine people here.

And another huge, rushing roar goes up, with whistles and shrieks and yells tumbling headlong across the sky towards the ship like the rumble of a huge human motor. In a small wave at first, then massing thickly, the customers start to mount the gangways and pour like lava on to the decks. A small stocky man who looks like a keg of explosives is among them. The throng swells and roars, a cyclone of humanity.

On the streets of Harbourville, the looting has begun.

Hannah's been telling me how when she met Benedict Sommers at her mother's in St Placid, she thought it was the end.

– And it would have been, if Benedict hadn't read the document in Leo's envelope. He did some research, and found out that Leo –

She stops, and her eyes fill with tears. I squeeze her hand.

– Dead?

She nods.

– That's when we knew I'd need to disappear. I went to Dr Crabbe's surgery, and Benedict stayed close to Pike.

She looks across at Benedict; he's with Fishook, at the wheel. They're studying a map. He turns and smiles and she smiles back, first at him and then at me.

My heart's going crazy.

The smile has spread to a grin. In Head Office I never saw her smile. She's so pretty. Her face is different from how I remember it. It's all flushed and – I don't know. *Free*. But suddenly, a horrible fear hatches: will she still want me?

– Hannah, are you still, you know, *you*?

There's a stretch of silence.

– I am, she says finally. If you are.

– But your Block . . .

– Well, I *was* blocked, once.

– And then? Did Dr Crabbe –

– No, you.

– Me?

I'm gobsmacked. Proud of myself.

– I did that? I say. Without even knowing? Just by . . .

– By loving me, she says.

There's another little pause.

– But it was so easy! I blurt. Anyone could've done it!

I'm blushing. Like a jerk.

– No they couldn't, she says.

And I take her in my arms.

In her tilted apartment, Tilda tingles with pride and a loose, disjointed bewilderment. It's not every day your daughter pops up alive and well on national TV when you thought she was a piece of calcium at the bottom of a crater. Not every day that you check the cassette they gave you, and discover it's not Hannah committing sabotage and falling to her death at all, but a promotional video for the Liberty Trust Scheme, showing how you can save twenty-eight dollars a month by pledging your assets to the Corporation in perpetuity.

On the streets outside, some of her neighbours have pumped up inflatable dinghies and are setting sail in little clusters, clutching maps and compasses. Good luck to them.

Tilda holds her glass of Vanillo high, its silver liquid gleaming in the fading light. She sips, and the warm glow spreads and deepens, cushioning her like a cosy internal duvet. She's seen the future. She's seen how her daughter and that grey-coloured man will sail away somewhere and get as far as they can but never be safe, because the United States is run by Them now, and it'll be re-named Liberty and the world will somehow overnight be – well just bigger and better and . . . Oh, she's too old to think about all that nonsense. Let the young ones worry. She doesn't have courage or ideals, she isn't a fighter; she can listen to the sounds of panic outside and the little screams, without being too disrupted. There are plenty of ready-meals in the freezer, and she's got the telly.

She's always been a bit of an armchair person.

Yes, she's seen the future. And she'll stay put.

The satellite predictions that now litter the Temple floor show how in a matter of weeks the land to the west will have saturated like soggy bread. How the plantations of mango, guava, coconut and lemon-grass will dissolve into swamp, more liquid than solid. Swamp that itself will effervesce, sucked down by the seductive lure of physics. Deep down below the tilted coast, geology resists feebly the pressure of the inevitable. The purity zones ravaged by filth, the waste channels blocked, the volcanic fissures bloated. Over the months to come, Atlantica will relax, loosen the corset of her geography, let what will buckle buckle and what will sink sink.

Gravity has outlined its agenda.

Urgent hoofing noises thunder in the corridor outside the Temple.

– She knew all along, murmurs Wesley Pike. The echo of the machine's high shriek still rings in his ears. Treachery tastes like sour iron in his mouth. *She knew*. Knew, and knew he'd buy whatever she said, knew he'd buy it because he was used to buying and it was all about buying.

His heart twists as he reaches for the lever that calls a halt. The software has already taken up office in the United States and it's over for Atlantica, it's been over for a long time, so whatever gesture he makes – the only gesture left – can mean nothing.

It's a smooth, cool, decisive slide. It's the work of a second.

It means nothing. It means everything.

When it's done, he is surprised to find himself a man again.

Bewildered faces turn to catch the last rays of the dying sun, and we breathe deep, inhaling the peppermint breeze that bears the ugly lurch of grief. The sky swarms and buzzes with helicopters peeling away from the city, thistledowning in all directions. There's a loud boom, and then a protracted honk from the funnel as the gangways lift.

Minutes later, to the sound of screaming panic, the ship has pulled slowly out from the dock and Fishook is steering eastwards from our steadily crumbling shore. As we leave the estuary behind, the waves in our wake seem to foam and curdle and the cloud-mass above us echoes with the high thin cries of the island we're abandoning. Gradually, the darkening silhouette of Harbourville grows smaller and more precarious, shuddering to a pinprick in the gusting wind.

Hannah and I stand in silence, in the first clobbered stages of shock, the tears running freely down our cheeks. On the horizon, the sunset glows a hectic red, fringed with the toxic blue haze of an all-seeing sky, and from the distant island, an orange-and-blue firework bursts and blossoms across the bubbling seascape, filling the sky with a fierce and bloody light.

I'll never lose sight of this tiny, intense split second, this little numb splinter of grace. The future is rushing in to swamp us, I can already feel the concave ache of it. I have no idea where we will sail to now, or where the human world is headed. But I know there is more gullibility than wisdom and more greed than kindness and more darkness than hope and more fine wares than anyone can ever pay for.

How easy we are to seduce.

Survival is our burden and our treasure.

Our treasure: a tiny guttering beacon in the whirling sea.

Let us not sink.

A NOTE ON THE AUTHOR

Liz Jensen is the author of *Egg Dancing* (long-listed for the Orange Prize), *Ark Baby* (short-listed for the *Guardian* Fiction Prize and long listed for the Orange Prize), *War Crimes for the Home* (long-listed for the Orange Prize), *The Ninth Life of Louis Drax*, currently in development as a major motion picture by Anthony Minghella, and *My Dirty Little Book of Stolen Time*. She divides her time between Copenhagen and London.

My Dirty Little Book of Stolen Time

Charlotte supports herself and her lumpen side-kick, Fru Schleswig, as a prostitute in *fin-de-siècle* Copenhagen. But the course of harlotry never runs smooth, and Charlotte's life is altered irrevocably when, one hard winter, she stumbles on an exciting new source of income. A dark mansion, home to the disagreeable Fru Krak, is in dire need of a top-to-bottom scrub – and the wealthy widow is hiring.

Transformed into cleaning ladies, the squabbling duo attack the dark abode – but soon discover that mysteries abound. The basement appears to be haunted, and there are rumours of desperate souls entering it – never to emerge. Meanwhile there have been odd sightings of the dead Professor Krak, master of physics, walking the streets as a ghost. Charlotte decides to turn detective – but finds herself outwitted by the mysterious controller of a demonic Machine which wastes no time in catapulting her and Fru Schleswig into the baffling world of twenty-first-century London. And beyond . . .